THE HUSTLED

Saga of a
21st Century
Pool Hustler

DAVID SUTTER

The Hustled : Saga of a 21st-Century Pool Hustler
By David Sutter

ISBN (hardcover) 979-8-9921146-3-8
ISBN (paperback) 979-8-9921146-2-1

Published by:
David Sutter, P.O. Box 1877, Clearwater, FL 33757

Front Cover Photo: Freepik
Cover and Interior Design: Maggy Graham
Author Photo: Maggy Graham

Printed in the United States of America

This book is dedicated to the countless players and fans of pool everywhere.

Introduction

This story has been a passion more than anything about pool, gambling and the artform and skill of the game. Fascination of the game impinged early on in my life from around age 10, 1963, growing up in a small town in Kansas. A friend told me about a local pool hall Grand Opening with free pool one Saturday, all day, which meant an out-of-school *rampage*. We proceeded to the pool hall. Nice room. Around 20 big tables, 9 footers. And that's what I grew up playing on.

Pool hadn't taken on a life of its own until into my 20s and 30s. In the 1970s I left Kansas and moved to Los Angeles. I went through the pain of complete madness that one goes through at the culture shock of a small-town Kansas boy suddenly finding himself amidst the grandeur of a monster-size city like Los Angeles. A square 500-mile concrete jungle, second largest US populated city beside New York to this day. It was a supersize of everything I found important at the time. Pretty women, fast exotic Italian sports cars and on down the list.

I stumbled around working at various jobs, and that evolved to owning a furniture business that took off like a rocket, and I finally had some walking-around money. I imported furniture from the Philippines, bamboo and rattan, designs not seen in America at the time. That Philippines experience would come full circle later as it relates to pool. Now blessed from a lot of hard work, in the 1980s I moved to Australia for about two years, me and my 1967 convertible Corvette.

That's another story. My trip to the Carnival in beautiful Rio De Janeiro in the 1980s played a huge part in this pool story. Macau was originally written as part of this journey, given my travels from Tokyo to Bali and Jakarta, Indonesia, and everywhere between. That was replaced by the seductive shores of the South of France, beautiful Monte Carlo-Monaco.

I moved back to L.A. in 1990. In 1992, pool enjoyed a revival and its popularity brought me back to the tables. The Hollywood Athletic Club opened on Sunset Boulevard. It enjoyed a complete facelift and was transformed into the most beautiful pool hall I had ever seen. Two floors with around 40 brand-new Brunswick 9-foot pool tables, a snooker table, bar, and restaurant. I played there almost daily for about 3 years. I heard of a pool tournament around 1993 featuring the world's best at "The Bike"—L.A.'s Bicycle Club Casino. "Earl the Pearl" Strickland and some of the best players in the world played "The Rifleman" Buddy Hall, Johnny Archer, star players from the Philippines, Efren Reyes, Francisco Bustamante and many others.

I had been in about 10 earthquakes, being in California half my life, but nothing like the 1994 quake. After that earthquake, I moved back to Kansas City. In 2017 I again returned to L.A., and did a study about life and livingness. This was the game changer. It answered deep age-old questions I had. Creative imagination and art were a few of the concepts I gained a complete understanding of. It worked! Upon finishing this study, I put pen to paper for 45 days straight. I wrote this story—as a film script—between 250 and 300 pages of action and dialogue. This was my first time attempting to seriously write the story I had been carrying around for 20 years. I saw this as a film from the very first day of writing. I never thought this would ever be a book. Script to film is all I could ever see. I later learned I only needed 120 pages to do an hour-and-a-half film. My excuse is, "Hey, I'm new at this!"

I hired the best I could in Hollywood, expert film consultant Eric Sherman, a marketing & public relations firm who surveyed seven American cities to shop the content: Is this story sellable? What of interest draws you to the story? The questions were very specific to people who go out and see a movie at a minimum once a month. I hired experts in editing. Could never have done it alone. I spent two years from 2017 to 2019 streamlining the script down to 120 pages. Never could I claim to have been a professional writer when I wrote the screenplay in 2017. One year ago, November 2023, I adapted the screenplay to this book. The industry does the opposite, from book to screenplay.

People ask me what this story is about. My answer is: "The Color of Money" on steroids going global. It should go without saying it was the original film that inspired me to write "The Hustled."

Enjoy the trip!

Prologue

On a hot and humid morning in June, 2014, the usually peaceful atmosphere of college town Lawrence, Kansas, was suddenly shattered by alarm bells and police sirens, followed by screams of frightened citizens as a tough-looking man in jeans and a black t-shirt wearing a Halloween mask slammed open the glass doors of the First Bank of Kansas and raced away up the street towards a car at the curb.

Only a second behind him, a determined security guard appeared on the steps, aimed his pistol at the fleeing man and shouted, "Stop! I will shoot you!"

Convinced that he was all out of chances, Kansas "persistent offender" Dwayne McTavish decided to keep on running. It was the last bad decision the two-time robbery ex-con made in a lifetime of bad decisions.

The explosion of the guard's pistol echoed around the plaza as the promised .38 Special Hollow-Point sizzled through the hot summer air and delivered the final ending to Dwayne McTavish's pointless life.

The cops swarmed towards the fallen thief with guns drawn, but the brutal husband to Patsy McTavish and cruel father to 16-year-old Cavalier "Cav" McTavish lay sprawled and lifeless beside his rusty 10-year-old Ford pickup. A plastic sack of stolen cash lay beside him in the gutter, untouched by the violence.

Later that day, the name, face and tragically pointless life of Dwayne McTavish was splashed across a special edition of the Lawrence Journal-World, and led off KMBC 9's "News at 5."

Dwayne McTavish's widow Patsy and his pale and sullen son, Cav, had little to say to the media clamoring around the door to their cheap apartment. Given Dwayne's lifelong history of drug abuse and crime, neither of them expressed surprise or even regret by this wretched ending. For them, the man had "done a nickel" in the state pen for robbery twice, once before Cav was born and again before his son was old enough to understand. A third strike would have sentenced him to nearby Leavenworth penitentiary for a very long time.

1

Building Character

Dwayne McTavish, a daily abuser of drugs and alcohol, frequently beat his wife Patsy, herself a habitual alcohol and drug abuser. But he had often beaten his son Cav as well, and for no reason apparent to Cav or anyone else.

In fact, Cav's relationship with his dad had never been one of shared experiences, never mind respect for the man. Cav felt only raw survival instincts when around him.

As the years passed and Cav matured, he had come to understand the truth of some things—mainly that his father was more of a punk and a bully than a husband and father, and certainly was nothing like the few thoughtful and kind parents of school friends he'd met. Cav had often considered running away but had stayed only because school seemed so important.

Three days after the event, a small, brief funeral service was attended by Cav, his mom, and a handful of her friends. No other members of Dwayne McTavish's family showed up. And Cav wasn't surprised that his father's few friends chose to skip the service.

They were all crooks and probably agreed that he was better off dead anyway.

The preacher said a few words. No one else spoke. It was a closed casket.

Decades ago, the McTavish family purchased a family cemetery plot and basic headstones. It included a space for Dwayne. The day after the funeral, only Patsy, Cav and two gravediggers were present for the matter-of-fact burial. No McTavishes showed up here either.

Patsy, dry-eyed, stepped forward and tossed a small handful of dirt onto Dwayne's casket as it was lowered into the grave. No preacher, no words, just a quick goodbye, and the gravediggers tipped their caps. That was the bitter end of Dwayne McTavish, flawed husband of Patsy and lousy father of Cavalier.

Three days later, early in the warm summer evening, Patsy McTavish appeared alone at the gravesite, none too steady on her feet. She had a glass of wine in one hand, a cigarette dangling from her mouth and tears in her eyes. She glared at the headstone, at the freshly replaced sod, and shook her head. Choking with grief and bitter loss, she screamed a few obscenities at her late husband, and then, as if to punctuate her message, she hurled the wineglass, smashing against the headstone. Slowly, despairing, she turned and walked away.

* * *

Cav now faced the harsh reality of a basically unchanged life—a mother with little warmth and even less to say, a heavy drinker and substance abuser, and not above hustling for a few dollars to buy more drugs. It was far from a typical American family relationship.

On top of that, Cav could never be honest at home anyway. He had to lie to his parents just to survive. They wouldn't accept him telling them the truth about his life, they only accepted fairy tales and bullshit. So, to keep the peace, that's what they got from him. This was how he mastered the "art of bullshit" that, later, would help him up the road.

Cav watched a father who didn't work, was a con man and a thief. His mother was useless, too. She abused the welfare system and scammed the government out of anything she could steal, mostly to satisfy her habitual drug and booze demands. This home environment was education for Cav. It was a tough wake-up call for Cav to see his parents as losers, using drugs and consistently drunk, especially his father who was a belligerent, angry drunk. The pain he suffered from his father beating him for no reason became an unfortunate but invaluable life lesson that he would never forget and, at times, even embraced.

Most of his friends and classmates didn't know the pressures that Cav lived with every day. They had normal parents who had grown to adulthood in small American towns and cities—church-going folks who cherished the values of hard work and play and kindness to strangers.

In more recent times, Cav's small circle of friends all smoked pot and had for years. Some eventually went on to hard drugs. He watched a few of them self-destruct, succumbing to addiction or even dying from overdoses. Adding to this, a life with cruel and drug-addicted parents was enough to keep him very wary of doing drugs and alcohol. So when he declined offers to smoke pot and do other drugs within his circle of friends, he was heeding the two shining examples at home. He decided that, for him, their choice to do drugs would never be options for himself.

Cav, normally a little shy, was tall for his age and good-looking, with dark blonde hair which he wore a little long, and a ready sense of humor. Cav could share his thoughts and ideas with his most trusted friend, Janie, because he wouldn't get yelled at or criticized for being honest like he did at home. Also, like Cav, Janie had a great sense of humor and no tolerance for bullshit. Cav and Janie were tight, really good friends.

Janie had a makeshift "pool table" in the basement, and Cav and a few regulars often came over after school and would play for hours. This scene was Cav's escape and retreat for years. The table was roughly two feet wide and maybe four feet long, with small disks serving as make-believe pool balls. Small wooden sticks made do as pool cues.

Cav was addicted to the game and played it as often as he could. He desperately needed distractions, anything to separate him from his trainwreck home life, and this little makeshift pool game was the perfect distraction. Among their small circle of friends, no one could beat Cav.

A year earlier, at 15, Cav had realized he was big enough and strong enough to at least try to defend himself from his angry, drunken father. All the pressure from his old man's attacks on his mother and himself had built to a boiling point. He wasn't going to take it any longer.

One day as he arrived home from school, he walked in on a familiar sight, both parents raging drunk and calling each other names like "whore" and "bastard" and "slut." When his father started hitting his mother, something in Cav just snapped. Here was the breakout moment for Cav.

He grabbed his father, spun him around, and punched him in the face so hard that he knocked his front teeth out and sent him senseless to the floor. That day, papa got his much-needed wakeup call. The years of Cav's taking his father's shit ended that day. His old man never laid a hand on Cav or his wife again.

And now, the old man was gone for good. With the death of his father, Cav's worldview forever shifted. The funeral signified something pivotal was about to happen. And he sensed that a new chapter in his life was about to begin.

He was absolutely right about that.

2

Into the Night

As the night began to settle in on Cav and his mother's first evening alone together, the complex emotional pain of what had happened and their new lives without Dwayne screamed silently through the home.

Cav's mom seemed to desire solitude, avoiding Cav's attempts to talk about things. Cav didn't know that his mom's real concern was how to hide her secret life, unknown to Cav, which could become visible with Dwayne gone.

Still quite young and attractive despite her self-destructive nature, Patsy had long ago surrendered to a life of self-destruction. Sinking into her troubles with alcohol and drugs, she maintained a small roster of "clients." She had a handful of local businessmen who more or less "kept" her. If she fancied a brief engagement she'd make a few calls. Husband Dwayne, usually stoned on drugs and booze, mostly ignored it. And Cav had paid no attention to his mother's comings and goings. He had no idea what she was doing.

After another hour of drinking, Patsy unleashed a drunken rant.

"You're nothing but a disappointment to me Cav, you and your dead father. I can't handle this now. You have to go. I really need you to leave. Now!"

Cav was shocked. She gave no explanation. It was crazy. He pleaded for time, money, anything to lighten the metric ton of pressure he was under.

"I have nowhere to go, mom! No money! Nothing! What the hell am I going to do? Please don't make me leave. I didn't do anything."

Patsy lit a cigarette and poured herself another glass of forgetfulness. She looked up at him, tears in her eyes. "This is not going to get any better here, Cav. It's gonna get worse. You better go. I mean it. It's time for you to go, son."

They argued a little longer, but Cav soon saw he was running out of options. She was resolute and becoming seriously more bitter by the minute. No choice. Cav had never seen her like this.

He packed a few belongings in his school backpack and went to the door. With tears in her eyes but a grim look, his mom handed him $200 in mostly small bills and slid some bags of snack food into his backpack. She looked up at him, gently shook her head and touched his cheek, and then turned and walked away.

The new chapter in Cav's life began.

3

How to Catch a Rising Star

Alone in the heat and darkness of a sweltering June night, Cav roamed the streets pondering his fate. Now homeless, the first problem was somewhere he could go, where he could stay, at least for a few days. Getting some kind of a job and a chance at a new life was second, but a place to sleep was number one.

On top of that, what was going to happen with school? It was over for the summer, but where would he be in September? Would he ever get an education?

Janie's basement would sure be nice as a crash pad. But he rejected that idea right away. Everyone in town had seen the news about his dad. It was too embarrassing to see Janie or any of the kids.

He walked for over an hour, and eventually found himself closer to downtown than he had intended. It was almost midnight, the streets were mostly deserted, and very little was open.

Twice he watched police cars slow down, giving him the once-over, before speeding up and away again. They saw a normal high school teenager with his backpack on his way home from a date or a late basketball practice. If they only knew, he thought. He had to have a story. Otherwise they'd pick him up, take him home, and probably charge his mom with some sort of crime.

There were lights ahead twinkling in the darkness. As he came closer Cav remembered it was Jasper's Pool Hall, the only business in town lit up like a Christmas tree until the wee hours every morning. For no understandable reason, he decided to take a bold approach and hit Jasper's up for a job. And out of that he might even find somewhere to stay.

Cav confidently walked into the pool hall and was struck at how much dimmer it was inside than it looked from outside. Well, when you looked towards the walls and corners that is. To Cav, who'd been walking in the dark for over an hour, the lights over the rows of pool tables were as bright as the noonday sun. He stepped further in and paused to look around. A few men sat on stools at the bar. And a dozen or more were perched on benches against the walls. Music played faintly overhead, but Cav was struck by the clicking of the pool balls and the aggressive "thunk" of cues striking cue balls and balls hitting pockets. To Cav the sounds were thrilling, real pool games were under way, so much more exciting than the silly clicks of playing stick-ring in Janie's basement.

Stand straight, be bold, he told himself. No one seemed to pay him any mind. Cav walked up to the counter and addressed the tall, middle-aged fellow behind the bar.

"May I please speak to the chairman of this noble institution?"

The man looked Cav up and down, and decided to play along jokingly with this kid to get a stir out of the dozen or more spectators at the bar and nearby benches.

"That would be me boy," the man said with a twinkle in his eyes. "They call me Jasper in these parts. I am the owner and 'chairman of this noble institution'."

Jasper was rewarded with chuckles rippling across the room. The customers—called "railbirds" in pool halls across the country—welcomed this unusual little drama. He continued to look with interest and an amused expression at this young buck, out and about long after his bedtime.

Jasper reached under the counter and flicked a switch, and the background music stopped playing. Play at the tables continued, most players unaware of the little drama underway up at the front. The nearby crowd, appreciating the distraction on this hot summer evening, quieted down to watch and listen as this underage newbie with attitude talked straight up to Jasper.

Quick to catch the spotlight, Cav picked up on most of this and seized the moment. He sensed that he had only one real shot at making a good and honest impression. Underage, no job, no home and on the edge of disaster, Cav came up with a crazy approach. He decided to just go all in, give it everything he's got like his life depended on it, which it pretty much did at the moment.

"The governor of this great state of Kansas told me to come and see if you needed any help here."

The locals leaned closer, smiles wider, intensely interested in how this would play out.

Jasper continued the back-and-forth with Cav, testing his claim. "Oh is that so, and who might that Governor be," Jasper asked, testing this boy's claim.

Cav was quick to respond. "Oh sir, that would be Samuel Dale Brownback, known as Sam to most folks."

The crowd, and Jasper, smiled and chuckled. Cav was winning them over. He had broken the ice and warmed up a bit, and boldly stepped even closer.

"Jasper is it?" he asked. "May I call you Jasper, sir?"

Jasper's expression softened slightly. "Yes, do please call me Jasper."

Now, unknown to Cav and all but a couple of his closest friends, Jasper shared a similar past—the tragic loss of being abandoned as a kid. Jasper's parents were killed in a car crash when he was a teenager, and that tragedy kept him locked in a situation similar to Cav's current crisis. Jasper suspected the same type of problem might be what brings Cav here at this very moment. Helpless, homeless, and desperate. Why else does a teenager ask for a job, and probably a place to sleep, in the middle of the night, and at a pool hall of all places?

"Okay. Well, boy, you got a name?"

"Yes, sir, I am Cavalier, but they call me Cav." Not revealing his last name to avoid the problems with his dad. "I won't let you down, sir. I will do my level best. At all times. Sir."

"Alright, Cav. How about we clean this joint up?" Quick on his feet, Cav said, "I'm on it like a duck on a June bug, Jasper, sir."

Jasper came out from behind the bar. "Follow me, Cav."

For Cav it was a lottery win. He was thrilled and thankful for Jasper's acceptance.

Jasper showed Cav the supply closet, brooms, mops, dustpans, assorted rags and sprays. Set him to work sweeping, and said he'd show Cav how to clean the tables later, after closing time.

"When is closing time, sir?" Cav had asked, as he began sweeping, wondering where and when he was going to sleep tonight.

"When it's time to close," Jasper answered, suspecting exactly those questions from Cav and not fully decided yet on how to deal with them.

"Okay," Cav said, and got straight to work sweeping the floors and emptying the trash baskets.

As Jasper was returning to his customary spot behind the bar, one of the regulars pulled him aside.

"Jasper, this boy has had it super tough. My girl Janie and he are best friends in school. She comes home crying so many days about how Cav was treated at home. That was his father, McTavish, killed in that bank robbery downtown the other day. And his mother is said to be a drunken whore. Tragic. He looks like a nice kid. I've only heard about him. He often comes over to the house but I've never seen him until now. Maybe his mother kicked him out of the house, or it's the pressure of losing his father. Or maybe he just thought it was better to skedaddle on his own."

Cav's story hit Jasper like a ton of bricks. He was at a loss for words. It was just as he had imagined.

"Thanks, Archie," he managed. "That explains a lot."

Jasper went into his office to recover from this sad news, so similar to his own experience as a kid. It affected him deeply. He shut the door and sat at his desk, wondering what the hell he's got himself into. This is a young boy, obviously desperate. Now it's confirmed what he suspected. This event sparked all the old memories of his own trials as a youngster, the sudden loss of both his parents at about Cav's age, and nobody and nowhere to run to for help.

After thinking about it, it came clear. Jasper decided he would help Cav—he had no other choice. The obligation and responsibility was right in his face, front and center: this boy was now his responsibility.

The decision weighed heavily on him, there could be legal challenges and so on with Cav being underage. But Jasper decided to do for Cav what Cav desperately needed—the kind of help that Jasper had never received himself when he lost both his parents. He wasn't going to let that happen to young Cavalier "Cav" McTavish.

Jasper came out and told Cav to leave the sweeping for a minute and follow him. In less than two minutes, Cav had a key to a small storeroom with a cot, blankets and a pillow, a lamp on an overturned crate as a side table, and a screened window opening onto the alleyway behind the building.

"This is yours as long as you need it," Jasper said. "There's always sandwiches in the fridge at the bar and Mason's Grocery is right down the street. We'll get more stuff in when we need it. Sound okay?"

Jasper put his hand out. For a few seconds Cav was speechless with surprise and gratitude. He took Jasper's hand and they shook hands. Looking into Jasper's eyes, Cav caught a glimpse of the father he'd always looked for and never found.

"I don't know what to say. I'm, like, just..." Cav stammered.

"I got it, Cav. I know," Jasper said, patting Cav's shoulder. "I've been there. Trust me. I understand. Just work hard and stay clean and believe in yourself. It won't be long 'til you have your own place. I'm sure of it." And he wasn't just blowing smoke. He sensed a strong center in this kid.

Cav McTavish was over the moon with gratitude. He had gotten a job and a place to stay all on the same night he lost his real home. So this was going to be his new home. And family. For a while, at least. Cav went back to sweeping with a new determination to make more good things happen in his life.

Jasper, on his part, made a mental note to make sure no one ever revealed to Cav that his friend Janie's dad had played a vital role in helping Cav get a new handle on his life. He called his assistant manager Harold over and explained the situation, and said Cav would have access to the snack bar and frig.

Harold nodded and smiled.

"I'll help look after the kid when you ain't around, boss. Don't worry. And I'll make sure he don't live on candy bars."

And with that, the new chapter in Cav's life began to take on real form.

4

Jasper's, Inc.

Jasper's Pool Hall was a famous high-stakes pool room, a hotspot for big cash games. Seasoned pool hustlers who crisscross the country looking for high-dollar pool action always visited Jasper's.

Whereas unlicensed gambling is generally against the law almost everywhere in America, and can sometimes lead to legal problems in larger towns and cities, in this little town Jasper's was left pretty much alone. And it didn't hurt that Clarence, the local precinct captain, nicknamed "the Sheriff" by the railbirds, was a big pool enthusiast, a close pal of Jasper's and a regular when big players were in town. In fact, when a high-interest money game shaped up, Jasper always called Clarence to get on over and enjoy the action.

Jasper's Pool Hall, however, was also where Cav was hoping to "find a solution to his immediate personal problems..." as well as create some long-term stability and promise of a real future. Cav had no personal aspirations or thoughts about the game of pool, never mind gambling on the outcome. But on his second night at the pool hall, he was introduced to an important aspect of the game he couldn't have imagined.

Cav was carefully mopping the floor near the bar when an interesting looking character sauntered over, ordered a beer from Harold, and carried it back to his bench where he resumed watching a couple of local amateurs playing 9-ball.

Cav realized that this same guy had been sitting there all last night and again tonight—same seat, quietly watching other guys play. Cav had thought he was just a fan with no home life to speak of.

What Cav didn't know was that this guy, Surfer Rod, was a money player who had a reputation for skillful play and a real love of gambling on pool. The important thing here was that Cav didn't know how Surfer Rod's lazy lack of action for two days was really pissing Jasper off. It took a sudden outburst from Jasper and a few comments from the patrons for Cav to learn this first lesson about pool, money, and pool hall denizens:

It's money action on the tables that gets more money action going in the room, so everyone has a chance to score big. That's why we're here!

So that's what made Jasper's popular to the local railbirds. Side bets, increasing odds, excitement, the stuff of life.

So here was Surfer Rod, walking in nearly two days ago with his leather cue case and attitude, and Jasper had immediately called Clarence the Sheriff who came right on over, along with a ton of railbirds. And here they all were, nearly two nights gone by, and Surfer Rod still just sitting there on his ass, and the guys playing 9-ball had already left.

Raising his voice and not so politely, Jasper demanded Surfer Rod better get his ass into some action but soon.

To which Surfer Rod, still with some attitude, replied, "Jasper, man, I just ain't ready."

So pointing to the sign on the wall that reads "No—No Gambling," Jasper fixed Surfer Rod with a dark look and told him he was "going to gamble or be arrested."

Surfer Rod just chuckled. "Let me get this straight. You're going to have me arrested for not gambling?" And he shook his head with a big smile and chuckled some more.

So Jasper looked over at Clarence and pointed to Surfer Rod and said, "Sheriff, arrest that man."

Clarence got up off his bar stool, pulled his handcuffs off his belt and started walking towards Surfer Rod, twirling the handcuffs around a finger so the steel sparkled in the lights from the empty table.

And young Cav watching all this with interest.

Surfer Rod wasted no time, got up real quick and pulled his cue out of his cue case. Clarence stopped twirling the cuffs and paused, watching.

Surfer Rod rested the cue against the wall, pulled a big wad of cash out of his pocket, slapped it on the table, and yelled, "Okay— so who wants to gamble?"

And that was the end of that little drama.

For Cav, it wasn't over. In fact, a new idea instantly found its way into this new chapter of his life. It bounced around in his head for the rest of the evening. He, Janie and their pals sometimes played Janie's toy game for nickels, dimes and quarters. It was fun without that, but somehow the dimes and quarters made it even more fun. A lot more in fact.

But this here at Jasper's was different. This was serious pool for serious money played by serious people. And the problem was that it looked too serious to ever be fun.

Really, anything worth doing should be fun. Right?

5

A Hustler's Education

The days at Jasper's passed into weeks, and the weeks into months. Cav grew acquainted with the Jasper's Pool Hall community, and he began to build real friendships with some of the regulars. Best of all, he formed a close bond with Jasper who became a real father figure. And Jasper seemed to enjoy the role. Cav especially appreciated Jasper's handling the school board (with help from the Sheriff) so that he wasn't on a list of wanted truants.

In his off time late at night, Cav was hitting balls around and his skill was increasing by leaps and bounds. Before long, he was playing informal games with some of the regulars, and he began winning many of them.

Jasper recognized great potential in Cav. It became obvious that he possessed a natural skill for pool, particularly 9-ball.[1]

---

1 "9-ball" explained: 9-balls shot in order 1 to 9. The goal is to pocket the money ball, the 9-ball. A 9-ball on the break wins, a combination that makes the 9-ball

He started daily coaching sessions, and over the span of several months as Cav's mentor, transformed him from an average player to pretty damn good.

Jasper also encouraged Cav to pay attention when money games were played. As well as shooting accurate pool, Jasper also took Cav through elements of high-stakes pool. He explained what was really going on, from the expected and accepted to the secrets of real hustling. Soon Cav understood the different levels of gambling and playing both good and bad pool for money.

One day, as they sat in a quiet corner chatting about winning pool, Jasper tapped his finger on Cav's forehead and said, "I sense there's a lot of noise up here."

"Yeah, I know what you mean—all those distractions inside my head and stuff. Sometimes it's annoying."

"That's right. You're playing toward perfection. It's called "the zone.' It's an area few players have ever experienced in their life. While the world's moving in super slow-mo, you are in super-fast mode! Nobody can catch you! You're making your own world,

---

wins, a luck shot that makes the 9-ball wins. Example, if my next ball, the object ball is the 3 ball and if I hit the 3 ball and pocket the 9-ball I win that game. A foul or "scratch" gives your opponent a free shot anywhere on the table. Example: My object ball is the 6 ball and I hit the 6 but no ball touches a rail, it's a foul, and a free shot for your opponent.)

"Roll-Out" Explained: After the break the first shot is allowed a "roll out"—I can strike the cue ball to stop anywhere on the table and give my opponent the option to shoot it from that position or give it back, and I must then shoot it at the one ball. The player must announce "rolling out" before he shoots this option, and state exactly what his intentions are, or it's a foul.

so to speak. A freight train could run through this joint and you wouldn't notice, you're that laser focused."

"Yeah! I know what you mean," Cav exclaimed with a big smile. "Sometimes when I'm practicing alone late at night I just can't miss. I play so good for hours like that. It's the most amazing feeling I ever had in my life."

Jasper nodded, "That's it."

"Really, man, my whole world changes," Cav said. "I don't think about, y'know, all the family stuff. Missing school. Not seeing Janie and my other friends. Like, I just see what I'm doing and see the future—like see the balls going in before I shoot, and then they do. It's kind of mysterious. But that's how I feel."

He looked at Jasper and added, "Weird huh?"

"I understand," Jasper said. "Yes, I've seen you in the zone a few times. It's rare; few players can hit that gear and rise to that skill level. But you clearly have the potential. Just keep doing what you're doing."

Cav saw that Jasper explaining the "zone" thing carried some weight. It was important.

"So," Jasper continued, "can you see how that noise in peoples heads gets in the way of accomplishing what they set out to do? How it interrupts concentration? It's usually some upsetting or annoying stuff in their life. If they can clean it up a bit, well, everything gets a whole lot easier. See?"

"That totally makes a lot of sense!" Cav really got it.

In a quieter voice, Jasper asked, "I've got a personal question for you, son."

That calling Cav "son" was like a little bomb going off for Cav. It really meant a lot even though he knew Jasper wasn't trying to be a father.

"You've told me a little about how rough things were when you left home. But it's been a while now," Jasper said. He leaned forward a little and asked, "How are you doing now? About all that?"

"A lot better Jasper. I don't worry about it anymore. When I do think about it...well, it doesn't seem to bother me. I don't know, I'm, like, I guess I'm getting past it."

The "son" and the question and the emotions of the moment really caught Cav by surprise. It had been many months since he'd left home and found a new life, new friends, a new family here at Jasper's.

"It's just like it's in the background of thinking. I don't sit and think about it. And it's totally gone when I hit the zone playing. So, like, it's cool."

"Good to hear that, Cav. So listen, just keep working on those center ball stuns and draws today. Ok? And if those bad feelings show up, put them into your shots. Blow them away."

"Okay? Thanks."

Jasper turned and walked back towards his office. Cav sat for some time, just buzzing over everything they'd talked about. He took to heart everything Jasper had said.

So much to think about. So much to learn. But Jasper was right. Everything felt better already. For the next few days, Cav worked like a madman getting through his chores so he could get to a table and practice with new determination. He was unlocking new levels of potential every day. Jasper was always there with encouragement and advice.

Also, from what he'd been witnessing on the tables some nights when money games were played, it sure was starting to look like making a pile of money shooting pool could be plenty of fun after all.

His dream of becoming a really skilled money player was more alive than ever. This was the new chapter in Cav's life, and it was really opening up and defining itself. He could see great things coming, and they seemed just around the corner.

6

From Zero To Hero

Two years, two months and 14 days had passed since Cavalier McTavish walked into Jasper's Pool Hall looking for salvation. Cav was noticeably taller now than that lost but hopeful 16-year-old boy, thanks to a late teen growth spurt. He still favored the longish dark blonde hair, and in fact he had become a good-looking young man who noticed the young ladies noticing him when they came in on the weekends to shoot pool with their boyfriends and girlfriends.

Not only was he a looker, he was a hell of a lot smarter. And sharper. And meaner. Young Cav had learned a trade that offered to make him seriously wealthy long before middle age. All he had to do was keep his nose to the green-felt grindstone and pay attention to Jasper's master lessons in the variations of pool playing and pool hustling.

Thanks to a suggestion from Jasper, Cav had reached out to his mom over a year ago and they sort of repaired their relationship.

Sort of. She'd been genuinely happy to learn that Cav had landed on his feet. But there'd been no apology or any indication that she'd mended her ways. They didn't talk again and a visit seemed out of the question. For Cav it was just okay, another lesson in how to toughen up and put it all into the shots.

This was his home. Right here was all the love he needed. And the future was whatever he personally decided to do with it. At last, Cav felt like he was in charge of his life. It was all up to him.

This morning, like most other early mornings and late nights, Jasper was coaching Cav on various aspects of gambling and winning at competitive pool. It was early, and quiet, still a couple of hours until the doors opened. No customers. No tables in play. Like every morning, Cav loved the atmosphere. There's something very special about the silence and the smells of a pool hall when it's empty, before all the lights are on, when it's still dark and nobody's there shooting pool. It's a kind of magical time machine where all of life has paused, silent, waiting for the first rack of balls, the whack of the break, the beginning and resumption of life as we know it.

They were sitting at the bar, Jasper nursing a mug of coffee, Cav with his usual morning bottle of Coca-Cola.

"There's something else I want to go over with you again. I want to go over it one more time."

"Shoot," Cav said, sipping his Coke. He loved learning all there was to know about playing and hustling.

"The score's tied. You have one ball left on the table. Make it, you win. Miss it, and you blow $10 grand." He paused, watching Cav closely.

"See what I'm sayin'?"

Cav nodded slowly. He knew Jasper was driving home the importance of the mental aspects of the game, playing a make-or-break money shot under tremendous pressure and not caving in to it.

But what was the essence of the lesson today? Surely Jasper would have some additional new insights to help Cav's game in such a situation.

Jasper started going over some new ways to help overcome the "noise," the mental stress, the thought disruptions that translate into a tenth of an inch tightness in the arm or hand or fingers or eyesight that mean a missed shot, and can send some pool players looking for another career. And Cav soaked up every bit of what Jasper had to say.

Of course they had covered this subject many times from all sorts of angles. But for 20 or more years, Jasper had studied this from every angle. His understanding of the depth and different layers of the mental states connected with this game was without question. To Cav, it was absolutely vital to his life, the new life he was set on creating. This was crucial knowledge, the kind that offers the clarity and confidence that makes or breaks careers.

Here's the bottom line, he thought for the thousandth time: Many players can learn to put most balls in pockets—making far more than they miss. But the tip-top 9-ball players can go through 3, 4 or 5, even a six-pack of racks, never missing a pocket no matter how tough some of the shots might be.

The great straight pool (also known as 14.1) players back in the day could pocket 10 or 20 racks in a row, 15 balls in a rack, 100 or 200 or even 300 or more balls, non-stop. What was their secret? It wasn't just accurately shooting balls into pockets. They had incredible focus and split-second decision-making under fantastic pressure.

"For example," Jasper said, "the great straight pool player Willie Mosconi set a world record back in 1954 pocketing 526 consecutive balls in a row, that's 35 racks plus 1 more ball, while people watched, some of 'em not too friendly, coughing, talking, all the little noises, people coming and going, Willie having to sit and wait 35 times for the reracks, and each time demolishing that rack, 35 of them, nonstop."

"It's the mental game," Jasper said. "That's where the real action takes place." And Cav really got it.

As the weeks went by, Cav dedicated every spare minute during his off time to playing and practicing and sliding into the zone. His game was improving by leaps and bounds, with each passing day mastering every kind of shot, pocketing balls from all angles, bank shots and playing position. The crowd at Jasper's witnessed Cav's progress, admiring his beautiful banks and long cut shots and his power breaks. Impressed by his skills, they encouraged him and cheered him on, recognizing this was the beginning of a true professional about to take on the world.

Over the months and years, with Jasper's help, Cav transformed himself from a rookie to a professional level hustler. He engaged in heated arguments, hustled older players, younger players, road players and local players. With each successful hustle, he earned the needed cabbage and established his reputation as a legitimate, certified money player.

The new chapter of the pool life had fully arrived.

7

Say Hi to Bongbong

One cold winter evening, Cav received a wake-up call from hell, and he was brutally humbled. This event would carry him forward for years.

A couple of guys showed up for a money game. You could always tell the player from the handler. The player was the one carrying the cue case.

They looked foreign and spoke English with an accent. Jasper introduced himself and Cav to the unknown entities. The player introduced himself as Bongbong. Bongbong's partner, his money man, stepped forward to negotiate a game. He pulled out a fat wad of cash and said he wanted to bet it up.

Bongbong asked to hit some balls to feel out the equipment.

"Sure, go ahead," Jasper advised. They wanted to see something before he put his boy in this match. This would give them some idea of his speed (meaning skill level in pool parlance). The room came to a halt, all the games finished up in the room, all the railbirds, everyone gathered round to watch the match.

Jasper pressed for a last name so he could make some calls and get a line on this stranger, get some kind of an idea of what speed this guy played at. Jasper called all his contacts and couldn't find out anything. No one knew anything about a "Bongbong" or had ever heard of this guy. A total stranger. They had no idea who this player was.

Bongbong opened his cue case, assembled his cue, and started hitting some balls. He played above average, a speed just better than a shortstop. ("Shortstop" is pool slang for a better than average player.)

Jasper and Cav watched every missed ball, looking at each other like they had the nuts, an easy win. It was decided that they would play 3 sets of 9-ball, a race to 20, best 2 out of 3 sets would win the money.

A set is 20 games, a "race to 20" is the first player to rack up (win) 20 games wins that set. Three sets, 60 games split 3 ways, best 2 out of 3 sets wins the match, and the cash.

They agreed to freeze up $10,000. Best two out of three sets would win the money. Jasper went back to the office and got his cash. Looking at each other's stack, they placed the cash on the lampshade above the table.

Bongbong won the coin toss. He broke and strung three racks together, an impressive start. Cav answered back. They played deep into the night, back and forth, hours passed, and they were both tied one set each.

Nine out of ten times when he did miss, he left Cav in a bad spot, hooked, snookered, forcing a very difficult shot. Was it luck or skill? Who knew. This wasn't the easy opponent Cav and Jasper calculated, but he was beatable as far as Cav was concerned. It was gambling, but at least they had a chance to win some money, maybe.

After tying the match at 1 set each, Bongbong's associate approached Jasper and asked if he would like to double the bet. He pulled out another $10,000 and laid it on the table. He told Jasper, "It's all we got."

Bongbong looked at Cav, and Cav gave Jasper a tiny nod like he was going to run away with it. Jasper agreed to another $5,000, not $10,000, the associate took $5,000 back, and now $30,000 sat on the lamp, $15,000 from each side.

Jasper was nervous, not showing it but not as confident as Cav. He suspected something, but he just didn't know what it was.

Yet.

So with the bet raised, and about five hours into the final set, everyone, including the railbirds, watched with increasing nervousness and Bongbong slowly crept up, overtook an amazed Cav, and won the third and final set, and all the cash. Not by a landslide but a decidedly favored win. Bongbong and Company had left nothing to chance; they were going to get the cash.

Well, these boys no doubt traveled a long way to get a good money game, and unfortunately Cav and Jasper were the victims. They got scalped, completely undressed—a huge loss for Cav in particular.

This was a wakeup call. Bongbong and Company grabbed the cash off the lamp and asked Jasper and Cav if they'd like to do another set. Jasper was inclined to say no thanks, and looked over at his pal Clarence the Sheriff, who gave Jasper a serious no-no head-shake to put a stop to it.

Bongbong and company politely said good night and left the pool hall $15,000 richer.

Now it was time for the after-game analysis.

If Jasper and Cav had been hustled, to Jasper it wasn't clear how, while to Cav it was a 100% mystery. Cav was shocked into disbelief.

In fact, it seemed as though no one in the pool hall had a clue what had happened. Cav had missed shots and lost position here and there, and it looked like the loss was all his fault, not some special skill of Bongbong's.

So if it was a hustle, it was brilliantly staged and executed to perfection.

While discussion went on among the railbirds, Clarence the Sheriff called Cav and Jasper over to share his findings and observations.

"I am sorry, but I didn't realize what they were doing until it was too late," Clarence explained. "You had already raised the bet. Then finally, late in that last set, too late, I saw what they were doing. Everyone was so hypnotized with the match, in a trance, including me, that it was really difficult to notice."

Clarence continued: "Bongbong played most of the time left-handed. But if Bongbong had a difficult shot, a shot that counted on him winning, a shot that really mattered, he always shot it right-handed. He wasn't a southpaw as we were led to believe. He was right-handed. Very clever system he employed. He perfected the art of switching left to right and it all looked perfectly natural. If he shot most of the three sets left-handed, as he did, how good was he really, full-on right-handed? This guy was an invader from another planet, an extra-terrestrial, some kind of ET motherfucker. Cav, you may have been playing one of best 9-ball players, if not the best, in the world. And nobody knew it."

Jasper licked his wounds and asked, "Who's next."

But this loss troubled Cav for weeks. His passion for winning pool had become his hope, guiding him out of the gloom and doom of his disastrous past. His dedication to the art of pool was evident in his unique style, his artistic form, and the masterful execution of his stroke. The surprising loss to Bongbong may have been the best motivation for Cav going forward. Playing pool was Cav's ticket, a path for him to rise to heights he could only dream about and become world-class someday. Having played Bongbong and suffered a tremendous loss, not because he played badly but because he was hustled, it demanded Cav to bring his skill level up a few balls better.

It was a tough lesson to learn for Jasper, as well.

Cav started working furiously on perfecting the art of the jump shot. He'd blown two of them in the match against Bongbong. He practiced every night increasing his ability to jump balls with his main cue, 57½ inches (148 cm), not just with the shorter jump stick.

Jasper was very impressed with Cav's progress, and with just how serious Cav was about his pool and winning.

A few weeks after the Bongbong fiasco, he made something of an announcement to Cav.

"Well, kid, as you know, this is the time of year when pool slows down here and heats up back east. I pull the plug here for a few months and leave the establishment in the capable hands of Harold, and go on the road to pick up some of that loose money back east. You've seen me go and come back with a happy smile and sometimes a not so happy smile. But always a smile.

Cav was waiting for the punch line. He was delighted when it arrived.

"So, my boy, it's about time you accompany me, and we get out and enjoy ourselves and go get some cash. I say you're ready, kid, as ready as you'll ever be. Nobody knows of you back there. You, for the most part, are an unknown person, and we can trap a whole bunch of chumps back east."

Cav really lit up. "Hell yeah, Jasper! I'm all in. Let's go make some money."

"I'll tie up some loose ends, and we can beat a path to Philly in a few days," Jasper said.

Cav was over the moon about his first road trip as a pro money player.

A couple of days later, as they were packing Jasper's beautiful old Caddy convertible, Jasper yelled into the wind, "Gonna show y'all my tail lights."

They drove off into a beautiful sunrise, heading east for Philadelphia, setting the stage for another new chapter in Cav's journey.

8

History Revisited

Three days of pleasant driving brought Cav and Jasper to the busy streets of Philadelphia. In the heart of the city, they found themselves at Mosconi's, a downtown pool hall known for high-dollar pool action and named after the famous player of the past, Willie Mosconi, himself a native of Philly.

As Jasper handed over the convertible at a full-service gas station, he instructed the attendant, "Fill 'er up, and oh, can you check the oil?"

With the car attended to, Jasper and Cav set their cell phones to "vibrate." They were going to replicate an old hustle of Jasper's that, he explained to Cav, used "pagers" long before cell phones were even thought of. And then he had to explain what pagers were.

They made their way into the old pool hall, greeted by the familiar haze of smoke and the clicking of pool balls striking other pool balls. It was late afternoon, drifting into early evening. Men were playing poker at a side table, the bar was loaded with the usual suspects, and a couple of guys were arguing about a pool shot—the typical and so familiar pool room atmosphere that Cav had spent the last few years growing up in, and that Jasper owned and operated for profit.

This was Cav's first real hustle, and he was almost vibrating with excitement. But he managed to rein it in and appear calm and relaxed, just as Jasper had trained him.

The bartender, eyeing Cav and Jasper, offered Jasper a drink. "You just drivin' through?"

"Give me a JTS Brown and give the kid a Coke," Jasper said. "Yeah, we're headed to Poughkeepsie. The family hired me to drive the kid to his uncle's. How far is it?"

The bartender, wiping down a glass, said, "Oh, it's about three hours up the road, two-and-a-half if traffic's light."

Cav looked around the room as the duo plotted to make their mark in the City of Brotherly Love. That Cav was an unknown entity led to one thing: get in quick, fast and loose, "get the cash," and get out.

The timing was calculated by Jasper, around 6-ish when the stiffs got off work and arrived, looking for action. Cav pretended excitement at the sight of an empty pool table, one he seized as the perfect site for the takedown and hustle. Easy access to the exits, bathroom, and perfect visibility, typically the money table in most rooms. Cav rolled some balls to see the high-low spots, how level the table played, and how balls rebounded off the rails.

Jasper, the pretended wise man, reminded Cav, "Now kid, you remember what happened the last time we saw a pool table." Jasper whispered to the rail and the bartender, "He blew $3,000."

This carefully arranged scene was a show, a method to build excitement and get the crowd thinking, wake 'em up, get the gambling started, get the money moving.

Cav shouted to Jasper loud enough for the room to hear, "Come on, you have to give me a chance to win my money back!" Jasper looked at the crowd and the bartender. "You see what I mean?" The room started buzzing with a little excitement as the duo engaged in their drama, setting the stage.

While Cav was messing around the pool table, Jasper shared with the bar just who this golden boy was. Barely 20, tall and good-looking, even wealthy looking!

"This kid is the grandson of that big shot business tycoon, y'know that chairman of Union Carbide, who was the kid's grandfather; he recently passed away. The kid and his parents inherited the fortune, the entire estate. The kid was tight with his grandfather and Gramps never forgot it."

Now the railbirds were really waking up.

"He's got $25 million waiting for him in a trust fund when he grows up," Jasper said to the bartender while everyone nearby listened. "Meanwhile, the kid was given enough money monthly to choke a horse. I feel a little guilty gambling with him, it's so easy to win money and he doesn't care."

Jasper turned and watched Cav trying a tricky bank shot, over and over. "You're going to lose all your money on that damn crazy shot. Now knock it off."

After a dramatic pause, Jasper declared out loud, "Kid, you got one shot at getting back a thousand." The greed factor and the idea of all that loose cash began to show potential among the railbirds.

Jasper had planted the seed, and the room was now suddenly interested. The slightest mention of $1000 action, and loose money to be made, drew the room in like a magnet.

Games started quitting, the poker table folded up, and everyone drifted toward the action. It was now all eyes on the kid and the cash.

The bartender, eager to be part of the action, asked to be included in the betting. With a loud cash register ringing, he opened the cash register, revealing a substantial wad of cash. This was exactly the response Jasper wanted. The bartender's involvement instantly added credibility and built trust instantly with all the gamblers, laying the groundwork for their perfectly organized hustle. With no words, Jasper had properly identified the bartender as the owner; the bartender proved this when he offered up the cash from the cash register as "his money." All very good signs.

Playing his part to perfection, Cav pointed at Jasper and snapped, "No, hell no. I want his money. He has my money, and I want it back." Cav pulled out a large wad of cash, about $10,000. Counting off $1000, he placed the $9,000 on the table in one stack and the $1,000 in another separate stack.

This calculated move raised the idea from betting hundreds of dollars to thousands of dollars. The other move in plain sight was the loose $9,000; it represented possible money to be won by gambling with the kid. This awakened the rail and the bartender's greed for a big score. They saw that stack of cash and went to dreamland.

Cav refusing the bartender was a move; this only intensified the bartender's impulse, demanding to get in on the easy money.

A railbird, frustrated and all fired up, yelled, "Who gives a damn where the money comes from?"

The idea of getting a piece of this easy money seemed even more possible every second. The urge to get a part of that fat wad of cash from the kid was irresistible. The room was consumed with getting the kid's money. The con was making it look like the old man and the kid were together but both independent of the other. In this sense, outsiders saw the old man as a guardian, not a father, which was easy because it was true.

Cav lined up a pool shot between him and Jasper for the $1000; the kid blew it. Missed the shot, made a mess out of it. Jasper walked over, collected his thousand dollars, flashing it to the crowd. That simple act, betting and winning the $1000, established that the two of them were not related, just traveling together. What did matter was that the kid was loaded and wanted to gamble.

Jasper just proved the easy money. With a wide smile he announced to the crowd, "Like shooting fish in a barrel!"

Cav, pretending to be frustrated and playing the pissed-off sucker to perfection, added a touch of drama to the scene. The rail responded with laughter, eager to bet faster and with more cash.

Jasper needed some time to let that rumor about the golden boy and his wealth grow arms and legs amongst the crowd. That whisper campaign would spread throughout the room like a wildfire. Jasper told the kid out loud he was going to check on the car and asked the bartender to watch out for the kid, establishing a fake, phony trust between Jasper and the owner/bartender. Jasper left and gave it about 10 minutes for their story to spread.

9

Get the Cash

Jasper and Cav both knew the railbirds needed to get more cash down there for it to be a good score. Their hustle was starting to make some progress as the railbirds were on the phone calling in friends, family, in-laws, and outlaws to bring in the cash. Half the people in the place were pulling out their cell phones and making urgent calls to friends and family to bring some cash over here now! Fast!

One of the railbirds was overheard shouting into his phone, "There's some loose money that just showed up from out of town. This kid is down here with a ton of cash; I just saw him lose $1,000. He put $10,000 on the table, I ain't fuckin around here, you need to get your ass over here fast or you'll miss out; bring me five grand now!" Another railbird was heard on his phone, "Some kid over here has $10 grand, he just blew a thousand, easy money. How much cash can you get me over here at the pool hall and fast? Bring all the cash you can, quick." And another said, "There is some kid over here with a stack of cash to blow, easy money. Hurry up, or you will miss out."

At this phase of the hustle, it was running on automatic.

Cav pocketed his $9 grand and slipped into the bathroom, intentionally stalling to allow for the chumps to arrive with the big cash. As the big money started to roll in, Cav returned to his table and set up some hundred-dollar bets with some of the locals to show and demonstrate to the bigger money, sucker bets. With the wad of several thousand dollars back on the table, it confirmed what they were told over the phone—the kid was a sucker with a lot of cash.

Cav set up a shot that he missed and lost a few hundred dollars to a few railbirds. He did another round of investing/losing a few hundred until he was certain all the big money had arrived, they had seen him losing, all that money moving, and that stack of cash sitting loose on the table for the taking. The energy and excitement was moving in the right direction.

Jasper, aware of the timing of this hustle, knew the "go time" was near. There was a small amount of time once the bigger money showed up for this particular hustle to work. If it dragged on too long, people would start to wake up out of their trance of easy money. Jasper came back in from allegedly going to the garage next door, and set the stage for the final act of this very-well-executed hustle.

"I'm leaving for Poughkeepsie," Jasper declared loudly to Cav. "Don't waste your money on that damn fool shot!" And he turned and started back out the door.

Following the script, Cav followed Jasper out the door, leaving his stack of cash on the table for the crowd to see what could be won.

With Jasper leaving, the kid on his own established it was the kid's own money. All of a sudden, it all became clear; the kid was on his own with all that cash to bet and to lose as he wished.

The railbirds and small-time-hustlers in this pool hall hadn't ever seen a couple of real polished professional hustlers like Jasper and Cav. A hustler could only be hustled by a better hustler. And as the pressure built, Cav returned. His task now was to get to the final big money shot, get the cash, and get out of there unharmed. Cav was there alone with a ton of cash; it was a gamble. He had been very well educated. This was his very first really big hustle. But he knew exactly what to do and when to do it.

He was strapped with a .38 revolver around his ankle just in case anything got crazy. Jasper had taken him to the range regularly, and he was well trained in using his pistol.

He looked around and was sure all the money had arrived. Cav could now get the bet made and perform the final act, "the money shot."

Now the center of attention, Cav announced to the room, "Okay, this is all I got, and I got no more." He piled up the cash for them to bet, "I will bet it all on this shot." He lined up the cue ball frozen against the 8 ball, with the 8 ball tight on the rail, for an impossible looking bank shot into the far corner pocket. "I will bet it all I can make this shot for the rest of my cash." Pulling another wad of cash, $6000, out of his pockets, money he got when he followed Jasper outside, Cav added the $6000 to the $9,000, setting the $15,000 on the table. He stacked it all nice and pretty for everyone to see what they could win from the kid. Cav started taking all the bets placed. The room was filled with explosive excitement as they counted out $15,000 cash; it was all on the table, setting the stage for the brilliant climax of this carefully organized hustle. They sorted out all the bets and amounts.

As Cav was approaching the maximum amount of the opponents' bets, one from the crowd chirped, "I want in; I'll do 7 to 5 for $500."

Cav, with unwavering confidence, answered, "Honey hush, no dice, even money, mister." The guy walked over and handed Cav the $500.

All the thousands of dollars kept pouring in; everyone demanded to get in on the action, and soon the bartender was slapping his money on the table. This all built up to this impossible bank shot. Cav took each bet and started piles of bets stacked around the table on the rails toward the exit in plain view.

Adding a sense of urgency, Cav explained, "My ride is waiting, and I have to be in Poughkeepsie in three hours. All this cash is yours if I miss this bank shot. But if I happen to make it, I'm leaving with that cash. Right? 'Poughkeepsie—or bust!' The crowd all looked like trained seals, nodding their heads yes to the kid. The bartender stepped in as the representative for all the house bets, to clarify and confirm the bet for all his customers and for himself.

The bartender asked the $15,000 question: "So, we're all on the same page here, and we all understand this, you're going to bank the 8 ball that's frozen to the cue ball against the rail, and pocket it here," he pointed to the designated opposite corner pocket. Cav confirmed, "Yes sir." The bartender immediately responded, "I'll take that action for another $3000," placing that $3,000 on the table.

That big, tall stack of cash Cav started with was now a little stack. Cav counted it out to the crowd, "I got $700 left, and that's all I have." Of course, the bartender wanted that too and took the plunge. All monies were now all in, all $30,000. There it all sat, $30,000 wide open on the table in small stacks.

Cav excused himself to go to the bathroom. In private, he texted Jasper to call the cops and Jasper got the text. As he came back to the table, he heard Jasper honking his horn once, signaling the police had been called.

This honking of his horn had a two-fold effect. It meant there was an urgency now to get the hustle rolling or lose out, because Cav might have to get out of there in a hurry. And it also demanded he get the crowd to bet everything they've got quick, or they might lose out. Cav knew that Jasper had now called the cops. And it looked like everyone, the entire room, was all in with their cash.

Just as all the bets were set, Jasper signaled the arrival of the police with another 2 honks. Cav, under tremendous pressure of their hustle going bust, shot and made the shot, pocketing the 8 ball in the corner pocket.

"Sorry, boys. I got lucky," Cav announced, and quickly scooped up all the stacks of cash and stuffed it in his jacket pockets. The crowd was speechless. They couldn't believe what just happened, but they saw it: he did it, he made the shot, and they lost the bet.

Outside, loud sirens blared, announcing the arrival of the local cavalry, like clockwork. The cops burst in as Cav was making his quiet exit, a couple of the police passing him by, unaware that the hustler they passed by had just pulled off one of the most strategic, brilliant con jobs in the history of Mosconi's.

The cops approached the bartender. "I hear you boys are gambling in here."

The bartender, exhausted and fully aware of the masterful hustle that had just played out, which he approved and co-signed, paused for a minute and told the cops, "No sir, not gambling, but I feel like we just got robbed."

After a brief inspection of the room, the cops decided there was no violence and no gambling to bust anyone for. But suspecting the nature of the situation, they chuckled among themselves and finally left, giving Jasper and Cav plenty of time to leave town.

While the cops were snooping around the pool hall, Cav raced to the car and jumped in, spilling all the cash on Jasper. As they sped off they were both laughing like maniacs, leaving behind a confused crowd in a pool hall that was only the first stop of many in the coming months, a great start for their tour and one of the great pool hustles ever pulled off in "The City of Brotherly Love."

Jasper had masterminded this plan very well. He had to figure a way out for a young Cav, holding a ton of cash, about $30,000, by himself. How could they provide a safe exit amongst a crowd of pissed-off hooligans and thugs? How could he ensure absolute 100% safety? There was only one way; he needed the cops to provide Cav's security and a safe exit with all that cash. It was brilliant!

Great score, great start, great confidence booster.

For the next couple of months, they traveled up and down the eastern coastal cities from Boston and New York to Miami. They ended up back in Kansas with about $80,000 cash profit, "no new taxes," and the memories of five-star accommodations and fine cuisine at each stop—a first-class, highly-paid vacation.

10

The City Of Angels

As the years passed, Cav and Jasper continued to score big wins as well as occasional losses, fixing Cav's reputation as a highly-skilled money player. He evolved to a point where he was expected to "spot" handicap most opponents just to stay in action, proof of his exceptional skill level.

Having matured and reached adulthood at Jasper's, with occasional road trips hustling in other cities and states, Cav decided it was time to bust out of Kansas and seek new opportunities and challenges across the country and even the world. He set his heart on visiting California first, and then seeing where life would take him after that.

As the years went by, Cav made many friends among the regular players and railbirds at Jasper's. Good fortune had smiled broadly in the person of Jimmy Jones, a regular at Jasper's and an enthusiastic and fairly decent amateur player and lover of competitive pool, especially 9-ball. Jimmy and Cav were about the same age, and over the last couple of years became best friends. They played pool for fun, but Jimmy became an excellent coach and training partner, helping improve Cav's 9-ball game even more.

Sometimes, the two young men would sit with a couple of beers and just fantasize about cashing in on that big, life-changing hustle of all hustles. It always prompted big smiles, but make no mistake, it was also a dead serious subject of discussion. And Jimmy was all for Cav trying his luck in Cali.

Not one to miss anything going on in his pool hall, one evening Jasper called the two young men over for a chat. He wanted to make a proposition that, to him, made perfect sense.

"Listen up, you two. I'm getting too old and in fact I'm too busy running this joint to handle the kind of year-round travel that's certainly in Cav's best interests," Jasper said. "So why don't I share some of my experience with Jimmy here about handling the road hustle, and you two just go ahead and manage your future as business partners?"

Jimmy and Cav exchanged smiles. "Sounds perfect," Jimmy said. "In fact, me and Cav have already talked about something like that."

"Yeah, Jasper, I'm all for it," Cav agreed. "But only as long as you're near a phone when we need you. And I'm sure we will."

"I'm always near a phone somewhere," Jasper said. "Call any time."

Over the next few weeks, for a couple or three hours a day, Jasper shared his 25 years of experience—about setting up super-smooth hustles, managing bankrolls on the road and dozens of small details that help keep players winning and out of local jails and emergency wards. Jimmy quit his no-future job at the warehouse and concentrated on soaking up everything Jasper had to say. As the lessons grew even more detailed, and Jimmy asked all the right questions, Jasper said he was "shaping up to be a good road manager."

Planning for the escape to California—lining up contacts, a place to stay, scouting potential matches—was fairly easy. Saying goodbye to Jasper was tough. Cav's mentor had taught him everything he knew about winning pool and pulling off successful hustles. Best of all, he had also shown Cav how to be a man, to be kind and be tough and have standards, and true to oneself and one's friends.

As for Jimmy, by the time they were ready to leave for L.A. he was already lining up matches with West Coast players.

Things were really starting to heat up.

The night before their planned escape, the crowd at Jasper's threw a big Goodbye Party to wish Cav and Jimmy success on their new adventures in California. No tears, just a lot of back-slapping and hoots and hollers to "kick some SoCal ass and score big" and "watch out for them earthquakes spoiling your shot on the 9-ball!"

And so, they left Kansas and began a great new journey. In a slightly beat-up older Toyota, Cav and Jimmy arrived a few days later in Los Angeles, California—The City of Angels—11 million people living, loving, and dying in a 470-square-mile concrete playground of endless sunshine and wishful dreams. The streets of L.A. became the new frontier, a perfect setting for this new chapter in Cav's pool hustling journey—bigger games and greater scores in the volatile world of head-to-head high-dollar 9-ball.

In the first few weeks, Cav and Jimmy made some serious cash in several pool halls around Greater L.A. But as word got around, they scored even more in the private billiard rooms of some very fancy Beverly Hills mansions.

Good news travels fast. Within just a few weeks, Jimmy was getting calls and offers from not just around L.A., but across the country. Word was spreading, backers were hungry for games. They wanted action. Cav was being offered matches with some of the world's best and biggest money players, really tough muscle matches—not hustles, just head-to-head pool for serious stakes.

One day, Jimmy received a very special offer that rose far above the rest. It was the biggest purse they'd ever played for. And Cav would be heavily favored. For Cav it would be soft action. But there was a problem. It was way down south—in beautiful Rio de Janeiro, Brazil. That sounded great, but neither of them had ever been out of the country. They knew nothing about passports, and they'd need travel visas—whatever the hell those are.

Jimmy didn't tell Cav about any of this. They still had a lot of action lined up in L.A. Instead of filling Cav's head with worrisome details, he needed to consult with Jasper. It would be fun calling and reporting on their latest successes.

11

Great News From Rio

It was a perfect California day as the two pool bums, Cav at the wheel and Jimmy looking out the window, drove relaxed up glitzy Rodeo Drive in Beverly Hills, a million miles from their country bumpkin life back in Kansas.

On their way to meet a potential private player, Cav and Jimmy were enjoying their drive through the expensive streets of Beverly Hills, admiring the beautiful half-dressed, wanna-be hotties from around the country and the world, all hoping to be "discovered." Cav, blond hair flying in the breeze, smiled and waved at the cuties and got plenty of smiles in return in spite of the clunker they were driving.

Jimmy had been waiting to surprise Cav with the explosive south-of-the-border news. Now seemed like as good a time as any to tell him.

"Hey Cav, guess who called and wants to play some real high-dollar 9-ball?"

Cav, curious, was all ears: "Who?"

Jimmy, enjoying the drama, revealed the challenge from another high-stakes pool player: "Fred!"

"You mean that guy Fredrico from Brazil? That me and Jasper hustled in Boston last year?"

"Yeah, the very one!"

"Why didn't you tell me earlier?"

Laughing, Jimmy said, "I just wanted to surprise the hell outa you!"

Cav, in disbelief, pulled over and stopped the car. He looked Jimmy straight in the eyes. The mention of Fredrico screamed the sexy sounds of money-counting machines in the back rooms of banks and casinos, of million-dollar slot machines rolling million-dollar jackpots, alarm bells and police whistles.

They both knew that if Fredrico could be trapped in a real money game, it's the lottery!

There had been rumors swirling around about Fredrico and some billionaire backer for months, a backer that spelled a bottomless pit of money.

All cocky and filled with excitement, Cav actually yelled, "Get that motherfucker up here! Tell him he's got the 8!"

In 9-ball, the 8 is a spot, a handicap of one less ball to pocket to win the game, giving the opponent now 2 money balls, the 8- and the 9-ball. Offering the 8 is used to attract opponents who play at a lower skill level.

Jimmy couldn't contain his laughter. "You're not going to believe this shit. I already set it up tight. Fredrico sounded hungry for action, even desperate! Get this. He told me he would play you even, no spot. But there's a catch. He won't come here. That's the only catch. He says we have to go there."

Cav's expression was like, So what? Where do I sign?

Jimmy had more: "Listen to this shit. I negotiated if we go there, we freeze up $200,000, do a best 2 out of 3 sets and they pay all our travel expenses."

"When was all this?" Cav demanded, smiling. "We've got a little more than 200 stashed now, right? So why didn't you tell me?" Still all smiles.

"Never mind, man! In two weeks we're goin' to motherfuckin' Rio de Janeiro and win us 200 large!"[2]

Cav was blown away, and they both started shouting, "Fuckin' Rio!"

Cav was overjoyed, more excited than ever up until now. "This is crazy, bro! The nuts! Say bye-bye to the nits, hello Brazil!"

The possibility of a high dollar game in Rio de Janeiro sparked their imaginations of an exotic fantasy land, impossibly far away, yet now becoming a reality. And only two weeks away!

Cav knew if they could pull this off and win, they'd be flush, no, actually rich, no need to worry about money again for a very long time.

If they could win. If.

With $400,000 staring both of them in the face, the path to receiving it was the easiest, because Cav had the chops to go into any pool room on the planet and win most of the time. He was playing real good, real solid.

---

2 "Large" means $1000; "200 large" = $200,000.

If ever there was an adventure, all-paid travel, hotel, food, everything comped, free, this was the big one. A city known around the world to be the most beautiful. The beaches as far as you can see. Music in a class all its own, the samba, bossa nova.

As an additional bonus, the focus for Cav and Jimmy would be the search for "The Girl From Ipanema"—or anything similar. Rio was Fantasy Island on steroids. This was the chance to make the score of a lifetime or bust out broke but happy.

12

The Billionaire Backer

Word on the street had been that Fredrico's big-shot, ultra-wealthy Brazilian backer controlled the emerald trade in South America. The very seductive possibility of a big fat score in Rio kept Cav and Jimmy up all night, fantasizing about everything this trip promised for their future.

A couple of days later, Cav and Jimmy were driving up Rodeo Drive again, this time with Jimmy at the wheel. Cav started putting the pieces together and raised a concern.

"Wait a minute, Jimmy. What about the cash? We can't carry that kind of cash down there."

Jimmy, ever the problem-solver, assured Cav it was already set up. "I spoke to my banker friend. The bank here notifies the bank there and wires the money from our bank to the bank there. Problem solved, easy cash transfer. We just have to show it to the IRS. You pay your taxes, right?"

Cav, trying to play it cool: "Oh, hell yeah. I pays some taxes."

Jimmy knew Cav didn't pay any taxes and that Cav was completely shitting him. Just for fun, Jimmy challenged him: "Okay wigger, what's your social security number? Come on, quick."

Cav, with a grin, responded, "I don't fuckin' know, never knew my social security number. But I gots a website. ... What a country. I love this country."

Jimmy pulled over and parked the beat-up Toyota right behind a yellow Bugatti. They each took a moment to admire the expensive car.

Jimmy turned to Cav and laid out the plan. "So I got this shit all set up, flights, hotels. And the special handling of the bank transfer avoids complications. Just to test Fredrico I asked for first class flights and the fuckin' guy said hell yeah. I figured Mr. Billionaire was payin' for it so what's it matter. We gin it in Rio, and we are set for life!"

Jimmy had tightened up the business side of things, organizing everything for their trip to Rio. Seriously jacked, Cav asked, "When do we leave? Where do I sign? Lock it down! Let's go!"

"We play our cards right," Jimmy said, pointing to the yellow Bugatti, "and it won't be long before we can buy two of those. One each. They're a mill and up used."

For the next week-and-a-half Cav and Jimmy wormed and weaseled through the red tape and managed to get passports.

Jimmy informed Cav they also needed to get visas to travel to Rio. Neither of them had ever traveled outside of the USA and they both were clueless about visas.

"What the hell is a visa, anyway?" Cav asked Jimmy. "I'll call Fredrico and see what's what." Jimmy called
Rio and left a message for Fredrico asking about visas.

Within an hour Fredrico called Jimmy back and told him to go straight to the Brazilian Consulate in L.A. and speak to the receptionist. He explained that his backer had special connections at the Consulate and that the visas would be issued on the spot. True to his word, as soon as the pool bums showed up at the Consulate, their passports were stamped and each was issued a 60-day visa.

Cav's life took a new turn in a direction that no one had even imagined.

13

In the Wind, Due South

The two weeks were up, and Cav and Jimmy took a cab to LAX and boarded their plane to Rio. They had all their papers in order and were on a direct flight from Los Angeles International to Galeão, Antonio Carlos Jobim International Airport in Rio.

It was a long 20-hour flight. They settled into their first class seats and immediately started discussing what they were going to do with all the money they would win from the big-shot billionaire in Rio. They were wined and dined on the flight and rested the best they could.

As the plane descended over Rio, they looked out the window at the breathtaking view over Copacabana and Ipanema Beach coupled with a close up view of Christ the Redeemer, the world-famous 98- foot statue of Jesus. The captain announced the final descent to Antonio Carlos Jobim International. Upon arriving at the airport, they were met by a very pretty lady carrying a sign with their names on it.

She escorted them to immigration, where the immigration officer was waiting for them. Everything was pre-arranged ahead of time as if they were diplomats. Immigration stamped their passports without questions, and the lady then escorted them to baggage claim, where they collected their luggage. She then escorted them to customs. Every move was pre-arranged.

Just who was this lady, who could whisk two pool hustlers through customs with privileges reserved for A-list celebrities and diplomats? Customs didn't check their luggage, the customs officer just told them to go ahead. Little did they know this would have been the safest customs counter in the world to smuggle in guns, heroin, cocaine, explosives—no questions, no search, good to go.

Their guide escorted them outside to a waiting chauffeured car which promptly dropped them at an upscale-looking hotel. As far as Jimmy and Cav were concerned this was just the way things worked down here. They were essentially clueless to what had just happened.

They settled into their hotel suite, and Jimmy called Fredrico to let him know they'd arrived. Of course he already knew because he had set everything up including their very pretty escort. But Fredrico provided them with the address and a start date for them to meet and play some high-dollar 9-ball.

The next morning, they asked the desk clerk to call them a cab to take them to the bank recommended by Jimmy's banker friend, and then on to the pool hall. All they had were two addresses from Fredrico that Jimmy had scribbled down on a piece of paper.

The taxi picked them up and waited while they went into the bank and withdrew the "cabbage" they had wired before leaving L.A. Concealing that much cash between the two of them was no small feat.

When they got back to the cab with $200,000 cash stuffed into their pockets, they realized they were in a cab being driven by a total stranger who spoke no English, and they sure as hell didn't speak Portuguese. Jimmy pointed to the second address for the driver, and now they began a confusing ride through unknown streets to an unknown destination in a strange city in a foreign land they had never been to before, carrying enough money to make them targets to be robbed—or worse, killed—if anyone knew. Most men would have needed balls of steel to attempt such a risk, Jimmy thought, like, well, gambling men, like two high-dollar pool hustlers from the U.S.A.

Hopefully, the driver could read Jimmy's scribbly handwriting on that slip of paper and knew where to take them.

As they drove away from the bank it became a nerve-wracking ride from hell to the pool hall. Reality started to get to them about how stupid it was to even attempt to do it in the first place, carrying all that cash. But it was too late, they were carrying all the money they had to their names, savings from their gambling that took two years in L.A. to win and save, just sitting here in their pockets.

The ride just seemed to get more intense with every minute, but went insane when the driver sped up and pointed at a dark car following, trailing their taxi. This went on for about 15 minutes, with the driver cutting in and out and going in circles, obviously suspecting trouble. Thinking he had lost the car behind them, he pulled over to look at the address again and they all looked around, scanning the streets. The driver just shrugged. He was lost. Suddenly the car that had been following them pulled up alongside. Jimmy and Cav froze, their hearts just stopped. They knew this was it; they'd been set up, and this was the shakedown for their $200 grand.

A burly, tough looking man got out of the dark car and, stepping closer to the cab, tapped on the driver's window. The driver, clearly afraid, lowered it slowly, and the big guy leaned in and explained in Portuguese, with intermittent translations in decent English loud enough for the boys in the back, that they'd been tailing the cab all the way from the hotel because they were ordered "by the boss" to "provide security." He apparently gave the lost cab driver directions to the pool hall and then actually managed a weird smile.

The security guys jetted off into the wind with the cab driver close behind. Cav and Jimmy were breathing normally again, both feeling as if they'd just got their first experience with what could only be called "fear of death."

As they climbed out of the cab at the pool hall, Jimmy handed the driver $200, probably a month's worth of cab fare, and got what seemed to be a profuse thanks in Portuguese.

The pool hall was just that, a pool hall—thick with smoke and echoing with the old familiar sounds of billiard balls clicking against each other and the exciting crash of an 8 ball rack breaking and then the slightly lighter sound of a 9-ball break. They were home again.

It was an old room and had had a lot of use with typical pics on the walls—framed movie posters of "The Hustler" with Jackie Gleason and Paul Newman and others of Tom Cruise as Vincent with Paul Newman in "The Color of Money."

Fredrico and Davi, the pool hall manager, were there to greet them. "Guests! Welcome to Rio!"

14

Flip It

Jimmy took the lead after exchanging handshakes and greetings. "I thought we were getting jacked on the way over here from the bank. This fuckin' car was following us; we were holding all that cabbage in the car, a major scare for us. Cav was sure it was a shakedown. The cabby tried to speak English, we couldn't understand a word. I'd never do it again. Anyway, we made it."

"You see we do things a bit differently here," Fredrico said. "You're not in Kansas anymore." They all had a laugh.

Back to the business at hand, Jimmy asked Fredrico, "Let's see the color of your money." A bagman appeared from the back with a green duffle bag, dumping the $200,000 on the table right in front of the boys.

Cav looked at Jimmy and Fredrico in fear: "Did we land on another planet? You would just expose all this cash to any and everyone, right here in broad daylight?"

"Cav, people around these parts here know their limitations," Fredrico explained. "Besides, the owner has a reputation that pretty much says don't fuck around in here. Every punk robber that made that fatal mistake of fucking around here—about five guys over the years—have been hunted down and whacked by the owner. We enjoy a private justice system here."

Cav and Jimmy had a good laugh at that one.

"Okay, so, Fredrico, we brought the 200 large." The boys followed Fredrico's lead and emptied their pockets, spilling 8 smaller bags of cash on the table. Jimmy examined Fredrico's money, and Davi, the pool hall manager, examined Jimmy and Cav's money. With all the cash accounted for, the 400 large was put into the green duffle bag and the four of them were escorted back to the office where all the money was safely locked up in a sizable vault.

Jimmy confirmed the match structure. "We're doing a head-set[3] to 10 games each set. Best 2 out of 3 of the head-sets wins the cash. Is that what we agreed to, Fredrico?"

Fredrico agreed. "Yeah, that's the way I understood it, Jimmy."

All set for some high-dollar 9-ball. Everything was established and set in motion.

Cav suggested hitting some balls to get a feel for the table. He tossed some balls on the table, checking for any weak spots, testing the rolls, and ensuring that the table was straight and level.

---

3 Head-set explained: The goal is to be the first to win 10 games in a row; reaching 10 games ahead of your opponent is one set. For example, 10 to 0, or 14 to 4, 23 to 13, etc. A player wins a set by getting 10 games in a row ahead of the other player and wins the match by taking two out of three sets. This is typically used by high-dollar gamblers.

Local railbirds gathered like hawks around a chicken coop to watch the upcoming match. This pool hall had rarely seen action of this magnitude.

Cav, ever the showman, announced he had some cash left for the railbirds to bet against him. He held up a wad of cash, enticing action from the onlookers. A slick individual stepped forward, "I'm down for $2000 per set." Cav took his money, counted it loosely, added it to his stack, and placed it on top of the lamp. Still cocky, he encouraged more action.

"Let's do something even if it's wrong. I got this $4000 left if anybody wants this action."

A middle-aged black Brazilian stepped up, handed Cav $4000, and stated his wager. "I'll do that per set." After a loose count, Cav placed it on the lamp alongside his cash.

After about 15 minutes, they decided to flip a coin for the break. Fredrico extended his arm in front of Cav and flipped the coin. The coin landed, and Fredrico won the coin toss and first break.

The match began with Fredrico breaking and achieving an impressive first break—pocketing the 9-ball. Fredrico showed tremendous skill as he consistently ran multiple racks and executed very precise shots. He strung 4 racks together. Cav, a little cocky, commented, "I see you've been playing, Fredrico. We should have asked for some weight. Just joking." *Weight* means a handicap, a spot.

This intentionally fluffed Fredrico's ego a bit. Cav and Jimmy knew they were heavily favored; they considered Fredrico soft action, no real challenge.

After hours of intense play, Fredrico maintained a narrow lead of three games, but his lead was brief as Cav took over and put on a clinic, break-run, break-run. They played for about 8 hours, with Cav pacing the game, stalling. Cav was in complete control of the speed and pace of the match. He gave Fredrico enough rope to hang himself.

Late into the first set, Cav took a commanding lead. He hit a gear that proved to Fredrico he was way outmatched. Cav was there for the cash, and he was going to get it. He needed 3 games to win the first set and pounded it hard, relentlessly, freezing Fredrico out away from the table, marching on to victory, winning the first set.

Cav complimented Fredrico on his playing, again fluffing up his obviously improved skills. This was the part of the show where you bullshit your opponent. Cav knew Fredrico had no chance of winning; he had watched him play for 8 hours, and Cav could tell Fredrico's weaknesses compared to his own. No contest. So what do you do in this instance? You bullshit your opponent, pump him full of false hope, keep him in the fight.

The boys saw this as an opportunity, a gateway to more cash. Convince Fredrico that he's actually better than he thought he was, and get him to increase the bet—not out of the question, considering the big money behind Fredrico!

Cav and Jimmy ganged up on Fredrico by getting into a "wolf fest"—arguing back and forth about the game, a ruse intended to lay seeds of doubt.

Cav also pulled out a trick played on him once. He got into some of Fredrico's better shots, telling him how brilliant his shots were and the way he moved during the set, assuring Fredrico that he, Cav, didn't have a chance to win. He really pumped it up, referring to Fredrico's multiple 9-ball breaks. Cav pointed out the bank shots, caroms, and combo 9-ball shots Fredrico executed and won games on.

"You break better than me, Fredrico, we're in your house, in your room, you slowed down at the end of the set, and I sped up," Cav said. "Hey, I just know as this match continues you have an unfair advantage, I'm going to need a little bit of weight."

This might have been one of the most chickenshit moves in pool, but the boys had a purpose.

Fredrico became slightly angered at this nitty move. "What in the fuck are you talking about? You won the set, Cav."

Cav, desperately trying to hold on to his Hollywood performance and not laugh, came back with, "Yeah, I won, but I don't like the way I won." One of the nittiest moves you could make in a money game. It was difficult for Cav and Jimmy to keep from laughing, but they held a straight face.

Jimmy walked over knowing this nitty, chickenshit move by Cav was a ploy, a ruse to upset the opponent. They could never win this argument as the rules had already been established. But they did it anyway just because they could, and it was free; it allowed them something to laugh about later.

Fredrico held his position: "Sorry boys, you bet, you put down your cash, we agreed to the rules, no going back now."

The boys continued trying to plant a seed in Fredrico's head. He would be thinking about this when his head hit the pillow: "Maybe Cav and Jimmy believed I'm better than Cav, maybe, maybe, maybe...."

A nit would attempt this move in a gambling setting, rare, but it had been attempted before. Cav and Jimmy did it with a purpose and partly for entertainment. Strategic planning for the future. It was a guarantee they would be laughing about it on the way back to the hotel. The truth was the boys knew Fredrico was the one that needed weight; he needed the 8-ball minimum handicap. A spot giving Fredrico the 8 might possibly give Fredrico room to even have a chance. That was what the boys had concluded after watching Fredrico play for 8 hours.

Feeling the effects of jet lag, the 20-hour flight, and the time adjustment, 5-hour difference between Brazil and California, Cav suggested continuing the match the next night. Fredrico agreed, "I have no objections," and they decided to resume the match on the following evening.

Cav scooped up the cash left on the lamp from the side bets he'd won, and politely informed the losers of the side bets that "you can come back tomorrow night and continue as long as you like or at least until I go bust."

Back at the hotel, Cav and Jimmy discussed strategy and any concerns. Cav expressed the mental fatigue, pointing to his head, and Jimmy playfully suggested that meeting a Brazilian superstar might change his outlook. After enduring yet another marathon session, the boys succumbed to their jetlag, collapsing into a deep sleep, anticipating the continuation of the battle the following night.

15

The Prince Of Darkness

Late in the morning, the boys headed down to the hotel coffee shop, and while sipping coffee in an outdoor café, Jimmy took the opportunity to prepare Cav for the upcoming night's match. Like a prizefighter's trainer, Jimmy addressed any concerns Cav had, fine-tuning their strategy. Insurance.

With pool being a mostly mental game, Jimmy recognized that the most important element was Cav's mental state. If Cav was focused, he played well and won. If he was distracted, it was less certain. It all came down to getting the mind right.

As evening fast approached, they made their way to the pool hall to resume the match. The night began with a powerful break from Cav, resulting in an impressive run of four racks. Cav was now ahead by 4 games, needing 6 more games to win all the cash. The momentum was clearly in Cav's favor. However, on the 5th rack, Cav's break was so powerful that the cue ball jumped off the table. Fredrico responded with a break, pocketing five balls, including the money ball, the 9-ball.

All of a sudden, the gates of hell opened, and the pool world shifted inside that room as the Prince of Darkness, Marco, made his grand entrance. He was dressed flawlessly, sporting his $10,000 Savile Row suit. Cav leaned over to Jimmy and whispered, "What the hell is going on here, is this the grim reaper or the President of Brazil?"

Marco projected a tremendous presence and commanded immediate attention with his charisma and obvious wealth. Accompanied by his two handlers, Marco's appearance at the match added a new intensity to an already highly charged scene. Cav and Jimmy had no choice but to be ready for their close-up with Mr. Black Magic.

Marco, with a distinct Brazilian accent, said, "Gentlemen, please excuse the sudden intrusion." He extended a warm welcome, expressing his appreciation for having guests from America. He introduced himself and inquired about their stay. Marco had class, and he was the ne-plus-ultra in confidence. He obviously had a very powerful effect on people he came in contact with. The boys stood respectfully and shook Marco's hand, expressing their honor and appreciation for his generosity in bringing them to Rio.

Little did the boys know their close encounter with Marco was, in reality, a job interview. Marco knew what he was looking for. In his line of work, he had studied an assortment of different personality types: thieves, murderers, con men, and women of the same type. But it was the pool player, the high-stakes professional specifically, that he had singled out.

The professional gambler, the pool player, had a mental state that rose above most for his specific needs. He had looked at different sports types; boxers were of interest. Fast on your feet, quick analytical thinking. He had bigger plans for these boys. This so-called meet and greet, TTM (table-top-meeting) at the pool hall, was a job interview, a casting call of sorts. These boys had no idea what was about to play out.

Cav and Jimmy were star-struck, intimidated, not quite ready for such a shock. The last thing they could have expected was a billion-dollar titan walking into this pool hall, a sharp contrast. It didn't add up.

We have always heard the importance of first impressions; Marco mastered the art. It was a showmanship act he had performed hundreds of times on a grand scale. He figured to overwhelm your opponent was the game—let your opponent know who was in charge, gently, with a smile.

Fredrico, quietly listening on the sidelines, stepped closer and with a smile at the boys, gestured towards Marco as if to say "He's the man!" making it clear that Marco was his backer and the one in control.

Marco assured Cav and Jimmy that other opportunities existed by which they could win more than $200,000. This triggered the greed instinct in Cav and Jimmy. If they could somehow trap Marco, here was an opportunity to win hundreds of thousands, even more.

"If we, or rather, I, lose the first match, are you still on board to keep gambling until we decide to throw in the towel and quit?" Marco asked. It was a foolish question but one that had a deeper purpose than it appeared.

Marco looked at Fredrico, awaiting his agreement. Fredrico nodded to Marco, and Cav, slightly confused by Marco's proposal, whispered to Jimmy, "What do we do?" Jimmy advised Cav to "go with the flow." Cav assured Marco, "Yeah sure, Marco, we will stay with you until you want to quit, or we go broke, you have my word on that."

Marco, satisfied with his initial observation that he had the correct two guys for his plans, extended a very generous offer of having them stay at his resort in Rio.

"Let me say this, gentlemen, we have a tradition of showing Southern hospitality from the far south. I will have you moved to our resort here in Rio. This property was a former Rock Resort; I purchased it from The Rockefellers. It's an old property; it used to be the best of the best, the shining star of South America. They had done a complete renovation, spared no expense, then put it up for sale."

Marco continued bragging: "I own 23 five-star properties throughout South America. I have a lot of vacancies this time of year in Rio, so you would be most welcome. I'll have my driver pick you up and handle your move tomorrow afternoon." Cav and Jimmy thanked Marco and expressed their sincere appreciation.

Marco's work was done. He said his parting line, "I own the emerald trade here in South America and would like you and Jimmy to come out and see the property tomorrow."

"Thanks, we will see you tomorrow," Jimmy said.

Fredrico was not amused but he hid it well. Marco treated him with disdain and manipulation. Cav and Jimmy didn't know that Marco had set a chickenshit split with Fredrico, a forced split of 70/30 take it or leave it. If Fredrico won it would net him

$60,000 of the $200,000, while Marco took the entire remaining $140,000. Backers and players always split 50/50. Marco knew that Cav would likely win, but he didn't care—he had darker plans for Cav and Jimmy.

Cav and Fredrico resumed play to finish the game. The 2nd set was back and forth, Cav slowing the pace of the match a little, like a cat toying with a mouse.

They decided to quit for the night, Cav ahead by 3 games.

Cav and Jimmy said goodnight to Fredrico and headed back to their hotel.

16

Gentlemen, Welcome
To My House

Just before noon, Jimmy answered a knock at their door. As promised, it was two of Marco's men for the move to the fancy resort. One of them announced: "We're here on Marco's behalf to get you transferred to his property."

Jimmy motioned the men to wait a moment, but as he and Cav reached for their luggage one of the men stepped in and picked up the suitcases and headed for the elevator. When Cav and Jimmy saw the Mercedes limousine waiting by the hotel entrance, the reality of their situation really hit home. "Are you fucking kidding?" Cav exclaimed with pure joy. "Why me?" He and Jimmy had to laugh.

The limousine whisked them to the new property—a 5-star resort surrounded by picturesque floral gardens, fountains and waterfalls. The setting was like something out of a movie, post-card perfect.

Marcella, Marco's beautiful wife, warmly welcomed them and led them through the stunning property to a dining room, where she mentioned a special luncheon was being prepared especially for them. Marcella gracefully guided them through, the staff standing at attention, representing a high level of professionalism.

Their flawless uniforms and the care of the staff left the boys hypnotized. This level of hospitality far exceeded anything they could imagine.

Marcella explained that Marco was currently at the mine, attending to urgent business.

"We own 30 emerald mines and various other interests throughout South America," she announced, as if it was a routine detail that must be shared.

Marcella then introduced Carlos, a staffer who would assist them in settling into their rooms. She invited them to relax by the pool and mentioned that Marco would like to meet with them later, extending an invitation for them to visit him at the mine.

The gracious hospitality and the breathtaking magnificence of their surroundings left Cav and Jimmy feeling a mix of thankfulness and disbelief. They extended their gratitude to Marcella. The boys began to realize that their lives had taken an unimaginable turn, entering a world of luxury and privilege.

Carlos showed them to their suite, and as they entered, the view took their breath away. Cav walked to the open window, where a gentle breeze stirred the curtains as he gazed at a picturesque view of the Atlantic Ocean, mountains to his left and right. It felt and looked like a painting that had come to life.

Carlos answered a knock at the door, and in walked Valentina, a tall, slender woman with stunning dark features who could

easily pass for a model. Speaking English pretty well, she introduced herself as their chambermaid, and took them on a tour of
the suite. Cav's mind seemed to wander in a different direction.
Jimmy noticed Cav checking out Valentina and he frowned and
shook his head, "no-no."

After the tour—mini-fridge, tv remote, walk-in wardrobe, extra
bedding etc.—Carlos asked if there was anything they would need
before he and Valentina left. Cav attempted to tip with a fifty but
Carlos politely waved it off. "No sir, we do not accept gratuity."

As soon as they left, Jimmy reminded Cav not to mess with the
help. Cav said he wouldn't, but the hungry glow in his eye about
Valentina suggested otherwise. They settled in and relaxed.

Hours later, Marcella warmly greeted Cav and Jimmy in the
lobby and introduced them to Luiz, the Concierge. She praised Luiz
as the best Concierge in Brazil and left them in his capable hands.

Marcella was a woman of great wealth and power. She dressed
and appeared to employ only the top European and American designers. With her wealth, of course, it was what you would expect
from being a billionairess. There was more than the eye could see,
something a bit mysterious going on in that pretty little head.

Luiz led them to the restaurant where two waitstaff guided them
to a table with a special carefully prepared lunch. Luiz informed
them that a driver was outside to take them to the emerald mine
to meet Marco "whenever you're ready."

They finished their meal and, excited about meeting Marco
again, met their driver and climbed into the back of the Mercedes
limo. The driver said it was many miles to the mine outside the
city, but there were refreshments in the cabinets.

They passed through at least 20 miles of neighborhoods of all kinds, some quite rundown. About 45 minutes later they left the city behind and entered an area of low forested hills and small farms.

The car approached a turn and stopped at a gated checkpoint. The driver lowered his window to speak with an armed guard. The guard stepped close and looked in at Cav and Jimmy. He nodded at the driver, the windows slid closed and the car moved off. Cav and Jimmy were a bit uptight and watched every move closely, wondering what they had gotten themselves into.

They approached a parking area in front of the entrance to an old, scruffy-looking building. A dozen or so older-looking cars were parked in a tidy row. The limo stopped at the main entrance and the driver ran around and opened the door for Cav and Jimmy.

Strangely, there had been no sign at the turn-off and security checkpoint identifying the mine. And again no sign on the building or by the entrance.

Surprise. As Cav and Jimmy were about to discover, this large, run-down old building and its several equally shabby paint-peeling outbuildings was no longer a functioning mine. In fact, no mining had taken place at this location in decades. It was, in fact, a luxury 5-star hideaway.

17

Don't Go Inside, It's A Trap

Cav and Jimmy approached the double-door entrance to the building and noticed a sign after all. In gold lettering on the glass window of the right hand door it said:

"South American Emerald Mining Company"

Before they could push the door open, it was opened from inside by Marcella, who greeted them with a smile and gestured for them to enter.

Off the busy crossroads of Rio, this building was where she and Marco conducted their business in quiet seclusion with minimum interruptions. Quite unlike the scruffy 19th Century exterior, inside everything was immaculate.

Marcella led them across the grand reception area, designed as an even more luxurious version of their resort. The sprawling reception area was more like an upscale, polished art museum, featuring a collection of what looked like Old Grand Masters, paintings worth millions of dollars hanging on every wall. Luxurious, thick carpeting enhanced with expensive Persian rugs.

Jimmy and Cav felt like they'd approached an old rundown building that had its own dedicated driveway at the city dump, and then it's transformed into Buckingham Palace as soon as you go inside. It was really bizarre. They exchanged a "what the hell is really going on here" look as they followed Marcella.

Marcella ushered them into Marco's private office, just a few steps off the reception area. Marco rose to greet them from behind a huge, stunningly handsome desk. It was an intricate hand-crafted multicolored Brazilian wood inlay masterpiece, forming a majestic centerpiece for the office.

Overhead, enormous hand-made European crystal chandeliers ostentatiously suggested grand castles and palaces of the past.

Marco gestured for the somewhat awestruck boys to be seated in the two chairs across from him. Marcella shot a quick smile at Marco and then sat at a small side table.

Before a word was spoken, an attractive young woman walked in pushing a cart stocked with drinks and hors d'oeuvres. Cav and Jimmy accepted graciously and looked inquiringly at Marco. They were eager to discuss matters concerning their stated purpose for being there—9-ball.

Before they could ask a question, Marco, with occasional input from Marcella, launched into a long and boring history of the South American Emerald Mining Company. The guys were both soon yawning, about to be bored into a coma. They struggled to be attentive as their hosts continued to spew more nonsense about their wealth and power. Cav daydreamed about his match last night with Fredrico, while Jimmy was stuck thinking about that "girl from Ipanema" in the bikini he'd spotted earlier by the pool back at the resort.

Finally, Marco arose and shifted gears. He beckoned for the boys to follow him, and led them to a large vault, or wall safe, in the corner of the office next to where Marcella sat. He swung open the vault door and stepped back to showcase a massive display of cash, emeralds, diamonds, gold bars, rhodium ingots, coins, and shelves piled with official-looking business ledgers and documents.

Marco held up a one-ounce rhodium coin and handed it to Cav, explaining its extraordinary rarity and value. "Rhodium is more valuable than gold, Cav. That one coin had reached $29,000 at its height in value for one ounce."

Cav whistled his surprise and handed it to Jimmy, who hefted the tiny treasure and gave a low whistle. Marco then put a roll of 10 one-ounce rhodium coins on the table in front of Marcella. "There's your $200,000 if you win the match. I could pay you in these rhodium coins if you like."

Marco knew the boys would never accept these coins as payment. But for Marco, it was all about planting seeds and shifting thoughts and ideas.

Cav was surprised and troubled when he noticed in the vault neatly packaged blocks of what appeared to be white powder. That suspicious image left him questioning if it could be what he thought it could be.

The vast wealth displayed in that office—the art, rhodium, gold, emeralds, cash—along with the luxurious resort and Marco's lifestyle, were calculated and served as a form of predictive programming, a tool to shape perceptions of those people one wished to manipulate in the future. The luxury and power were intentional components employed to influence others. Marco understood the power of attraction associated with such displays. The 10 ounces of rhodium, everything, was all predictive programming. Cav and Jimmy were sucked in like a magnet at this point.

Once they were seated again, Marco laid out a very attractive proposal.

"Gentlemen, what I am about to tell you, you may not believe; you will have doubts. I am sure this will confuse you, but please hear me out. I am certain you both will do well at this project, and most of all, you will become rich. My North American territory for my emerald business has a vacancy. I am hoping you two, Cav and Jimmy, will help me fill that vacancy. Please let me explain. I have ready buyers in various countries around the world, everywhere but America and Canada. Simply put, I wish to establish an outlet through New York over to California."

Cav laughed, "Wait a minute, Marco, you're telling me you want a couple of pool bums who know nothing about gems and emeralds to take your goods to America and Canada and just show up and sell something we know nothing about?"

Jimmy added, "Don't we have to have some kind of special registration or special certification, like import licenses?"

Marco asserted his authority with so-called facts to coax the boys along. "I will have everything certified, the stones graded and appraised, all the documents very carefully prepared by the government here. All of your documentation makes you completely legal. You will receive first-class travel. I provide you with the buyers, and all you will be doing is delivering the merchandise. We would make you presentable, no offense. New suits, new wardrobes, and you would earn approximately $1,000,000 per year each. If you're hungry, $2,000,000 per year each, meaning multiple shipments a month. Cav and Jimmy, to become my number one emerald importers in North America, I like the sound of that. I had a good feeling about you boys when I met you at the pool hall. Honest, hardworking Midwest American boys. My boss, Marcella, mentioned the same. She has a hunch you two will do well. We have discussed it at length, and we believe we can trust you; we don't think you will steal from us."

To install more predictive programming, he handed them the shiny object, putting in Jimmy's hand the flawless 18-carat Rockefeller Emerald.

"This was sold at Christie's auction, owned by the Rockefellers, for $5.5 million." Marco pointed to a large batch of beautiful emeralds, putting it right in their face. "Any one of those investment-grade stones could secure a comfortable retirement."

Cav, still full of doubts, stood up and questioned the connection between their skills of playing pool and the emerald trade. "Marco, I am a pool player, not a gemologist, sorry I don't think we can honestly do this."

"Hey, cool off here," Jimmy said, "let the man speak his business, is that okay, Cav?"

Cav sat down, apologized, and asked Marco to continue.

In response, Marco reassured Cav, "It's all about the presentation. I will show you how easy this is, promising to teach both of you everything you need to know. Everything is documented, all the banking is legitimate, I have accounting firms that work around the clock in multiple time zones, the world's best law firms on speed dial. Allow me to say this, gentlemen, you have before you an opportunity that will change your lives financially."

He emphasized the potential to transition from hustling thousands in pool to handling millions with this opportunity. "I don't expect you to quit playing pool, please just know there is an opportunity here you may like to consider that could make you both wealthy over the next year. Ponder your fate. Think about it, no rush."

As they wrapped up, Cav and Jimmy expressed their thanks and returned to the resort to weigh their options and prepare for the match with Fredrico in the evening. They soaked up their new spacious 2-bedroom suite, surrounded by a five-star, first-class living standard never imagined in their lives—food delivered on a silver platter, a postcard-perfect ocean view overlooking Rio's storied beaches.

They didn't know that Marco had met them face to face at the pool hall to confirm he had the perfect match for his job opening, his casting call. Putting them up in his five-star resort and getting them used to the feel of big money was all part of the predictive programming. He knew the power of persuasion, showing them, letting them live what it was like to live in pure luxury. It was all a planned move by Marco and Marcella.

Jimmy was thrilled about the possibility of becoming seriously wealthy in a year's time. "Cuz, I don't know, what the fuck, all I can see is dollar signs everywhere I look down here. We may have hit the lottery here."

Cav was more cautious, even skeptical, trying to spot the catch in this seemingly near-perfect proposition. "What is Marco thinking? Let's examine this shit seriously. I am only asking if there's a catch, what's the catch? There has to be a catch, but I just don't see it. I don't deny Marco sees something in us, or he wouldn't be putting us up here, flying us down here for a two hundred thousand pool match. Really? Fuck, I would give you 10 to 1 those paintings in his office are worth millions, bet me on that. Those stones, those emeralds, worth how much? Millions! What's the over and under, high/low on those chandeliers? Huh? A mill, 2 mill? You're telling me Marco is fucking around with us for $200 thousand?"

They both fell silent, contemplating Marco's business plan. The attraction of immense wealth controlled their doubts; greed seemed to always win.

Jimmy finally broke the silence.

"Ponder your fate," his voice cutting through the pressure. "Okay, I did, now where the fuck do I sign? I would do that in a New York second! I'm buying whatever the fuck he's selling! No risk, all documented. Okay, what's the problem?"

Cav's concern was evident as he looked at Jimmy. "Jimmy, we need to figure out what Marco's true intentions are. No one gives away millions like this without expecting something in return."

"True, true," Jimmy acknowledged. "But what if there isn't a catch? What if it's as good as it sounds?"

"There's always a catch, my friend. Let's meet with Marco, get more details, and then decide. Look, Jimmy, let's not forget why we're here, what we flew 20 hours to come here and do. We came to bust Fredrico and his backers, so let's just get the cash and then decide. Hell with the emeralds. Who knows how much money we can win here and not have to fuck with this emerald business or whatever he's selling."

Jimmy nodded in agreement. The idea of 2 million guaranteed was tempting, but caution and street smarts prevailed.

Cav took a walk to clear his mind. As he crossed the hotel lobby, he was urgently motioned to come to the front desk. A message from Fredrico with some disturbing news—the night's game was canceled. Cav picked up the desk phone and shared the message with Jimmy, wondering if they were being scammed out of their $200,000. Was that the move?

Jimmy came down and they exited the lobby in a hurry and flagged down a driver. They raced to the pool hall, anticipating the worst.

At the pool hall, with thoughts of being tricked and horsey fucked, Jimmy demanded answers from the bartender regarding their $200,000.

"Where the fuck is our 200 grand? Are we getting played?"

Cav, just as angry, demanded, "What's going on here? We need to know about our money."

The bartender attempted to ease their worries. "You guys didn't hear? There was an incident last night. Some troublemakers stirred things up, and the police shut down the games for the night to do an investigation."

Jimmy, still agitated, pressed the bartender, "And our money?"

Doing his best to calm the boys down, he explained, "Don't worry, your money's safe. It's secured in the back in the vault. You can pick it up with your match when things settle down. We'll reschedule your match when everything's back to normal. It's just a temporary setback."

The uncertainty about their money was not going anywhere. The atmosphere in the pool hall shifted as Davi, the manager, approached Cav and Jimmy. He handed the phone to Cav, indicating that the call was from someone important. Cav, nervous, answered the call.

"Cav, it's Marco. Fredrico called me. There's been an emergency. Davi is going to show you your money. Listen to me carefully. I guarantee every dollar of that $200,000 of yours with my blood. Do you understand that?"

"Yes, Marco, I do," Cav answered. Cav was taken aback by the sincerity in Marco's voice. He realized his doubts were way overplayed. He nodded reassuringly at Jimmy who was observing the conversation and had heard it was Marco.

Cav was relieved, and also a little embarrassed for sounding so doubtful. Marco's carefully crafted message eased Cav's skepticism and, more importantly, built new trust. At that moment, Cav's doubts were erased.

Marco knew exactly what Cav and Jimmy were feeling. He had decided to humor Jimmy and Cav with a bit of theater, casually downplaying the importance of the $200,000.

"Cav, I spend $100 thousand dollars just entertaining dignitaries in an evening. This is small potatoes," Marco declared. "Now go out and have some fun, compliments of the house."

Marco generously arranged for his driver to take them to one of his favorite nightclubs in Rio, promising encounters with some of the most beautiful women in the world.

"Careful in there, actresses, models, all types are in there. During Carnival, you can't get in; it's bought out for two weeks by some European bigwig. He has been reserving it for two weeks every Carnival and said he would until he dies, that's what he told me once."

"That sounds great, Marco," Cav said, "thanks so much for the ride, and the advice!

"One hundred percent," Marco continued, "you will finish your match tomorrow night. I'll see you tomorrow. Now go enjoy a special night in Copacabana."

"Okay, Marco. And please forgive me for suggesting you had anything to do with our money. We're wrapped a bit tight, you understand. That's all the money we have in the world. We got a little concerned. I hope you understand."

"Yes, I totally understand. I have instructed the manager to take you back to the vault with me on the phone," Marco said.

Davi took Cav and Jimmy back to the vault to show them their money. He reassured them as he opened the vault, "Verify anything you wish. We would never steal your money."

Jimmy reached into the vault and pulled out the duffle bag, opened it up, and picked out several stacks of cash to inspect it.

"It's all there, just like we left it," Jimmy told Cav.

Davi's simple exercise left little doubt about Marco and the company's sincerity. It established a bond that strengthened confidence in Marco and all the actors in this play.

As a gesture of goodwill, Davi handed Cav $1,000 and a piece of paper. "This is from Marco. This is the address of Marco's favorite club in Rio."

With Marco still on the phone, Cav was embarrassed, chomping down on some crow and attempting to cover his ass for doubting Marco.

"Marco, I can't tell you how easy it is to fall into doubt and feel you are a target. I guess on the positive side, we can use this experience to strengthen our association and set aside our doubts and weaknesses."

Marco acknowledged Cav and assured him that his comments and realizations were 100% correct and encouraged their mutual feelings to be upheld and followed going forward. He confirmed the trust before he hung up.

"So, gentlemen, are we good? If you will excuse me, I am walking into an important meeting and will see you both tomorrow."

Cav hung up, relieved. Jimmy was still trying to make sense of the situation.

"Guess it's on the square, straight up, Marco personally guaranteed it, 'with his blood.' It's chump change to him. Think about it."

Cav was also convinced of Marco's legitimacy. "Hell yeah, these guys are for real. No games, straight business." This event served to demonstrate to the boys that Marco was straight with them and there were no concerns going forward.

They left the pool hall and climbed into their waiting car. Back at the resort they retreated to their room, relieved and more relaxed, almost certain they were not scammed. But a legitimate question still remained: Did Marco intentionally stage this whole event for something more sinister? Was this all a small part of a bigger plan?

Cav and Jimmy engaged in a brainstorming session, tossing ideas back and forth. Cav, always the unpredictable thinker, proposed a theory: "I bet anything it's the yeyo, the coke they want us to run, not emeralds. Remember those large cubes of white blocks against the walls?"

Jimmy, with an air of disbelief, responded, "See, Cav, I believe you took some of that white stuff. You want me to find you a crack pipe? Come on, Cuz, you're dreaming again."

Cav suggested to Jimmy, "Okay, let's forget all about this, let's just let it go. Jimmy, get ready; we're going out to this club and see what shakes in Rio. I can't wait to see what Marco considers the best night spot in Rio. Pretty bold statement."

"Nah, Cav, I'm bushed. I'm just gonna lay low tonight."

Cav was eager to head off into the night. "Well, I'm going to Copacabana. Find me a Brazilian superstar to blow my mind."

Cav cleaned up and headed down to the car, handing the driver a piece of paper with simple instructions: "Copacabana."

With his window down, Cav enjoyed the scenery. He envisioned a fun evening, a great dinner, and the potential to meet the Brazilian lady of his dreams. He couldn't help but think that, if this was Marco's favorite spot, it must be the best.

18

You're the Beautiful Woman I Dreamed Of

As he walked along world-renowned Copacabana Beach, searching for a cool spot to pause and reflect upon the amazing view, Cav felt relaxed and relieved the $200K he had feared lost was safe after all. His timing was perfect for the coming sunset, and he could smell and feel the ocean breeze against his skin. The panoramic view of beach and sky unfolded before him, brushed with shades of orange, blue hues, and pinkish puffs of clouds.

The locals on the beach shared the sunset with him. Somewhere nearby, Brazilian music was playing—a samba. It enhanced the perfect setting. Still lost in his world of thoughts, Cav eventually made his way to the nearby watering hole that Marco had labeled his favorite.

The coming nighttime in Copacabana held untold potential for Cav. He was fascinated by the increasingly vibrant atmosphere as

Rio's elite, who usually only come out at night, surrounded him in this very upscale restaurant and bar.

He noticed a trio of stunning Brazilian women seated at a small table near the back. Taking a seat at the bar, Cav glanced back casually— and caught the gaze of one of them. She was watching him. He smiled; she returned it, her expression lingering just long enough to spark curiosity.

Before he could act on the moment, the bartender appeared, breaking his thoughts to take his order.

As he considered his drink, he felt a gentle yet unmistakable touch on his arm. Turning, he found her standing beside him, closer now, her smile warm and magnetic. He grinned again, and her returning smile deepened, lighting up her eyes. Their eyes locked. In that instant, time seemed to pause. It was unplanned, unspoken, and yet utterly undeniable.

This encounter would become another unexpected Brazilian turning point for him. He found he was genuinely curious about her, he needed to know this girl.

The barkeep came back and asked in accented English, "He has to decide what to order to drink?"

Under the guise of asking her advice, Cav shrugged and looked questioningly at the girl. She responded with a beautiful smile and suggested a caipirinha *(Kai-purr-reen-ya)*, calling it "a Brazilian masterpiece cousin to the Spanish mojito, but ours is better." The stunningly beautiful Brazilian spoke near perfect English.

Cav nodded and ordered two caipirinhas. And then looked back again at this vision smiling up at him. She was more generously proportioned than the usual fashion model, more along the lines of an Amazon goddess. She had long, naturally dark-blonde hair and unusual features for a Brazilian.

Of course she saw him looking her over, she was very used to that. "So, you are American!" she said, with a decided sparkle in her eyes.

"Yes indeed I am," he answered, "I'm Cav."

"I am Esmeralda," she said. "What are you doing in Rio?"

Instead of the truth, he joked and played on the probability that she was Catholic, answering, "I'm on a mission from God." This prompted laughter. He proceeded to tell Esmeralda how fortunate and blessed she was to live in Rio, because it was so beautiful. Cav had concluded to himself, starstruck, that she was the highlight of his trip down here. She made everything else in his plans pale by comparison in that moment.

Esmeralda stood at nearly 6 feet tall, and was already in a good mood after a couple of caipirinhas. She had heard it all before, but she was very receptive to Cav's compliments—of course, Cav's imposing 6 feet 2 inches and chiseled features surrounded by his own long dark-blonde hair didn't hurt his chances.

She got Cav talking a little about his life back in America. It wasn't long before Cav had her laughing with delight when he contrasted life in Rio with life in Kansas.

"You speak great English, far better than my Portuguese," he said, and they laughed.

"Well, I actually spend most of my time in Paris. And also London. And sometimes Milano. That's where most of my work is. I've kind of picked up a few languages. But everyone sooner or later learned English."

"Paris? Milano? Don't tell me. You're one of those 'supermodels'?"

She laughed and ignored his question.

"So that's why everyone in this bar has been looking at you all the time. It's not because I'm so gorgeous!" He laughed. "You're famous!"

And they just continued to smile at each other silently for several minutes, sipping their caipirinhas. Standing side-by-side admiring each other in the middle of one of Rio's most glamorous night clubs, Esmeralda became Cav's unexpected "best friend at the moment." And the feeling was mutual.

Cav was a little shaken. He had not suspected a chance encounter with a Brazilian beauty would have any kind of deep, almost overwhelming effect on him and his life going forward. Esmeralda's intelligence and beauty and straightforward no-bullshit way really fascinated him. It even challenged him. She was not only a stunning Brazilian, she was a real woman gifted with extraordinary charm and social graces and honesty that far exceeded the ordinary wordplay, the kind of silly banter he encountered in Hollywood. He realized that this bit of fate had brought him face to face with someone truly exceptional.

The perfect night, with bossa nova playing in the background, the ideal mood, sparked the mysterious connection that blossomed between Cav and Esmeralda. The need for banal conversation was replaced by the irresistible pull of mutual attraction. As the evening wore on, they enjoyed the best of Brazilian cuisine, endless cocktails, champagne toasts, smiles and more smiles, and dancing. All these worked their miracles in more intimate conversation, as social barriers, borders and taboo subjects gradually melted away.

Anyone watching from the outside who could see the two snuggled up would find it difficult to imagine they had not arrived together as a long-term couple. They seemed naturally made for each other. And when their heat had reached a boiling point, they left the club together, arm in arm.

At Cav's resort, the privacy of his room dissolved all inhibitions under the glow of moonlight through the big window. Each of them were like world champions in their respective fields, yet they were unaware of each other's fame. Their chance encounter evolved into an explosive and intimate connection. Later revelations of their professional lives would prove intriguing. But right now, Cav was as unaware about what Esmeralda really did as she was about him, other than she knew he played pool and he guessed she modeled.

His testosterone level could have lit Vegas. Clothes long gone, the two converged into his four-poster canopy bed beneath the sheets.

The following morning, room service delivered breakfast for three. Cav was anxious to introduce Jimmy to his stunning bedmate, and signaled his partner to come into his bedroom.

Jimmy walked in and managed to keep a cool exterior. Cav did the intros: "Jimmy, let me present Esmeralda! Esmeralda, this is my man Jimmy, the main reason I'm still alive and ticking."

Of course Jimmy was struck silent by Esmeralda's beauty, but managed a mumbled "Hi" before Esmeralda, taking the lead, greeted Jimmy warmly, expressing a genuine sense of familiarity toward him.

"Hi Jimmy, I've heard a lot about you. I already feel like we're old friends."

Esmeralda sat up, pulled a sheet over herself, and patted the bed, inviting Jimmy to sit there. She effortlessly directed her charm, well aware of the impact she had on men.

After chatting for a while, Esmeralda excused herself to the bathroom. She gracefully slipped out of bed, and her nudity caught Jimmy off guard, the sight leaving him numb and entranced. Unlike many other cultures, Brazilians are mostly unashamed of nudity. They have no preconceived fixed ideas and are free-spirited as a rule.

Cav's voice broke the trance when he phoned the concierge.

"I've got a favor to ask, Luiz. Would you bring up that beautiful sarong I saw in the display window? The one with the leather sandals?"

Luiz answered Cav's question with another of his own: "By chance, is this for Esmeralda?" Marco's influence evidently was everywhere.

"Why do you ask, Luiz?"

Luiz replied that several staff members had noticed Esmeralda enter the property the previous evening, and now everyone was talking about the sighting. When Cav asked why, Luiz dropped a bombshell, disclosing that she was a world-class supermodel currently residing mostly in Paris and part-time in Rio—and that she was even more famous because of her historic family background.

"You were very fortunate to catch her in town; she's rarely in Rio. Her parents are admired all over Brazil, nobility. She bears the surname Bolivar, the noble descendant of the great Simon Bolivar. Her-great grandfather eight times removed, nine generations ago."

Cav hung up the phone, feeling like a lightning bolt had zapped his head. It was a shock to learn who he had spent the night and shared passionate sex with. He felt outmatched as he ran a headline image across his mind:

"A nobody Kansas Pool Bum Has International Super Model Encounter In Rio."

Luiz called back to tell Cav that the requested package was on its way to his room. Almost immediately, the doorbell rang.

Jimmy answered the door, accepted the package from Luiz, and presented it to Cav, who now was quite nervous. The pressure and weight of the moment grew inside of him as he recalled practically begging her to show up at his evening match against Fredrico.

Wrapped in a plush white terry cloth resort robe, Esmeralda rejoined the boys in the bedroom. With his self-confidence shaken, given her world famous status and family nobility, he nevertheless bravely handed Esmeralda the package.

Esmeralda maintained an air of professional dignity as she opened the box and curiously examined the contents. She looked up at Cav and asked, "What's this?"

Cav encouraged her to try it on, stating that he believed it would look great on her. Despite her professional life wearing the finest high-end designer clothes, Esmeralda graciously agreed, and took the sarong with her into the bathroom.

She soon emerged from the bath wearing the sarong, surprising both Cav and Jimmy with her stunning appearance, including adding a touch of glamor with her high-dollar sunglasses perched on her nose. She playfully showcased her best moves for her private audience, eliciting fits of laughter and applause every time she struck an exaggerated runway-model pose, as only she could.

"Okay, boys, what time is the big event tonight, and where is it?"

Jimmy had prepared the room service, so they discussed the upcoming match while they ate. Cav had planned to pick her up and take her there, but Esmeralda explained that, due to prior commitments, she would not be able to join them until later.

Cav, concerned, asked her, "So is this where you head off into the sunset never to be heard from again?"

Esmeralda smiled. "No, not at all. I'll be there, I promise, Cav."

Seeing Cav's ill-disguised internal struggle, Esmeralda leaned into him, encircled him in her arms, expressed her gratitude for the wonderful evening they had spent together, and reassured him with a kiss that said she would be there later.

Truth be told, this Kansas country boy, whom Esmeralda had ensnared, was more than she could ever have hoped for. Cav was, for now, the perfect fixture she needed in her life. She could look beyond his probably lackluster past and formulate with him a magical, unexpected connection that was icing on an unexpected cake for both of them.

Cav also brought more to the relationship than he was aware of. Constant reminders of his father's and mother's failures, and his poor upbringing, troubled him. Happiness and good thoughts came and went with the roller-coaster highs and lows of his life to date, but an undercurrent of the rough stuff always remained.

For Esmeralda, the opposite held true because of her coming from an upper-class, high-society lifestyle of glitz and glamor.

Despite the disparity of their respective backgrounds and experiences, Cav still managed to hold onto his self-respect. If there were any others to credit how Cav had survived his train-wreck at home, those would be his high school friend Janie, and "step-dad" Jasper.

Thanks to Jasper, he was well-grounded and taught to excel in the games he had a natural talent for—a deep passion for pool games, hustling, and high stakes gambling. That pathway gave Cav opportunities that heretofore he could only have dreamed about, which in his new reality, he lived. His rise to world-class skill and reputation in pool had brought him renown, money, and a metric ton of respect from far-flung quarters. And now, opportunity and, of course, Esmeralda.

Esmeralda was accustomed to a world that glittered with paparazzi flashbulbs, attentive fawning media eager to see her beautiful face and figure on the covers of prestigious magazines around the world, strutting down catwalks wearing the world's most renowned designer ensembles. It made her the envy of the world of fashion and beyond and constantly demanded her time and attention.

The contrast between Cav's childhood and his current lifestyle, when compared to Esmeralda's glamorous world, generated a nearly perfect, classic case of opposites attracting each other like magnets. Somehow, perhaps like predestined meteors, they had found unexpected connection through their natural attraction, which rose far above the apparent challenges and considerations of each of their duties.

Esmeralda efficiently prepared her early leave due to her obligations. But Cav felt a need to express a few of his opinions to her before she departed.

"Hang on," he said, taking a step back to admire her. "It's perfect, you look stunning!" Seeing her broad smile, Cav offered her a heartfelt hug, a gesture she had expected and wanted. But his whispered, mysterious words, while assuring her heart, tugged at her mind:

"No matter what happens tonight, don't worry. All is going to be okay."

Carrying that message with her, Esmeralda, after leaning in for his kiss, disappeared like a fleeting wisp of a cloudlet.

"Ciao!"

Their anticipation for the night ahead added a touch of uncertainty in the air that left Jimmy and Cav reflecting on the incredible connection they had found through this serendipitous encounter with a glamorous celebrity.

Esmeralda's immediate impact on Cav was undeniable. He found himself engaged in some dangerous horseplay—jumping from the bed to the sofa, sofa to a chair, and attempting a backflip on the bed before bumping his head on the ceiling.

Having found humor in Cav's love boat excitement, a laughing Jimmy stepped in with a strict warning: "Dammit, Cav, you're going to break your fuckin' neck. Stop, please!" Laughing his antics off and then giving sobered reflection to the task at hand, Cav and Jimmy left behind their thoughts of the extraordinary turn of events and, instead, prepared for the upcoming pool match of their lifetimes. Sobered to the task, the two friends at last settled down.

19

A Brush With Death

U pon arrival at the pool hall, the boys found a sizable crowd of railbirds and others gathered for the highly awaited second round of the match.

Cav broke the balls first and took control of the game with impressive shots, gaining a significant lead. The clock ticked onward. Cav seemed to be the odds-on favorite to win all the cash. However, just as the tension built to a crescendo, Esmeralda walked in accompanied by a gorgeous female friend.

The room fell silent as everyone took notice of the two women, especially shocked to see Esmeralda, the international Brazilian megastar in 3-D living color. As one of Brazil's best and most famous celebrities, she was normally seen only on TV and in newspapers and magazines, or 40 feet tall on billboards everywhere. The two women looked stunning but somewhat out of place in the smoky and masculine pool-hall environment.

Cav was delighted and surprised by her arrival. He laid down his cue and warmly embraced Esmeralda before he introduced her to Fredrico. For his part, Fredrico displayed gentlemanly manners and greeted Esmeralda and her friend, Gisele, with gallant admiration. He added a touch of humor by welcoming them to the pool hall as his "humble abode" and "home away from home." His remarks momentarily broke the serious intensity of the match. Esmeralda, in turn, introduced her friend, Gisele, also a model with international connections, to Jimmy and Cav. Jimmy instantly stood and greeted the second woman with a warm smile, obviously very interested to know her. He then prepared their seating and ordered their drinks to his corner.

Cav took a moment to explain the 9-ball game to the ladies so they could easily follow the play. Follow they did, surprised at how well these pros managed their skills while playing this match.

Mindful of the situation, Cav apologized to Fredrico for the interruption. The match continued for about an hour until Fredrico miscued, causing him to badly miss his shot. Tension in the pool hall increased dramatically.

Cav seized the opportunity, extending his lead to five. He now needed five more in a row to win the cash. With his audience, the ladies, watching closely, he really bore down and unleashed break-run after break-run, shooting long, tough cut shots, jump shots, bank shots, astounding the ladies with his skill and control of the game.

Nearing the end for Fredrico, and a win and all the cash for the boys, a huge distraction—gunshots outside in the street. Did this signal a threat to the match? Would it lead to a possibly violent robbery? Had someone leaked the existence of the $400,000 match money in the vault?

Jimmy, Cav and Fredrico instantly paused the game. Everyone in the pool hall braced for a possible violent assault.

More gunshot blasts outside, even closer to the front doors, cause some real panic. Suddenly the entrance doors crashed open and several masked assailants dragged a bloody body into the pool hall and dropped it just inside the door.

Cav and Jimmy grabbed Esmeralda and Gisele and stood in front of them. The masked men waved pistols and steered the crowd into a back room. Another gunshot echoed outside, accompanied by a scream, intensifying the terror. One ruthless gunman started screaming orders in Portuguese demanding directions to the vault, asking who was in charge and threatening the crowd. Esmeralda whispered a translation to Cav and Jimmy, "Take me to the vault! Do as I say or you die!"

Esmeralda and Gisele were terrified. Cav and Jimmy stayed in front of the girls. A second gunman took the security guard hostage, demanding information about the location of the vault. When the staffer hesitated, they ruthlessly shot him dead in cold blood. Davi the manager stepped forward, attempting to stall the would-be robbers until the police might show up, offering senseless information while appearing to cooperate. Upon reaching the vault, the gunman got upset at the manager's stalling and shot the man at point-blank range, leaving him dead in front of everyone, including Jimmy, Cav, and the girls.

The bartender opened the vault. The lead gunman grabbed the green duffle bag, easily identifiable by the large orange decal, and checked inside. He nodded to the others, and they all raced for the exit with the cash, including Cav and Jimmy's $200 grand. Gunshots fired at the walls of the pool hall further frightened the crowd, adding to the already turbulent and violent situation. As soon as the gunmen were gone, the bartender was instantly on the phone to the police, and Cav urged everyone to immediately leave.

Outside, Cav yelled and waved for a taxi and it pulled to the curb. Safely sheltered inside with the ladies, Cav and Jimmy comforted Esmeralda and Gisele who were still trembling from the robbery. They all agreed to go back to Cav and Jimmy's hotel.

Finally back in their room, Cav reassured anyone who would listen that "no one in our party was hurt, we escaped unharmed and losing $200 grand isn't the end of the world," when in fact it would seem to be the end of their world if they couldn't get their money back.

Jimmy expressed doubts about Marco's guarantee, but Cav defended Marco, emphasizing Marco's assurance that their money had been guaranteed with his blood.

Jimmy was skeptical. "Good luck with that," he said. Alarm bells went off in Esmeralda's and Gisele's heads. "Marco? Marco who?" Esmeralda demanded.

Cav admitted he didn't know Marco's last name. Esmeralda was surprised. "If it's who I think it is, Luis Fernando Da Costa Jr., he's a very dangerous man!"

"What are you talking about?" Cav asked in disbelief.

"He's a gangster, a notorious criminal!"

Gisele joined in. "He's powerful, he's wealthy. He has killed many people and kidnaps anyone who threatens his power."

These revelations that their proposed business partner had a seriously dark and dangerous side shocked Cav and Jimmy.

Esmeralda asked how they had met Marco.

"Marco's the money behind Fredrico, our opponent in the pool match for the $200 thousand prize," Cav said. "He showed up at our first pool match and, well, things just developed from there."

Jimmy described their dealings and the offers, explaining that it was Marco who had them stay at the resort for free, paid their expenses to travel, plus the proposal to become his "emerald representatives for North America."

"You want money? I have money." Esmeralda reached into her purse, pulled out a wad of cash, and handed it to Cav. Gisele did the same.

Esmeralda flashed a Black American Express card at them. "Here, you want a plane, a house? I have unlimited funds with this card, no limits!"

The boys had never seen a Black Amex and didn't know what one was until now. Cav took the card and looked at it. "You could buy a house with this?"

"I can buy a department store. I can buy the Taj Mahal with that card!" She was livid. "Tell 'Marco' he can go to the devil, you don't need him!"

Jimmy and Cav exchanged looks. Esmeralda's Marco didn't sound like the Marco they thought they knew.

Cav thanked Esmeralda for her generosity and refused the offer of cash and cards. He tried to reassure both women that he and Jimmy would be okay, and that their association with Marco would work out okay, that they'd be careful.

Although he expressed appreciation for their concern, this new knowledge about Marco's serious criminal background added doubt and uncertainty to what Cav and Jimmy thought they were getting involved with. The truth was that Marco's emerald mines and luxury resorts, and all the wealth that Marco and Marcella showered on them, had Cav and Jimmy blinded to any suspicions they might have.

They both understood this now. It made walking away from the potential spoils very difficult. Certainly an enormous weight and pressure bore down on their shoulders.

For their part, the girls were not convinced at all that the boys fully understood the magnitude of this moment.

20

We Own Them

Feeling the weight of the previous night's events, Cav prompted Jimmy to contact Marco and confirm his promised insurance policy on the $200,000 prize. "Don't forget, he said he would cover that money with his blood."

Jimmy dialed Marco, despite his uncertainty about the outcome.

Marco enthusiastically answered the call. His sincere tone shocked Jimmy; he spoke with rock-solid, apparently genuine concern about the pain and sorrow his guests had gone through at the pool hall during the robbery. To Jimmy, those were surprising words, considering he had been called out as a cold-blooded killer and dangerous druglord by Esmeralda and Gisele. At this point, though, Jimmy and Cav really didn't give a fuck about that; they cared about the $200,000 they originally had posted.

Marco responded, "Jimmy, look, I will send my driver over. I do have something I want you to see, some good news that I think will bring your spirits back up."

Marco emphasized that their safety concerned him most, not the monetary or match-related gains. Cav, listening in, was somewhat reassured by Marco's words and agreed to the visit. Marco again assured them not to worry, stating that their lives were more valuable than a mere $200,000. He stressed that money, pool games and material objects were replaceable but their lives were not.

Cav, ever the hustler, thought that maybe this was all just a setup. The push-pull of their 200-large net worth being tossed around like a basketball, and people being murdered, could be a great way to manipulate someone's emotions and commitment. Nah, too crazy. He brushed the idea aside.

Marco hung up the phone and immediately affirmed the success of their plan to Marcella.

"Everything! We own them!"

They agreed that Cav and Jimmy now fully believed the entire scheme. They also were pleased that the second part of their plan took hold.

"Damn we're good! Part One was the emeralds and the greed seed. Now Part Two has them by the balls!"

Marcella smiled. "Well done!"

Cav and Jimmy, still shaken by the previous night's events, arrived at the mine site where Marcella, who also professed her heartfelt sympathy for what had happened, welcomed them. For their parts, Cav shared the brutality of the situation, and Jimmy recounted the terror they had experienced, emphasizing their good luck: "We're very lucky we didn't get killed."

Upon his joining the conversation, Marco reassured them with firm confidence and vowed to find those responsible for the brutal attack.

"When I find those sons-a-bitches—and I *will* find them...!" With increasing fury, he continued: "Let me explain. When I wanted to first put my name out there, I established a reputation to pay top dollar for information. I knew early on that people wanted to kill me because of my emerald business and then take it over. Now, it's a known fact in the underground and above ground that Marco pays a premium for information. Rest assured I put out a bounty on those fucks last night at the pool hall! I will find those sons of bitches! You watch!"

What Marco never expected was for Cav to strike solid gold by meeting the mega superstar of Brazil who, he knew, could trash talk him and Marcella. In pool hall slang this would be called "squirreling" his action.

Still, Marco and Marcella had prepared for this kind of thing to possibly happen, and figured that in the end, money could solve any bad publicity about the two of them.

Now Marco pivoted, taking a surprising turn by bringing up the interrupted match against Fredrico. He acknowledged that they all had lost the $400,000 to the violence and chaos. Despite this setback, as he put it, Marco reaffirmed his commitment to having the boys' backs and delivering on his promise: "Fredrico informed me that you were about to win the cash, all the cash, and that you only needed one or two games to end the match. Is that right, gentlemen?"

Jimmy answered, sounding mousey like he was still a bit spooked, "Yes sir." Left unsaid was that this revelation was Marco's challenge to Cav and Jimmy to re-evaluate their private ideas and opinions of him and Marcella.

Right on cue, Marcella took what looked like an unexpected firm stand. Mrs. Princess of Darkness got up and, acting upset at Marco, ordered Marco to "Pay the boys the money they rightfully won! It's not their fault we got robbed, is it? So pay them their money."

Marco, looking hard at the boys and at Marcella, stated, "Now you see what I mean by who is the real boss here!"

This unexpected move boosted Marcella's credibility, earning some new-found respect and trust from Cav and Jimmy. Meanwhile, Marco and Marcella, the skillful con artists they were, effortlessly continued their terrific performance.

Marco stepped up and declared, "Okay, you heard the boss!" He led Cav and Jimmy to a table decorated with beautiful emeralds and pounded home the emerald business details along with his plans for their involvement as partners for the product line in North America. Marco assured them that both he and Marcella had very thoroughly discussed their partnership together and trusted them completely for this new role in their expansion plans.

Marco pounded into their heads the $2 million dollars they could earn per year, making the idea almost irresistible, before he invited them to step forward and look inside the vault that revealed the promised and insured "with his blood" $400,000 cash. He tossed $200,000 into one pile on the emerald-laden table and created another separate pile with the other $200,000.

"There it is gentlemen, $400,000. It's all yours, I am a man of my word. Congratulations. In our minds, you won it. The boss ordered me to pay you, so there it is. I propose we go to the bank in the morning, and I will wire it to any bank of your choice, or you can keep it here in the vault where it's Smith & Wesson insured."

Cav and Jimmy were speechless. In front of them lay the pool score of their life, in cash right in their face, and it was theirs; they had won a monumental score.

The powerful move served Marco and Marcella, too, as they gauged Cav and Jimmy's response. This was pure entertainment for them since they often fucked off millions in a week! $400,000 was peanuts to them. Once Cav and Jimmy left, they would likely have a laugh and toast their own success, since manipulation of others was for them the real game they loved to play.

The boys woke up out of their trance with Cav suggesting they leave the money in the vault for now, to which Marco announced, "In that case, let's celebrate your win! Don't let us stop your success, let's get this party started."

Right away, a staff member entered the office with an eye-watering vision: a long cart with a half pound of cocaine displayed across its top next to a calligraphed sign on the side, "Blow Cart!"

The way-over-the-top presentation came complete with polished sterling silver utensils and a large high-dollar silver-framed mirror encompassing the entire surface of the cart.

Marco wasted no time beginning his ritual, a form of predictive programming, of intelligently planting seeds in Cav and Jimmy's minds. Marcella dimmed the lights as they put the blow in front of Cav and Jimmy to "test the product."

There were so many actions at play in this moment that the boys couldn't keep up with the dazzling con job. They had never seen so much blow so close to their faces. Maybe an ounce here and there, but a half pound of coke loose on a cart right in front of them, to have as much as they want...NEVER!

Cav's early childhood policy to never do dope eroded over time as he grew older and got around some bad people and bad relationships. Right now, Jimmy and Cav were dying to sample the goods, so when Marcella handed them each a polished sterling silver coke spoon, pointed to the powder and asked them to "indulge yourselves please," there was little to stop them. She even made a joke out of it, saying, "Eat all you want, we will make more!"

The boys engaged, swooped down, and scooped up samples while they discussed the emerald business with their new employers.

Still, "shocked" would be an understatement once they experienced the quality and purity of the product. Cav enthusiastically congratulated Marco and Marcella for such an amazing product.

"It's the best blow and highest quality I have ever tasted!"

Jimmy, likewise, congratulated them. "Marco, you have won the grand prize here. I give it the blue ribbon, Best in Show award."

Marco responded in kind, "Gentlemen, it's pure 999.9 fine blow. We give it the Good Housekeeping Seal."

Cav asked why they were not joining them in the celebration, and Marco responded, "Oh no, as you can tell we're wrapped too tight for that. We smoke opium to mellow us out. Let me show you, follow me."

Marco and Marcella led them toward a back room, opened the door and turned on the light—a dark red light. The room was decidedly upscale décor with a custom neon sign posted on one wall, "OPIUM DEN."

In the center of the room was a circular, high-tempered glass, five-feet tall hookah-like chamber lit up with a blue light inside. Inside lay 10 two-foot-square cubes of opium, the 10 blocks having roughly a street value of maybe $160,000-$170,000.

Cav was speechless with disbelief, but Jimmy was acting like, "Sign me up!"

They walked up to the massive chamber, disbelieving but examining the blocks of 100% pure, black-soiled opium cubes.

Suddenly, the chamber gas fired.

Cav joked to Jimmy, "We've seen logs on the fire, but this is a whole new level of shit up in here."

Surrounding the opium dispenser were six deeply cushioned luxurious chaise lounge chairs, each with a long individual hookah tube resting on a custom holder next to the chair.

Marco laughed. "It's a giant dope pipe for six!"

Marcella turned up the fire inside the chamber, instantly filling it up with smoke. She invited everyone present to take hits.

Jimmy asked for a rain check as did Cav. Since it was more blow that they wanted, they journeyed back to the office. There, Cav, for the last time raised some concerns.

"Guys, what do I know about emeralds? Jimmy, you want to weigh in here?"

Marco took over and continued, "Cav, it's all about the presentation, the appraisals, and the documentation. It's simple because it's just selling. The old story goes, you can lead a horse to water, but you can't make him drink it. Well, I led you to the water, to millions of dollars in your hands, easy money, and you still doubt me?"

Though listening, Jimmy and Cav continued doing more coke. The boys soon flew high in dreamland on the blow. They were soon coked out of their minds, which was Marco's design. As they reached a state of weakened reasoning powers, lost in a dream space, Marco dropped the hammer and got right to the real show: Part Three, the final act.

Marco raised his hands, rose, and quieted the room, offering more money in a shorter amount of time.

"Gentlemen, depending on how much money you truly desire, from the looks of it, two million doesn't appear to win friends and influence people. How about $24 million a year plus? Not 2 million a year. How about a million a month, each? Do I have your attention now?"

Cav leaned back in his chair and asked Marco politely to continue. "Yes sir, you have all my attention."

Marco raised his bet, standing up and leaning down over the boys while rising to a supreme level of confidence as he drove home the real play, the game he and Marcella had really brought them down to Rio for.

"Gentlemen, I call what I'm about to tell you 'the generational wealth insider trading tip of the day.' I have a way, a system, to take you to retirement in one year. You will never have to work another day in your life, in a very short amount of time. You can then do what you want when you want for life. Focus on your pool, play as much pool as you like, whatever. Life will suddenly be on your time, no demands on you, no one influencing you but you!"

Cav and Jimmy sat hypnotized by Marco's voice, mesmerized by his pitch and his persuasive personality. They were eager to believe in his promises of luxury and glamor. This was where Marco shone—the part of the show where he figured he must win them over. This was the final act that must be successful or all of his and Marcella's efforts would fail.

Now, with the fascination of the quality of their cocaine and the deep effect of dollar signs on both Jimmy and Cav, Marco unveiled his bullet-proof, iron-clad proposal.

"I will deposit almost $12 million in your bank account over the next six months—$6 million for you, Cav, and $6 million for you, Jimmy."

This was stupid money, a ridiculous amount of money offered to these pool bums who miraculously had only recently managed to have $100,000 apiece that represented everything they owned under the sun, moon, and stars, to travel to Rio to gamble it all on a pool match.

Incredibly, with everything handed to him on a silver platter, and in his current semi-dream state, Cav managed to push back. He expressed his hesitation.

"Marco, with all due respect, I won't like being locked up in a cage for a quarter century."

More receptive to the proposal, Jimmy interrupted, "I'm listening Marco. Cav, I'm going to let the man speak his business. Is that OK?"

Cav waved a hand and sat back to listen.

Using the persuasive effects of the cocaine on his prospects, Marco revealed a seemingly foolproof system.

"Gentlemen, I have a highly paid, trusted, US Federal Customs Officer at LaGuardia International Airport in New York on my payroll, and New York has proven to be my strongest entry point to North America.

"First, we are going to transform you, both of you. Marcella has hired the best Benny Boy designers in the southern hemisphere. From new designer shoes, $10,000 tailored suits, first-class flights...hell, even Esmeralda will envy you two!

"A polished million-dollar professional appearance, that's all a cover-up. Call it live theater, and you two are the stars of the legitimate high-dollar emerald imports portion of the show. Your suits are props, the emeralds are props. Documents you will hold may be the closest to anything legitimate in your possession and issued by the government of Brazil!

"You will look the part, act the part, and prove with all your certified documentation that you are what you present to the world. And if anyone outside our orbit asked, which is very unlikely, you would have the proof of your innocence right there in your lily-white hands."

Marco relentlessly painted a picture of a lifestyle filled with overwhelming financial and personal success.

"Gentlemen, you won. First, you won $400 thousand on a 9-ball match by default. Now, I'm offering you $6 million in cash each in the next 6 months for 30 minutes of work time. By the time you pick up your bags at baggage claim and hand them over to my man Mr. Anderson, less than 30 minutes of possession for a cool million will have passed."

Marco was winning the sale.

"Sorry I got so tied up in all the excitement I forgot to give you two other props, here take this." Marco handed them each a box.

Cav asked, "What's this?"

Marco replied, "More props, damn expensive ones. Brand new El Presidential Rolex watches to go with your high-dollar suits."

Marco then insisted they take $10,000 each for walking around money, and handed them $10,000 each as if money was so easy to come by around them. He jokingly remarked, "There's a money tree around back," which prompted laughs.

If Cav and Jimmy only knew what really was outside!

Marco continued, "I show off all my agents to appear rich and successful; this throws off prying eyes and suspicion. Now, strap on those watches. Let's see how they look."

Jimmy commented, "Damn, Marco, you sure about this?" Marco responded, joking in his style, "Not too sure about it, but I would bet my life on it."

This proposal came wrapped in the temptation of wealth and a shot at entering the upper class, placing Cav and Jimmy in a challenging position at a crossroads, still not fully decided. Their integrity was being tested by the appeal of unlimited wealth and never-ending abundance. And by this time, the same test had almost 100% proven success among other recruits.

"Oh, before I forget, I'm hosting a party tomorrow night for my niece's 16th birthday," Marco added. "You're all invited, of course. I will share with you some of my most sensitive, classified, foolproof methods of getting the goods past the gatekeepers. I promise you, gentlemen, after tomorrow night you will have zero doubts or concerns. But, for now, I ask that you both just hang on to what I have shared so far, and keep it under your hats between yourselves. Keep an open mind until I show you everything tomorrow night. Tomorrow night I will leave you with no doubts, and you will be able to make a rational decision with all the facts known to you."

Agreement was obvious, although not a word was spoken from that point forward about the proposal. Marco confirmed their attendance at his niece's 16th birthday party the following night. He also handed Jimmy a card, and said: "Gentlemen, please visit my tailor tomorrow and pick yourselves out a couple of nice suits for the party. My tailor is already expecting you."

You could call Jimmy and Cav stunned, incapable of thinking up any more questions.

The following day was to be a big day in paradise.

21

You Look Marvelous

Upon that polished finish and with perfectly tailored suits in hand, the tailor handed Cav a card for the barber and a final coat of polish, after which, transformed, they headed back to the resort to relax before preparing for the evening's coming events.

Early in the evening, the girls arrived, Esmeralda and Gisele turning heads as they walked through the lobby. Each had poured on the beauty for the evening, knowing it was a formal event to be attended among many of their friends, dignitaries, and other local celebrities.

They knocked on the door to Cav and Jimmy's suite and found the boys immaculately turned out on a par with their own wardrobes. Delighted, the ladies said the boys were almost unrecognizable. Esmeralda asked laughing, "Is there a guy named Cav here?" Laughing with Esmeralda, the boys presented the ladies with fresh flowers.

In the late afternoon, Marco's driver arrived at the resort to escort the quartet, Esmeralda, Gisele, Jimmy, and Cav, to the niece's 16th birthday party. As they approached the Marco mansion, it became evident that this wasn't just a party. The wealth and luxury on display rivaled the grandest of affairs. The evening promised to be a glittering affair attended by such notable figures as Richard Nunes, the Governor of Sao Paulo, and Carlos Magarinos, the Ambassador of Argentina. The guest list alone testified to the wealth and prestige of the unusual event. The presence of dignitaries, socialites, and influential figures was an exclamation point to the influence and power wielded by Marco and Marcella.

Cav and Jimmy, transformed by their new tailored suits and Rolex watches, appeared to belong within the circle of influential figures and other usual suspects. The idea of wealth, and the promise of a lucrative partnership with Marco, was still pending but a likely conclusion.

All eyes were on "Miss International," Brazil's proudest daughter, the showstopper of the evening—Esmeralda. Draped in pink chiffon, her entrance captivated the attention of the other guests, media reps and the ever-present paparazzi. She was instantly surrounded, the center of attention. Such occasions were nothing new to her at this point in her career. She graced the scene with seasoned confidence, poise, and natural beauty.

The media, orchestrated under Marcella's directions, focused its lenses on Esmeralda and her companions, determined to capture every move in a flurry of flashes and clicks. Beside Esmeralda, Gisele exuded her own brand of raw elegance that complemented the superstar's presence. Guests and media reps asking who Esmeralda and Gisele's handsome escorts were would have been amused to learn they were just a couple of no-name pool sharks from Kansas. Marcella's crew had worked wonders transforming Cav and Jimmy to fit the roles designated to them in flawless high dollar suits and accessories, and fed the media "influential sportsmen, our guests from America."

This affair was certainly one of the country's most notable exhibitions of excess and indulgence of the year. And in this realm of privilege and power, those with questionable backgrounds but the right connections were afforded special treatment.

Marco and Marcella themselves were masters at appearances and generosity all while simultaneously engaging in unlawful activities. They donated sizable sums to high-profile charities to advance their public relations, any causes that cast them in a positive light. Yet they secretly participated in fraudulent charity swindles, supported phony research foundations and fake fundraising events from whatever direction the wind blew, as long as it attracted crooked politicians and the likes of South American Emerald Mining Company tycoons, while the media perpetuated the hype that they were decent and even noble people.

The sweet sounds of bossa nova floated through the mansion as Marcella and Marco warmly welcomed their prime guests for the night, Esmeralda, Gisele, Cav, and Jimmy. A waiter appeared and presented each of them with a glass of champagne.

Esmeralda inquired about the whereabouts of Marco's niece, the birthday girl. In a moment of staged bravado, Marco summoned his niece and introduced her first to his superstar of the evening.

"Graziela, please say hi to Esmeralda, Gisele, Cav and Jimmy!" The pretty teenager extended her hand to them and curtsied—a paparazzi moment, for sure. Even Marco's thick coat of machismo appeared to melt a little by Esmeralda's dazzling presence. But a look from Marcella reminded him he had a larger agenda to attend to tonight.

Esmeralda, covering her deep hostility towards Marco, presented the adorable young Graziela with a small, beautifully wrapped birthday gift. Speaking in Portuguese, she introduced herself under an imagined assumption that Graziela probably didn't know who she was, or her global celebrity reputation. However, the youngster was a big fan who had followed her career through magazines and the online media. The personal gift from one of her idols touched Graziela's heart.

Esmeralda asked her to open the gift now. With the crowd watching and paparazzi snapping picture after picture, Graziela opened the gift and was moved to tears. Esmeralda had given the niece her first-ever tiara from the first beauty pageant she won at 16. After the initial shock, Esmeralda set the tiara in place on the niece's head. Of course, dozens of guests snapped pix on their cell phones while the paparazzi went ballistic with flashing cameras. Everyone congratulated Graziela, who smiled through tears of happiness.

Marco and Marcella were entranced by Esmeralda's social graces, on a level they could only dream of doing themselves. Rare it was to see Marco humbled in this way, but he had no choice. At his side, Marcella looked on with envy.

Esmeralda introduced Graziela to Gisele, Cav, and Jimmy with the elegance of a diplomat presenting esteemed guests. She intended this experience to have a profoundly positive effect for Graziela, one that would, in a sense, pass on the torch of poise and social refinement under the pressures of frequently unwanted public attention, something Graziela would surely experience more of in her life.

The night's festivities progressed, and eventually Marco took the stage.

"I request my distinguished guests to raise their glasses in a toast to my niece's birthday celebration. Here's to the radiant soul celebrating 16 glorious years of life. May every moment ahead be as bright, adventurous, and extraordinary as the beautiful journey that was. Cheers to a future filled with joy, success, and endless possibilities. Happy Birthday, Graziela!"

Enthusiastic applause followed, a fitting tribute for the young girl of the hour.

With her typical impeccable grace, Esmeralda introduced Gisele and the boys to the Ambassador of Argentina. She showcased her linguistic finesse, conversing fluently in Spanish, as did Gisele, further illustrating their sophistication and cultural appreciation at the highest level of their culture.

Cav and Jimmy, caught in the midst of this grand theatrical production, were impressed by the polish and pizzazz of Marco and Marcella's world. The promised moment came when Marco summoned Cav and Jimmy to follow him down a hallway, away from the party, until he paused in front of a life-sized statue of Buddha. He reached out and lowered one of the statue's arms, which opened a door hidden in the wall. They entered another hallway, the door closing behind them, and followed Marco to an underground hideaway—a secret lair that concealed sensitive information. The boys were impressed by rows of gadgets, a table of bottles and dishes and test tubes, what looked like an X-ray machine, and whatever else he might need, all apparently for his cocaine business.

Marco walked over to an empty desk, sat down in the chair, leaned back and smiled. Cav and Jimmy stood quietly, watching and wondering what was up.

"Do you know how many people have been in this room? I can count them on one hand," Marco said. "This speaks to the trust we have put in you two gentlemen. And there's no catch. If I make you wealthy, what does that do for me and the boss? It only empowers us more. You bring in the emeralds, pay any fees, and our paid federal agent at LaGuardia ensures everything goes smoothly as planned. I've been doing this for years and now we really are foolproof. You're not risking anything. I told you that I would demonstrate this tonight and I shall."

Cav, still a little skeptical, questioned Marco.

"But why us? Why bring us into all of this? There's a thousand guys out there. What do you get out of it?"

Marco was all too happy to accommodate Cav's doubts.

"I see potential in you two. You've got street skills, and I like winners. Plus, it's always good to have reliable partners. And, of course, there's the matter of loyalty. Can I be completely honest with you? I brought you down here because I did a process of elimination among several different professions: boxing, soccer, baseball, many different types of sports, even lawyers, you name it. None made the grade or survived the, shall we say, cut!"

He leaned forward and pointed at Cav and then at Jimmy. His smile disappeared, replaced by a matter-of-fact seriousness.

"Professional big-money pool players have some unique qualities. Street smarts. Ability to make creative decisions under pressure, quickly! You are con artists, like it or not. And you're actually part of an art form and an international sport, which is pool. Money action pool is an extension, and that's the deal, my friends. I could go on but we're wasting time. I've decided on you two bums and that's that."

His smile came back. They all laughed. Cav and Jimmy exchanged glances, sensing that loyalty to Marco involved far more than a simple partnership.

Marco continued, "I'm offering you a chance to play in the biggest of leagues, gentlemen. The real question is, can you have it, can you do something with it?"

Cav hesitated, weighing the risks and rewards, but Jimmy seemed more inclined to take the plunge right away. The appeal of unimaginable wealth and the fascinating lifestyle Marco promised was tough to pass up.

Jimmy tossed out a question.

"Marco, what about the coke? Won't that show up on the x-rays?"

Marco smiled. "Allow me to demonstrate. The trick is that we use a specially designed lining in the luggage that masks any presence of the coke. Our own lab perfected it. No x-ray can detect or see the coke. We have proven this many times."

Marco then asked them to examine some luggage. "There is a secret compartment for the emeralds that you will expose to the eye in the sky at the airport upon your arrival for the optics scan. We let them see you take out the stones from the secret compartment, but we planted the 'yeyo' (cocaine) in the other hidden compartments."

Marco then walked them over to an x-ray conveyor machine, identical to the ones used at the airports.

"Walk around here so you can see the screen when we put the luggage through. You see exactly what they see.

"First, examine the contents with it open: toothbrush, clothing, shaver, underwear, shoes. And here are the emeralds in this 'secret' compartment. Okay, now I put back the stones in the special compartment. Close it and run it through.

"You see there is no sign of anything except my clothes, contents and the stones in the special compartment."

Marco then opened the luggage, removed the contents and took a military-style knife and cut open the lining at the bottom, the sides, and the top of the luggage and pulled out the packet with the blow. He opened it and showed the boys, making believers out of them, having driven home the fundamental proof-positive principle of this business model.

Jimmy asked, "What about the dogs?"

Marco explained, "That's a good question. This wrapping material insulating our product in the luggage puts out a scent that temporarily numbs the dog's ability to smell the product.

Cav, still hesitant after his partner's request, asked, "And what about the risks? What if we get caught?"

Marco leaned in with a serious expression on his face. "Gentlemen, that's where my connections and human protections come into play. My resources extend far beyond this mansion. You play by my rules, and I'll make sure nothing happens to you. Remember, loyalty is everything. And from what I can see before me, you're under my wing now."

Still processing the information, Cav ran his hand through his hair. "It sounds like a well-thought-out plan, Marco. Let's talk about the money. How do we get our share, and how much are we talking about, really?"

Marco ignored the question and went on, "Another significant development in our labs is our breakthrough to condense the product and maximize space and quality. Over three years of research by the best chemists in the world, from Switzerland to Germany, has led to this breakthrough. You two are among the very few who will know this, but the quantity in your luggage can be processed at a ratio of 1000 to 1. One gram equals 1 kilo. We have a secret lab set up in New Jersey for all our processing—a state of the art facility equipped with AI and $10,000,000 worth of equipment for its use. The reduction process is done here in Rio for transport and, later, the expansion of the product is done in New Jersey."

Jimmy and Cav exchanged a look: "Impressive."

"One more thing. When you arrive at the airport, my contact there receives the goods. Once you hand over the luggage, it's zero risk to you at that point. Your hands are clean. You technically take less than 30 minutes possession, and you're done. Once it's out of your hands you're free and not liable legally. There is a small section between Customs and ground transportation where you hand over the luggage after you leave Customs. My man, Mr. Anderson, will be waiting for you where there are no overhead cameras, confirmed with each arrival by our confidential staff there."

Marco continued: "All money is electronically handled and by the book. We deposit the funds from the phony sale of the emeralds to honest, legitimate registered businesses who purchase the emeralds. They are all shills—phony, fake buyers in Thailand, Hong Kong, and Tel Aviv, who wire the funds for the emeralds' purchase, which goes directly into your bank account in Los Angeles. You keep the profit after wiring the other funds due me, back to my bank here in Rio."

By now, Cav and Jimmy were 100 percent engaged, listening carefully to every word.

"That money you wire back to Rio is made to look like your next order of emeralds. The money you get wired to your account is what I am paying you to transport the product, but the totals match exactly the value of the sales of the emeralds.

"Example: We wire you $4 million for your emerald sales, and you keep $2 million and wire $2 million back for your next emerald purchase. It's that simple and all funds match receipts, internet net auction bids, sales, and expenses all done by our accounting firm. Air-tight, nothing left to chance. Our accounting firm will track and account for all the taxes, deduct it and place it in a private pool for them to pay the IRS."

Marco's final pitch:

"This operation is 100% foolproof, and it works every time. If my previous asset had not gotten greedy, you wouldn't be here. Greed is not good. Be straight with me, follow the carefully documented, proven route, and you will be rich. Fuck with my money and I will fuck with yours, a simple proven successful rule in my business. I'm very sincere and fair."

Cav expressed his final concern and a counter-offer. "Marco, please, you are asking us to risk our lives. It's 25 years if we get caught, gone, poof, our lives are over. Make it a straight $4 million per shipment."

Turning toward his partner, "And, Jimmy, if you accept, we are all in."

Jimmy agreed. "I have no objections."

Cav, a good, smart negotiator, had more to say.

"This is a hell of a risk, Marco, and you know it. You could lose 100 shipments and it wouldn't change one damn thing for you. You know we're serious. You know we are trustworthy. Trust is currently a valuable commodity, and I know you appreciate that. Let us prove ourselves to you and the boss, Marcella, that we can do this regularly. And I hope we can do this until we have enough money to retire early. That way you're happy, we're happy and life moves on."

In this delicate stage of the negotiation, Marco and Cav engaged in a strategic back-and-forth. Marco, protective of his carefully designed system, countered Cav's proposal.

"I spent millions developing this system. I pay my Customs Agent a seven-figure annual salary. The risk is zero."

Cav, unshakable, remained unyielding.

"Nothing is zero risk except for you and Marcella, Marco. How many grams can you get inside that custom pouch? Times eight pieces of luggage? $20 million-$30 million per shipment for you and a measly $4 million to me and Jimmy. That's a win-win Marco. There will always be risk. $4 million per shipment to prove myself, ourselves. Soon, you will be a believer." Cav then raised his glass and proposed a toast.

"Here's to our success. I extend to you in advance my most sincere gratitude to you, Marco and Marcella."

Marco looked hard at Cav, then looked around the lab and thought for several moments. Then he stood and, with a smile, stuck out his hand to Cav and Jimmy.

"Deal!" Marco said. "Now, our work is done here. Cav you are one tough son of a bitch!"

They shook hands, everyone smiling, Marco especially delighted at what he had accomplished—getting the boys' agreement—and at the price he was secretly prepared to pay all along.

"Shall we go back and join our friends at the party?" Marco suggested. "But Cav, before we go, I want you to have this for your beautiful new lady, whom, I hope, will soon be your wife."

He handed Cav an unexpected gift.

Cav opened the package from Marco and held it up, feeling the weight of an expensive emerald and diamond necklace. He was visibly taken aback by the generosity and value of the present.

"Marco, this is truly stunning," Cav said with a mixture of gratitude and hesitation in his voice. "I appreciate your kindness, but I can't accept such a generous gift."

Marco insisted, "Nonsense, my friend! Esmeralda will love it. Consider it a token of our friendship. Besides, she deserves something as beautiful as she is."

With the necklace in hand, Cav soon contemplated the best way to present the magnificent gift to Esmeralda as they all departed the secret office and lab, ready to celebrate their new alliance and the possibilities it could bring. As they walked back to the party, Cav couldn't shake the feeling that they had just stepped into a world that would either make them or break them.

They arrived back at the lively atmosphere of the party with its music, laughter, and clinking glasses. However, Cav sensed some tension and even suspicion from Esmeralda, wondering what he and Jimmy were up to, disappearing with Marco for nearly half an hour. He attempted to downplay the situation and instead reassured her by telling her a story manufactured out of desperation—the need to recover their lost money from the robbery.

Esmeralda, with her intuition and understanding of the world, sensed that there was more to the story. Her concerns spilled out as she questioned whether they might have made a deal with the devil and sold out their souls. She turned to Jimmy and demanded the truth.

Cav and Jimmy struggled to convince Esmeralda their dire situation was real, the difficulty Cav struggled with just to make enough money consistently to live, and how he had suffered most of his life. Anything but admit any deals with Marco.

Cav saw that Esmeralda wouldn't be easily swayed to accept the whole deal right now. So he suggested they say their goodbyes and leave the party and move to somewhere farther away from Marco and company. Esmeralda yielded a little, acknowledging that perhaps she had overstepped with her earlier objections, and agreed the foursome should find a more relaxed setting where they might set aside their differences—at least for the evening.

They found Marco and Marcella and thanked them for the lovely party, and accepted Marco's offer of a limo back to their hotel.

Once they were comfortable in the limo, Cav felt the need to lighten the mood and make things special. He playfully teased Esmeralda about having "something very special for her."

Esmeralda laughingly said that she already had the key to the city, what more could she possibly want?

They chuckled a bit, and then Gisele yelled out, "It's honestly true, she does have a key to the city."

Their laughter marked a return to normalcy and friendly relaxation.

"Can I have it tomorrow night instead of tonight?" Esmeralda asked Cav. "And would you like to know why?"

"Have what tomorrow?" Cav responded. "Sorry, I'm lost knowing that you actually have a key to a city." This got a new round of laughs. "Yes, sorry, please do tell me," Cav said. "I would indeed like to know why tomorrow night and not tonight."

"Well, if you insist," Esmeralda teased, "it's my birthday tomorrow."

They all took turns reaching over and hugging and congratulating Esmeralda.

"I have reserved somewhere special I would like us all to go to, a very exclusive private restaurant," she announced. "The reservation is set for 8:00 tomorrow evening. It's a place Gisele and I have treasured for a long time. I truly believe you and Jimmy are going to love it."

Looking into her eyes, Cav said: "And I promise to make this the best birthday you've ever had."

Esmeralda was deeply moved by Cav's promise. He embraced her again and tenderly wiped away a tear with his thumb. He placed a gentle kiss on her cheek and whispered in her ear, "You are the most amazing woman I have ever met!"

22

Happy Birthday, Gorgeous

The following evening, Esmeralda and Gisele stopped at the hotel to pick the boys up for the birthday dinner party. As they entered the lobby, they were met with a delightful surprise—rose petals scattered across the lobby floor creating a magical path for them to follow. Posters on the walls announced: "Happy Birthday Esmeralda!"

Luiz, the concierge, warmly greeted them. "Welcome, ladies. This way, please."

He had dolled up the resort for Esmeralda, a conspiracy that he and Cav had come up with. The entire staff was gathered to extend their best wishes for Esmeralda's birthday.

Esmeralda and Gisele were genuinely surprised and touched. They expressed their gratitude to each member of the staff as they walked past.

More surprises. Cav and Jimmy's suite was also transformed, candles flickering, bouquets of flowers beautifying every surface, and a huge "HAPPY BIRTHDAY" banner above everything.

Cav and Jimmy, impeccably dressed, waited with champagne in hand. Cav greeted Esmeralda with a big smile and a "Happy birthday, gorgeous." She looked stunning in an emerald-green dress with matching accessories, making her every bit the appropriate birthday icon.

Gisele was also glowing and beautiful and ready to celebrate in an equally stunning outfit. Jimmy presented her with a bouquet of orchids. Touched by the beauty of the flowers, she thanked him with a heartfelt kiss.

After enjoying some champagne and banter, Cav glanced at his new Rolex and said, "Shall we go? We don't want to be late."

The quartet stepped into a waiting limo to make a night of incredible memories. At the restaurant, they entered a world of grandeur and class touched by a breathtaking sunset view of Rio spread below. The waitstaff was there to greet them, and the witty owner, Gilberto, immediately hugged Esmeralda and joked about her age as, "21 and holding."

The party was settled into a private dining area with elegant décor that added to the celebratory mood. A stunning, breathtaking view of the city stretched out before them. As soon as the guests took their assigned seats at the family-style table, the hors d'oeuvres began arriving like clockwork, and laughter set the tone for a delightful evening.

Gilberto, acting as the sommelier, personally brought the first wine to accompany the first course. He bragged about the neighboring Argentina vineyards. After pouring the wine, however, he changed his message: "Let me shut up, and you tell me what you think."

Courtesy dictated that the first sip go to Cav. With great anticipation, everyone stared at him, and you could have heard a pin drop if it weren't for the beautiful Brazilian samba filling the airwaves in the background. Unfortunately, Cav expressed a distaste for the wine with a sour look on his face. Gilberto was embarrassed, as was their group, until Cav burst out laughing.

"This is the best wine I have ever had! It sure beats the hell out of Boone's Farm Strawberry Hill!"

Everyone laughed, Jimmy especially hard, as he was the only one who actually knew the Boone's Farm brand.

Pouring the fine Argentinian wine generously, Gilberto couldn't stop laughing at Cav's prank. Joy reigned from there forward, and the evening continued on a high note. Esmeralda, overcome by the surprises of the evening, couldn't help but feel grateful for the thoughtful gestures that surrounded her—even the restaurant staff had greeted her warmly, acknowledging her special occasion with genuine and sincere birthday wishes.

The waiter appeared to announce the meal.

"The courses have already been created and preparations are underway as I speak. If you would like to request anything special, go ahead and don't be bashful. Please have fun."

The courses unfolded, and each dish was a masterpiece of succulent flavors and brilliant presentation. Esmeralda, surrounded by familiar people who had become integral parts of her stylish life, was deeply happy and grateful.

Gisele, beaming with happiness, exchanged frequent glances with Jimmy. Jimmy wore a grin plastered across his face, a look that said he may have met his special Girl from Ipanema.

Cav tapped his wine glass and rose to make a special announcement to honor Esmeralda.

"A toast, to a celebration of my woman of the hour."

They all took a sip of wine, and Cav reached over and presented Esmeralda with the wrapped gift.

Esmeralda carefully unwrapped her present, revealing a beautiful emerald-and-diamond necklace that took her breath away. She was speechless, but everyone saw her love for Cav and the sparkle in her eyes as bright as the diamonds in the necklace.

Cav attempted to attach the necklace but his nervous fingers couldn't handle the tiny clasp.

"Damn it, I can't seem to get it!"

Esmeralda turned around to face Cav and quipped, "Well, you didn't have any trouble with my bra, did you?" loud enough for everyone to hear including nearby tables of strangers who of course recognized the beautiful model. She brought the house down with that one. Cav was laughing so hard he was rendered hopeless with the necklace. The laughter turned the moment into one of the high points of the evening.

Jimmy sprang to the rescue and attached the necklace. With Esmeralda's huge smile, it looked absolutely perfect on her. She appeared to be royalty. Cell phones came out everywhere and everyone took photos and loudly admired the beauty of the necklace, congratulating her and Cav and wishing her the happiest of birthdays.

In spite of all the joy, Cav found himself harboring an unspoken question: Was Marco so moved by the class Esmeralda had shown to his niece at the birthday party that he gave Cav something beautiful for Esmeralda? Or was there some other ulterior motive?

After the final course, a waiter arrived with a birthday cake decorated with candles and placed it before Esmeralda. Gilberto also arrived and stood nearby.

The room momentarily hushed, and then everyone sang the Brazilian equivalent of "Happy Birthday." Esmeralda's eyes sparkled as she made a wish and blew out the candles.

Gilberto presented bottles of Dom Pérignon and a waiter placed champagne glasses for everyone. This added even more class to the event, much to the gathering's delight.

After several more hours of champagne and various desserts, it was time to say farewell to the rare and delightful celebration. Everyone exchanged heartfelt goodbyes with the staff and fellow patrons, knowing as they left the posh restaurant that memories of the love, laughter, and the warmth of the evening would remain for years to come.

Back at the boys' hotel suite, they sat and chatted about the party, great food and wine and new friends, enjoying the quiet end of their night-long party together.

It was dawn when the house phone rang, and Jimmy picked it up. He had a brief exchange of words with someone, whispered "Marcella" to Cav, and excused himself from the group to speak with her privately in another room.

Esmeralda and Gisele were preparing to leave when Jimmy returned, his expression a mix of gratitude and sadness. He embraced both ladies warmly, thanked them for everything, and said how much he would miss them even if it was for just a couple of weeks.

Cav was also affected by the emotional farewells. "Let's walk them down," he said to Jimmy.

The four love-birds proceeded to the lobby. Under an early morning sun, Cav assured Esmeralda of his safety and urged her to call him that evening. The quiet exchange between Cav and Esmeralda spoke volumes, revealing the depth of their connection and the genuine love they already held for each other.

Esmeralda looked into Cav's eyes with concern and sincerity. "So, you're really working for Marco."

"I am not going to lie to you. I asked for your trust, and the assurances I gave you I meant. I gave myself six months, and that's it. I'm done, I promise."

Esmeralda maintained her poise and responded carefully.

"Cav, I said it's none of my business. That doesn't mean I'm okay with it."

Cav whispered, "Don't worry. I'll see you in a couple of weeks."

"I hope so," she said, tearing up a bit.

"Listen to me," he said. "I'm doing this so I can live comfortably and not rely on you or anyone. I need to stand on my own and use the money I set aside to make more money legally. I will have enough soon that I won't have to do this any longer and not worry about money any longer. I want to do something legit, something we can do together."

The weight of Cav's words hung in the air as they embraced, and he kissed her goodbye.

Esmeralda managed a smile through her tears. "You take care of yourself. And Jimmy."

Jimmy and Gisele were having a similar conversation.

The ladies left and Jimmy and Cav went back to their suite and began packing their belongings, both trying not to imagine various scenarios involving customs agents and cops and prisons.

While the events of the previous day lingered in the air, Jimmy was unable to contain his curiosity.

"Really, how did Esmeralda do with the Marco connection?"

"She was crushed. But she'll be okay. She's a strong woman and far above average. How about Gisele? Did you two get into that?"

"I guess she's a little less bothered by it. I don't know. What do you think?"

Cav didn't answer. Esmeralda's doubt still lingered in the back of his mind. For the last time he asked Jimmy,, "Are we sure we want to do any of this now?"

Jimmy expressed the frustration that had been building inside him. "Cav, I'm tired of being broke and making a score when we can even get a fuckin' game. And for what? Hundreds, thousands, the rare 10-20 large? Playing muscle games where we work our asses off to hustle for what? Don't think for a second I haven't thought deep about this shit. I couldn't sleep night before last. Listen to me, the thought of us being locked down for a quarter century keeps me up nights. If we went down and got sentenced we would be released mid-century, think about that, around the year 2050, earlier if we're good boys. Maybe."

They came out of their rooms, dressed and ready, and stood in the living room, both deep in thought.

Jimmy, with a sweeping gesture, directed attention to the possibilities that lay ahead.

"I mean, look at us and look at what's in front of us. We can be in and out of this business in a short time and, like you say, go legit and say, 'Fuck them.'"

Moving forward to take the plunge, Jimmy asked, "How do I look?"

Cav responded, "Brother, you look like a million dollars!"

Jimmy, strapping on his Rolex, declared, "Let's roll!"

With that, the duo embarked on the path they had chosen, which would forever shape their lives.

23

A Grand Design
of Untold Wealth

Using Marco's influential connections, Cav and Jimmy acceler-
ated the passport process at the Ministry of Foreign Affairs
and obtained new work visas on the spot, normally a three-week
wait period. Marco could maneuver through bureaucratic chan-
nels, controlling his connections to secure certain advantages
others might find challenging. While it might be considered an
abuse of the system, Marco saw it as manipulating a free pass in
a free-market system.

Later in the day they met with Marco personally. Digging
deeper into the strategy, Marco again explained the schemes to
his newest partners.

"You'll be handling emerald sales, and the accounting for the
emeralds will serve as the heart and soul of both our legal as well
as, let's say, our sub-standard transactions."

He emphasized the need for the international accounting firm Finney & Brown to act as their shield against the prying eyes of the IRS and other government agencies.

"They're the guardians of our financial purity. With their stamp of approval, we're insulated from unnecessary scrutiny. The careful documentation of the capital flow is our insurance policy. Every dollar accounted for, every transaction, accurately recorded, forms a protective barrier against any potential legal entanglements."

As Marco further detailed the scheme, he introduced two key players in the operation—the Customs agent and the actual recipient of the goods on the ground.

"These are the essential parts in our machine designed for smooth execution of our plan. They are our eyes and ears at La-Guardia, ensuring that everything goes according to script."

With a casual yet confident demeanor, Marco handed over the documents that would serve as Cav and Jimmy's ticket to financial security.

"Here are photos of your contacts on the ground and your documents for the emeralds."

The photos showed Customs agent Bob Toomay, and Richard Anderson, who would receive the goods.

"Keep those. They have yours."

Cav reassured Marco that there would be nothing to worry about on their side. He expressed renewed confidence in their ability to direct the essentials of this operation.

The handshake that sealed the deal marked the beginning of a new chapter.

As they parted ways, Cav added, "You did a great job perfecting this trade route. Me and Jimmy are going to take it to another level. You watch."

The wheels were set in motion for a journey that promised the two unimaginable wealth, albeit dangerous twists of fate, too.

In Marco's world, manipulation of the system was an art, and he could paint with broad strokes. He envisioned a world where legality and illegality coexisted, and each element played a crucial role in the grand design.

24

The Big Apple

Manhattan's towers gleamed in the morning sun as Cav and Jimmy wheeled in the sky and landed at LaGuardia International.

Their first stop was Immigration in the Customs office, where Marco's insider officer took them in individually.

Marco was correct. Their polished appearance, Rolex watches, slick suits and the flash of their very professionally prepared papers provided the needed cover for them to get through in a hurry.

Stepping out of Immigration now was the big moment on which their future success lay in the balance. They searched for Mr. Toomay, who noticed them before Cav and Jimmy noticed him. With a nod from Toomay the boys gathered their luggage from baggage claim and proceeded to his specific Customs counter.

Toomay asked them to open their luggage and he did a quick survey of the contents, after which he requested to look at their paperwork. When he located the emeralds, he pulled them out and placed them further back, ordering the two travelers to close their luggage while he took their paperwork to another agent, who inspected the documents. Satisfied that Toomay had stamped their paperwork, he took the sheaves from his fellow officer, stamped them and returned the stamped paperwork to Toomay, also handing approved copies to the travelers, waving them off with his "Okay" to leave. The quick and efficient handover of the luggage to Toomay, combined with the signed-off documentation paperwork, further solidified the success of this operation and took a ton of pressure off the boys' nerves.

Still, the final piece of the entry puzzle had to be solved. The boys conducted a quick sweep to find the last relay partner who held their final ticket to freedom: the promised cool four million dollars handed to them as planned—the easy money. They walked out of Customs and quickly found Mr. Anderson holding up a sign with their names on it. They recognized each other from photos Marco had shown to them.

Mr. Anderson's uniform gave the appearance that he was a porter, a valet of sorts. This appearance, should anyone be watching from an eye in the sky, looked wholly legitimate since he appeared more or less like a hired hand working for Cav and Jimmy Enterprise. Later, the goods transfer occurred in a tunnel area of the airport where there were no surveillance cameras, where Mr. Anderson took possession of their luggage. Cav and Jimmy instantly rushed outside to ground transportation and took a taxi midtown to The Waldorf Hotel.

The choice of the Waldorf, expensive and exclusive, was a reward for their success at Customs and the larger-than-life experience they had just pulled off for the first time without a hitch.

Once in their suite, Cav called Esmeralda and reassured her that they were safe and that the whole operation was smooth as silk. Esmeralda's relief was replaced by excitement and anticipation for Cav and Jimmy's return, now a guarantee since they were free and there'd been no complications. Cav was already planning an early reunion, and asked Esmeralda to pick him up at the Rio airport when he got back. The notion of her picking him up at the airport added a personal touch to their relationship, emphasizing the closeness that had developed between them.

Time flew by. Their daily routine developed and ran like a smoothly tuned Ferrari. The boys traveled back and forth to LA, down to Rio, and delivered in NYC. This continued for the next several months before they went full throttle with a fury, picked up merchandise in Rio, delivered it at LaGuardia, and, later, celebrated with excessive private parades and parties. Their lavish lifestyle appeared to be never-ending.

In Beverly Hills, their newfound wealth transformed their lives into a luxurious lifestyle they continued to share. Their new mansion was a hub for luxurious pool parties that brought them drugs, more gorgeous women, a fleet of fancy cars that included Lambos and Rolls-Royces, shopping sprees, and a continuous, seemingly endless flow of money as long as they stuck to their routine. Their unrestrained lifestyle extended to anything and everything they had ever dreamed or hoped for. A private accounting firm in Los Angeles exclusively worked for Cav and Jimmy, which Marco had set up for them. Their cover company, World Premier Films, and everything else was accountable to Marco and prepared with laser precision.

The boys enjoyed credit scores of 800+ even though they didn't even know what that meant. Their 5A Dunn and Bradstreet rating on their company was the highest credit score for a business in the $50,000,000 range, and they didn't even have a clue what it represented. They did understand that each had Black Centurion American Express cards with non-stop, no-limits privileges.

Cav and Jimmy had reached the point where they could walk away from their high risk, dangerous business and live a life of luxury and wealth without ever looking back. But no, hell no! Greed will always be a motherfucker.

Not many humans ever overcome the greed factor when the money rolls in at the volumes they experienced nonstop.

They had more money than a show dog could ever jump over, and a beautiful mansion rental in Beverly Hills. One day, their wealth management banker asked them to come by. She explained to them the process of buying a luxury estate, everything: the terms, the process, the down payment of $10,000,000, and the stability it could potentially lead to. They were clean, so they took out a mortgage for the balance and its all-auto debit payments. All their payments were already on auto pilot. All signature loans on the house, cars, everything! They didn't even know they paid interest on loans, the car payments, house payments, everything.

They never saw the mechanics of having money; they just lived it to the maximum!

The boys lived a life that most could only dream of, a high-rolling escapade defined by extravagance, an uncontrollable appetite for thrill. Extended getaways to Las Vegas became their norm—not as mere tourists, but as VIPs of the highest order. To the casino management, these weren't just guests; they were colossal "whales," gamblers of extraordinary means, worthy of the finest.

It all began on a typical Thursday night in Beverly Hills, where the boys—Jimmy and Cav—would host legendary pool parties at their sprawling mansion. These weren't ordinary gatherings; they were grand events meticulously crafted to indulge every possible luxury. Fifty, sometimes even a hundred guests attended, all treated to an exceptional buffet that was prepared by the finest chefs in Los Angeles. The spread featured everything from the finest culinary creations to flowing rivers of fine wines, $5,000 cognac, and $10,000 single malt whisky. And for those seeking an additional buzz, the "blow" was as abundant as the hors d'oeuvres.

Word about these parties spread like wildfire. Soon, super-models, pole dancers, professional dancers, and high-class escorts clamored for invitations. The ratio at these gatherings was ideal for the boys: 70% female and 30% male. By 3 a.m., decisions were made. Jimmy and Cav would round up their choices, summon 15 of their hand picked guests, and head straight for the red-eye to Vegas. Their preferred method of travel? A Gulfstream G-550 private jet on permanent speed dial, complete with dedicated pilots ready to take off at a moment's notice.

Vegas welcomed them like royalty. The boys' reputation quickly cemented them as the crown jewels of the casino world. Tens of millions could evaporate in a weekend, and they didn't blink. To them, money was an afterthought; the adrenaline rush of the gamble was the true prize. The casino boss recognized their value immediately. Ultra-luxurious VIP suites were arranged for their entourage, complete with every imaginable amenity.

As top-tier whales, Jimmy and Cav were awarded an opulent, multi-room private villa, hidden from public view—complete with butlers, chefs, and private swimming pools. The sprawling sanctuary was outfitted with a sauna and a 24-hour team of masseurs. Nothing was off the table. Casinos would increase table limits (into the hundreds of thousands per hand) or customize games to suit their preferences.

They were provided with a Lambo on each visit for personal use. At Christmas they were each given a rare Patik Philippe watch valued at $125,000, and on rare occasions they would be given private concerts.

"Super VIP" programs or exclusive gambling rooms were provided for Cav and Jimmy. This gave them complete privacy, top-tier service, and the opportunity to gamble at unparalleled stakes.

The casino's seduction didn't stop there. To ensure their loyalty, management began dispatching the casino's private jet at all hours. If the boys showed even a whisper of interest, a plane would arrive within minutes to whisk them away. The allure of the gaming tables became irresistible. With Vegas only a 45-minute flight from Beverly Hills, it was too convenient, too tempting, and far too thrilling to ignore.

Weekends bled into weekdays. The boys' win-loss tally became the stuff of legend. On a good night, their bets could pay for an army's sustenance for a year; on a bad night, it barely made a dent in their bottomless reserves. The casino's strategy was masterful—entice them with luxury, romance them with exclusivity, and keep them in action. Jimmy and Cav didn't just frequent Vegas; they became part of its fabric, inseparable from the glitz and the gamble that defined Vegas. It became so silly stupid that the casino parked one of its premier fleet jets at nearby Van Nuys Airport for immediate shuttle service to Vegas at a moment's notice.

25

Choices

As the days, weeks and months passed by, Cav and Esmeralda, given their schedules—her staying in Paris and Cav on the road for the most part—finally set up a meeting in Rio after a long time apart.

Cav and Jimmy returned to Rio and headed to their resort, where Esmeralda and Gisele greeted them. However, the reception was not the loving reunion they'd hoped for.

Esmeralda was furious at their physical appearance. "What the hell have you both been doing with yourselves? You look horrible, losing so much weight! You look like skeletons with puffy eyes, and dark circles under them."

Gisele also scolded them. "What happened to you guys? Is this what success looks like? I don't think so."

The atmosphere in the room was anger and frustration so thick you could choke on it.

Gisele continued her rant: "This is embarrassing. Do you not look in the mirror? Do you think you see Cary Grant when you look in the fucking mirror? You both should be ashamed."

Unable to contain her feelings, Gisele stormed out of the room with Esmeralda in tow, expressing her outrage with a flurry of "Fuck this and fuck you."

Cav, feeling the desperate need to save the situation, followed them ahead of Jimmy and attempted to persuade the women to return. It took some effort, but eventually, he managed to coax the two of them back into the room.

The boys poured on the bullshit, enough at least to settle down the ladies. Once cooled down to a semi-normal tone, Jimmy opened a bottle of wine and poured four glasses, while making a request.

"With your permission, may I order some room service? While it's being prepared, me and Cav are going to clean up, it was a long flight. I apologize I didn't sleep much last night. Please excuse us. Twenty minutes, I promise."

The two men left to clean up and make themselves as presentable as possible before returning. Meanwhile, room service for four progressed as the ladies sipped on their wine, which seemed to settle them down, although they got to tipsyville almost immediately.

Jimmy and Cav were numb and lit by the coke they both did while getting ready. Making sense of anything became a challenging task. The basic choices in life at this stage were dangerously reduced to self-destruction, dragging anyone who might join them along for the ride—in this case, Esmeralda and Gisele.

As the girls relaxed under the effects of the wine, Jimmy tried to make things look better, spreading his special blend of make believe. "The operation is almost complete. We are in the wind-down of the final stage of the business, and then we will be done."

They say "misery loves company," and that company at the moment was Esmeralda and Gisele. Still, the mood gradually lightened, and an appearance of happiness returned to the room. The ladies, by now somewhat intoxicated from the wine, seemed visibly more comfortable and relaxed.

As the evening progressed, the room filled with laughter and companionship, albeit beneath the social banter lay a deeper, sinister plan. The initial targets, Esmeralda and Gisele, remained unsuspecting of anything amiss. The boys, however, had dangerous intentions and destructive plans.

Things took a dark turn when Cav made his move, suggesting as he set up a piece of cut mirror loaded with cocaine on the table in front of everyone, "Shall we celebrate?"

Esmeralda, shocked, questioned, "What the hell is that?" Again, she demanded: "What the hell are you doing? Are you insane?"

Cav responded, "This, my dear, is a little something to make us all feel like we're in heaven. Yes, probably insane, but one small hit, and I bet you're gonna be super happy you did it."

"Come on, it won't kill you," Jimmy added, speaking to Esmeralda as he moved forward. "Go ahead, Esmeralda."

Jimmy snuffed a hit, followed by Cav. This simplifies the process, they see them doing it and how to do it, making it easy for the ladies to participate.

Pretty drunk and feeling susceptible, Cav and Jimmy pushed them hard, almost begging.

"Come on, just once. If you don't like it, we'll stop and put it away, but I bet you'll like it."

Backed into a corner and feeling the pressure of the moment, Esmeralda looked at Gisele, secretly hoping for her approval. "Should I, Gisele?"

In a moment of weakness, Gisele surrendered and lit the fuse. "Well, I don't think one time is going to do any harm. Why not at least try it, once?"

Esmeralda paused, letting the room fall silent as everyone else watched in suspense.

"Fuck it, why not?" She snorted a hit, soon shouting, "My God, wow, this feeling is incredible. I feel indestructible, I feel like I can do anything!"

Laughter erupted, and she handed the straw to Gisele, demanding an explanation from the boys: "Why have you kept this from me? OMG! I feel like I can fly, this is amazing."

Gisele took the straw and joined in. They all waited for her reaction in silence. "Holy fucking hell, OMG!!!"

Jimmy confirmed what he'd said earlier: "I told you."

They all partied into the night, losing themselves in the joy and sudden initial exhilaration of the coke.

To bring their filthy business and drugged lifestyle to these two angels was cruel and cold blooded. The boys had fallen to a new low, unconscious of their actions and the possible long-term consequences. It would be a hell of a wake-up call if they would ever make the journey back to the innocence they had before visiting Rio!

The next morning, the group awakened and looked terrible— weak, numb, physically and mentally and spiritually drained.

Jimmy was sick, throwing up in the bathroom. The girls, while sensing something was wrong, wallowed in guilt and felt helpless.

Esmeralda suddenly realized she had missed a meeting with her agent and new clients, and a press interview. She desperately searched for her phone, and then called Eliza, her agent. She apologized profusely, but Eliza expressed serious regret because the opportunities she'd arranged with Chanel and Ralph Lauren would be lost. In fact the representatives "are here with me now and leaving shortly, and they came mostly to meet with you."

Esmeralda tried to do damage control, saying she thought she might be coming down with the flu or something. She promised to make it up to her agent, and they ended the call.

The chaotic mood in the room was evident to everyone: scattered clothes, half-empty wine glasses, and leftover lines of coke scattered on various tabletops—a complete disaster.

But this one night was far from the end of it. The coke parties continued, night after night and day after day. Esmeralda and Cav, Gisele and Jimmy, they each experienced a rapid fall into the emotional and physical depths of hell.

Cav and Esmeralda were at the top of their games—Esmeralda a world-renowned supermodel, and Cav a celebrated pro world-class pool player. They were now in the compulsive grip of drug-fueled self-destruction. And the same was true of Jimmy and Gisele, each of them successful in their chosen profession. The impact of the drug on their lives was ruining them.

The toll on their lives and careers was undeniable and clearly visible to anyone with experience in drug addiction. Esmeralda eliminated her typically busy schedule of jetting off to photo shoots in London, Paris and Rome because that whole game no longer seemed important. That was par for the course anyway, because she was looking like hell. The same was true for Gisele, who was on the threshold of her own promising career as an international model.

As for Cav, he never practiced his pool skills anymore, and he had little interest in anything at all except getting more blow. There was no motivation to do anything beyond lines on a table and putting more millions in the bank.

Jimmy was just a shell of his former self. The idea man was now more of a walking dead man. He and Cav could crank it up when they absolutely needed to, like delivering to LaGuardia.

The effects of their destructive choices weighed heavily on each of them. They were past looking closely at what was happening to their lives. They just couldn't see how these choices were ruining their lives.

26

The Great Awakening

You might say that some time, something had to shake up the routine, and restore their awareness of reality.

Jimmy and Cav flew back to LaGuardia on one of their regular, well-rehearsed runs from Rio. Given their recognized status as frequent fliers, Immigration went smoothly without a hitch. However, when they approached Customs, they discovered their usual contact, Robert Toomay, was clearly absent. Jimmy immediately panicked, so Cav took over, coping with both the Customs problem and his shaky, coke-hungry partner.

"What the fuck do we do, Cav? We're in deep trouble here! We can't just tell these other federal officers that we're waiting on our special Customs agent. What's the plan, Cav?"

Then they noticed that trained drug-sniffing dogs were thoroughly inspecting everyone's luggage, and it looked as if security operations were visibly heightened everywhere.

Suddenly, federal agents and state police stormed past, scrambling towards what could be a major event unfolding in another part of the terminal. Jimmy and Cav paused, waiting and watching as their untouched luggage became abandoned at the baggage claim. They dared not let the bags get into the wrong hands, so they cautiously headed toward the claim area.

Suddenly, gunshots erupted from nearby where the agents had run. A frantic, panicked evacuation order echoed over the PA throughout the airport. Chaos reigned as people ran away from the sounds of gunshots. Amid the chaos, desperately seeking an escape route, the boys grabbed their luggage and joined the crowd of dozens of arriving passengers racing unchecked through Customs towards the exits. By some miracle, all the agents had also obeyed the emergency evacuation and left their duty stations. In fact, there were no agents anywhere in the vicinity inspecting any passenger luggage.

The duo raced straight through and past the empty customs counters, trying to get the hell out of the terminal, escaping bullets or worse.

Arrest for smuggling enough cocaine to put Cav and Jimmy behind bars for a long time was not an option in their minds. But none of their usual contacts appeared, leaving them alone and vulnerable, on their own for the first time without friendly contacts or protection, and still in possession of millions of dollars worth of smuggled, highly concentrated cocaine.

Nobody to turn to now. They had to think quickly and act on their instincts. FBI, NYPD, and special undercover agents with guns drawn swarmed the terminal, intensifying the sense of urgency among terminal personnel and passengers alike.

What were the odds Cav and Jimmy could make it outside free and unharmed? In the end, they cheated death and certain arrest. Had they been assigned another customs agent not on Marco's payroll, the outcome might have been far different.

Feeling invincible over time, Cav and Jimmy had started carrying private, personal-use stashes on themselves. They had gotten cocky and lazy. One patdown, one suspicious agent to check pockets and clothing, and their luggage would have been torn apart. It would have been curtains for the boys for a long time, like a minimum 25 years. One look at their fake financials by a tribe of IRS accountants from the Feds' enforcement arm would have put a microscope on everything they did. The evidence was there. The mansion, Lambo, Rolls Royce, any and everything, was out in the open if one knew where to look! An indictment would have included the RICO Act (Racketeering) almost certainly added to the drug bust. Unless Marco had a judge on the payroll in the Southern District of New York, these boys would face another 25 years, 50 years total, no doubt.

Federal agents selectively leak explosive stories to handpicked media allies. This one would have glorified the Feds as watchdog heroes. The media circus would sell a lot of hot dogs for a week, and advertisers would beg for more exposure, giving them extra time to sell more drugs, cars, insurance, whatever, during the longer media blitz—a guaranteed, 100-percent rousing story before the media moved on to a new calamity.

Cav and Jimmy would have been splattered over all media outlets internationally for a minimum of at least two news cycles. A good solid week of the colorful life story of two Kansas boys. And what a story it would make: two boys from Kansas hustling their way to the top of their pool game and eventually meeting up with a notorious crime lord and kingpin in exotic Rio de Janeiro: Marco and the real power behind him, Marcella.

The book would read like a modern-day *Evita*, the famous story about Evita Peron, the Argentinian rags-to-riches tale and famous Broadway musical and film.

Hollywood screenwriters, documentarians, and professors from top universities would jump in and join the feeding frenzy. If Esmeralda could be drawn into the story, as she most certainly would be, it would ruin her life and pristine reputation as well, for sure!

But, who gives a fuck, right? Just get the story out, never mind the lives wrecked. All the news that fits, yeah?

27

Escape to
New York's Waldorf

Outside the terminal, Jimmy flagged down a taxi and the two escaped with their lives intact. When they checked in at the Waldorf, they paid special attention as the bellhop piled their suitcases onto his hand truck, each bag stuffed with millions of dollars worth of blow.

Later, while watching the news on their TV, they learned that a high-level UN Security Council member had been assassinated in cold blood at the airport. The baggage claim area where they retrieved their luggage was a mere 50 feet away. Two assassins, foreign nationals, died in the exchange of gunfire with the cops.

"Damn lucky we didn't catch a stray bullet. We cheated death there, bro!" Jimmy exclaimed. "We could have easily been shot. You heard those bullets fly, sounded like a bad night in Beirut. We were right there ringside during the shoot-'em-up!"

The Swiss chemist from New Jersey eventually arrived at the hotel to collect the goods, taking the shipment and abruptly leaving without a word said. He was way outside of his comfort zone. For him, being forced to carry the goods put him at extreme risk due to someone else's incompetence. Playing errand boy was not in his job description. He was furious, and rightfully so. But he didn't cause a scene, mostly because it wasn't the boys' fault.

Cav retreated to his room and shut the door behind him, leaving Jimmy watching TV. Cav lay on the bed and stared at the ceiling, deep in thought. The memories of the incident back at the resort with Esmeralda and Gisele, the pressure he and Jimmy brought to Esmeralda and Gisele to do the coke, weighed heavily on his mind. The more he thought about it, the worse he felt about it. Adding to that the close, very close call at the airport built up Cav's worries and regrets to a near breaking-point.

Rapid-fire thoughts came at him: Getting caught for his drug trade, getting shot and killed over what? The cars, the money, the mansion, the parties and especially Vegas? They were fast starting to lose value. *How could I have fallen so far down so fast?*

He started to realize how cocky he and Jimmy had become, often being in trances from the blow they constantly sucked up their noses, never considering the potential consequences of carrying cocaine around tucked inside their suit jackets, special secret stashes of the white powder right through airport security. This had been going on for months, both of them considering themselves untouchable.

It really hit him: If agents had found that little stash, a full search would have been performed on every piece of luggage. They would have cut open the lining in all their luggage and their lives as they knew it would have been over. They would have lost everything! The Lambo, the Rolls, the mansion, and every pimped-out bank account seized. For Cav, far more valuable than any of the material possessions would be the loss of Esmeralda. The physical possessions were all replaceable, but not her. There was only one Esmeralda. And the whole affair would have crushed her heart.

The loneliness of his bedroom became a space of raw soul-searching. Cav realized it was not a prison sentence he feared. Instead, it was his life without her, and all because of destructive choices he made.

He got up and looked in the bathroom mirror, reflecting on the brutal comments Esmeralda and Gisele had made on their appearance. And now he also saw his weight loss, the dark circles under his eyes. These weighed heavily on him.

Back on the bed, a long time later, he eventually fell asleep. As sleep claimed him, the last image in his mind wasn't the chaos of the airport or the money —it was Esmeralda's face.

28

The Rise from Darkness to Light

Cav woke up and it was morning in a fancy mansion in Beverly Hills. *What the hell am I doing here? I'm craving cocaine more than pool, more than the girl I love, more than life itself.*

This has got to be over. Gotta make it be over. Get myself back.

Cav knew what he had to do. He always knew what he had to do. With his no-account father. His poor lost mother. His nowhere no-future life before he marched into Jasper's and got a real life over a decade ago. He always knew, and he knew right now.

The decision was made. Dry out. But how?

There's hospitals. Rehab clinics. Then there's cold turkey. That last one there is tough as hell. Even dangerous.

So...fuck institutions. Cold turkey it is.

Cav knew it was not going to be easy. He had to get Jimmy in on it too. *My man Jimmy can care for me for a few days or a week. Then I can take care of him.*

It was non-negotiable. It was now or never.

If he didn't cut it loose he was done. It was either bye-bye cruel world OR transform yourself into some superhuman state.

And he knew there was something else bigger and better in it for him, he just didn't know how to find it.

Yet.

But that was changing too.

His first challenge was to get Jimmy on the same wavelength. Would his partner make the same choice?

Would he be willing to go along with Cav? Otherwise, the plan was dead.

Surprise!

He braced Jimmy on the situation, and Jimmy was not only on the same page, he had been pondering the same thing for days and knew he would be dead far sooner than he could imagine if he didn't take hold of it right now.

They each had realized it was the death house if they didn't make the change.

The two worked out schedules, and promised to help each other through the worst of the physical and mental nightmares.

"I'll go first," Cav said, "and when I'm straight enough I'll get you through. And don't forget, we gotta call the girls."

Jimmy nodded. "Absolutely, but right now we gotta flush the stash. Right?"

"Yeah. And it ain't gonna be easy."

In spite of the decision to get clean it still was horrible watching all that blow go down the drain—not the money, knowing what was coming in a few minutes and hours and days. Hellish to watch but then actual relief, like better days are coming. He kept a little in a baggy in a shoe box for anything really seriously life-threatening.

For the first three hellish days and nights it was just that—pure hell. But they stayed focused on the long game, the end game. New territories to conquer. The loves of their lives down in Rio.

After nearly two weeks of pain and rebuilding, with proper diet and exercise, Cav and Jimmy had definitely put it behind them. There were more weeks needed, maybe months, and even more improvement to come. They welcomed it. It was all going to be better.

On the first truly drug-free morning they were sitting on their beautiful Beverly Hills patio enjoying a coffee and some early morning California sunshine. They weren't talking about anything, just feeling amazingly "normal" for the first time in months.

Jimmy sat up and put his mug down on the white-painted wrought iron table.

"Cav! The girls! We said we'd call when we were done, remember?"

"I was thinking the same thing!" Cav said. "We gotta call them. Right now! See how they're doing."

Cav whipped out his phone and dialed Esmeralda's cell, Jimmy listening intently.

After two rings Esmeralda picked up. "Cavalier!"

Jimmy pointing at his ears. Cav hit the speaker button. "Hey gorgeous." Huge smiles all around. "We're done. Fully shaken and baked. A birthday cake."

"We've been waiting on you! We flushed our little bit we had left and helped each other for over a week!"

"That's great, baby, wonderful! How you feeling?"

"Oh Cav. Welcome to the real world, honey! Never again. Right?"

"Never again, gorgeous. Onward and upward!"

Jimmy jumped in. "Hey Esmeralda, what-up with my main squeeze?"

"She's right here, Jimmy."

Gisele came on the line. "How is my favorite former nose-candy nut-job?"

"That's the truth right there, Gisele. Former! Forever," Jimmy said. "You doing okay?

"Missing you, that's what!"

The call went on for a grotesquely long number of U.S. dollars and Brazilian reals and no one gave a rat's ass. They finally said goodbye with promises of a reunion very soon.

***

Cav figured he had conquered already, with the accumulation of enough money to live comfortably from the coke biz, but that wasn't enough. He figured with what he knew and what he had done on the green felt and his love for the game, his hard-earned skill and his talent from the heavens, what he could do and accomplish was unlimited. Prior to that he could only imagine; now, he could actually do it for real.

Cav was firm about his choices and confident he could do the "impossible" on the green felt. For those lonely two weeks he had nothing to do but study his prior mistakes in his aiming system, his stroke, his execution of very special shots and banks and his jump shots. All of it; the whole process. He concluded that supreme above all was his mental game. If he could recapture and conquer the most important part of his game, the mental game, just like Jasper had taught him 10 or more years ago, the rest would be automatic, natural.

After two weeks of reflection, contemplation, and cleaning up his act, Cav decided now was the test. Time to get back to his roots, his proper domain.

He also realized that Esmeralda getting clean amplified his focus and mental game, sent them soaring to new heights.

Home in his familiar surroundings, in the still of the night, Cav strolled downstairs into his billiard room, flipped the lights on, and closed the door.

He prowled around the table, staring at the balls in silence. Cav was in his element. This is what he was born for, the payoff for all the battles and wars he had fought and won, all the high-dollar match-up successes.

Memories of past triumphs were returning to him with remarkable clarity.

Cav went into a nonstop play session that lasted for the next seven hours. He observed some very basic actions that hadn't been working for him. His aiming system lacked proper focus. He started lining up very difficult shots he had never quite mastered—and he had begun crushing them.

His mental game had undergone a sea change. Undisturbed and focused, he practiced his breaks, banks, and long cut shots, marveling at the transformation in his skills. Executing flawless shots, difficult combinations, and near-perfect breaks, he felt that something fundamental had changed.

Cav was experiencing a revitalization, a rebirth. He had to give himself up to the moment or lose it forever.

Jimmy awoke from a deep sleep and wandered into the kitchen. He could hear the sharp, crisp sound of pool balls drifting up from the billiard room. Cav was practicing. Jimmy quietly walked into the billiard room and stood silently watching as if in a trance. He wanted to cheer and celebrate. Instead he just found a chair and settled down to watch the magic.

Jimmy had watched Cav for years, every aspect of his game. This was different. This was a new, improved Cav, a new day for pool. In the dimly lit billiard room, there was a smoothness to Cav's strokes, an effortless precision that went beyond mere skill to something almost mystical.

Jimmy recognized that the world was changing. A revolution was unfolding before his eyes.

Sensing the weight of this revelation, Jimmy reached for his phone, stepped out, and dialed Jasper. He needed someone to validate what he was witnessing, to confirm that this wasn't some hallucination brought on by the chaos they'd been through. The call went through, and Jasper's voice crackled on the line.

Jimmy struggled to find the right words. "Listen, Jasper. Yeah, it's Jimmy. I have some breaking news. Cav's playing pool like… like I've never seen before." Jimmy stumbled, attempting to frame the moment. "It's like Cav's tapped into a different dimension, a new higher level of the game or something. It's fucking bizarro, Jasper. I've seen nothing like it in a lifetime of watching pool." He hesitated. "We slipped into a bit of trouble. You probably heard about it, or you will soon."

Jasper asked about their "health" and hinted at their "legal status."

"Yeah, Jasper, we're in the clear now. It's over and done with. Trust me, that's a metric ton lifted off our shoulders. Plus, Cav's met a lady. I'm telling you, it looks like he's in love for real. And if you met her, you'd understand why."

Jasper was overjoyed at the news.

"Well, that's fantastic, Jimmy. I've heard of this type of thing happening to players over the years, this 'new dimension' stuff, playing three or four balls better overnight. Never saw it myself. Urban legend shit, ya know, but what if we really are that lucky?

"If he is really playing as good as you say, let's get him matched up quick with that big-shot French billionaire casino owner in Monte Carlo. Word on the street is, he has posted a $10 million bounty to come to his casino and play a 9-ball match for a $10 million minimum. The Frenchman thinks his racehorse can beat any, bar none."

"Who, Junjun?"

"None other," said Jasper. "He is playing some of the best 9-ball in the world."

"He's the real deal."

"As real as they come. Check this out. They gave Rhode Island Red the Orange Crush,[4] (the orange 5 ball) handicap last year in

---

4 "Orange Crush" is a special handicap given by a stronger player to level the playing field against a less experienced opponent. Its name originates from the

Vegas and Red liked it a lot. When the Frenchman blows 50 large, that's like 10 dollars to me and you."

Jimmy smelled action. "Like I said, Jasper, the timing couldn't be better for us. This may just be our lucky break. Cav needs this right now. Me too. I have a good feeling about this. Mr. Monte Carlo is about to get a rude awakening."

"Tell me about it," said Jasper. "They say this Frenchman is cocky, he's got an attitude, an ego the size of Mt. Everest. Gustave LeBlanc is his name. He goes by 'Mr. LeBlanc' and sometimes 'Mr. Big'. This would be the perfect time to go trap him if Cav is hitting the balls as well as you say. LeBlanc has deep pockets and likes to bet high-dollar 9-ball. This billionaire has been trying to get any top-level, high-dollar 9-ball player to Monaco to bet it up high. He wants a ten-million-dollar match for his boy."

"Not a pool player in the universe with that kind of money," Jimmy declared. "However, Jasper, we're all pimped out. We're flush. We have the cash to take on LeBlanc. I'm telling you the timing couldn't be better for us, with Cav playing like a beast,

---

iconic orange-colored soft drink, as the handicap revolves around the orange 5-ball. In this arrangement, the 5-ball becomes a "wild" ball, there is no call shot; the standard rules of pocketing balls in numerical order, with the 9-ball as the game-winner, are adjusted to any pocket by simple luck or skill. The player receiving the handicap can win the game by pocketing the 5-ball or any ball with a higher number. This change is often called the "five out." Many versions of the "Orange Crush" exist, but the concept always centers on simplifying the win conditions for the less-skilled player to balance the competition. The player receiving this handicap wins the game by pocketing the 5 ball or any higher-numbered ball.

and we're the only ones who know. We got 'em by the nuts. We're stealing."

"All right, Jimmy. I'll call Rhode Island Red and get this in motion. Expect his call. I'm sure he will want in on the side. I'll keep you in the loop on any updates. We'll have to play this one close to the vest."

"Never closer," Jimmy agreed. "You're all receiving our monthly payments, yeah? And is there anything you need?"

"No, Jimmy, I'm good for now, and I really appreciate it. Give Cav my regards, and I'll get Rhode Island on the horn right-the-fuck now."

"One more thing, Jasper," added Jimmy. "You remember Texas Ted? I'm bringing him up here to spar with Cav for a couple of weeks, make sure he is shipshape for Monte Carlo. Later, Jasper."

Cav had made sure that Jasper was taken care of. Away from the crossroads of his questionable monies from the illegal trade, out of his own private money, Cav had purchased Jasper his dream home, a new car, furniture, and a lump sum of cash, plus generous monthly payments—a contingency plan on the off-chance that, God forbid, Cav and Jimmy got busted and they seized Cav's properties under some racketeering bullshit. The feds couldn't link Jasper to Cav and Jimmy's illegal trade. At the advice of his lawyers, Cav set up a bulletproof trust for Jasper. The guy was set for life, Cav made sure of that.

Jimmy made some calls to get a line on Gustave LeBlanc, and any information about him that could be had. Cav and Jimmy might know of Junjun from the old days at the Hollywood Athletic Club, a great upscale pool hall in Los Angeles while it lasted. Junjun was considered the best in Cali and one of the best in the world. Now there was a new star in town—the new Cav. Nobody knew it yet. Bless their ignorance.

Jimmy entered the billiard room at the house and gave Cav the rundown. "I just got off the phone with Jasper. He's steering us to a match. The guy owns a big hotel casino in Monaco. A bottomless pit of money."

Cav stopped shooting and stood up straight, listening closely. Jimmy continued.

"Name is Gustave LeBlanc, I've never heard of him until now. He loves high-dollar 9-ball action. He thinks his racehorse can beat anyone. So get ready. We're going to the French Riviera, brother. We'll scalp him.

"And get this—he has been promoting for anyone to come to Monaco to take on this Junjun at a $10 million minimum. Nobody but us has that kind of cash. The timing couldn't be any better."

But Jimmy didn't sound real happy. And Cav picked up on it. "But?"

"I won't sugarcoat it, Cav. Jasper's..."

Cav dropped his cue softly on the table and walked over to the window, staring out at the blackness. "How bad is it?"

Jimmy didn't answer.

"Lay it on me, Jimmy. It's all good, I understand, the circle of life, all that shit. We're all gonna make it to Amos Funeral Home someday, right?"

"It ain't like that."

"It's like what, then? What?"

"I dunno, Cav."

"You don't know what? Come on, man." Jimmy was silent, just shook his head a little.

"All right, fuck it," Cav said. "What do we do with Marco?"

Jimmy exploded: "Man, fuck Marco. What about Marco? We announce a vacation and that's the end of it right there."

Cav had a better plan forming in his mind.

"Look, we just gently advise them after the boondoggle, their fuckup at LaGuardia and what happened, we almost got shot or imprisoned because why? Because of their incompetence. Or how about this? Being less than 50 feet from an assassination on some UN bigshot by two Turkish terrorists. We almost caught the fuckin' bullet, we easily could have. Marco's contacts were not there, plain and simple, leaving us wide open to search and seizure. We were fucked and left to stand on our own. We got motherfuckin' lucky. How about that for needing a break from those sick fucks, perfect excuse. That clusterfuck at the airport, are you kidding me? We cheated death or life imprisonment by a fuckin' shoestring."

Jimmy was nodding vigorously. "And look at us now. We can win tens of millions in a week in the French Riviera. Maybe $50, $60 million? No limits. We throw down $25-$30 million, and who gives a fuck if we blow?"

"How well do you know these guys, Jimmy?" Cav asked.

"I don't," Jimmy said. "Jasper knows of them through Rhode Island Red." Jimmy shrugged. "He loves pool and loves to bet high. He loves the action. Word on the street is he will bet with anyone, but only high stakes. That ego and arrogance? They say it shows. He has no stop, no quit, he knows one speed, and that's stay. Stay in the action."

Cav slid back into the zone.

"That all sounds delicious, Jimmy, the great escape for us. Especially when I take down his boy. And by God, I will take him down. The balls look different, like I can see every angle at once. The world looks different. I've hit a new gear; it was always there for me but my head was never clear enough to see it. Cleared out my head from all that blow; I'm not a fuckhead now. I'm me.

"If I can hold this, from where I last played my absolute best, I can say I am playing at least 3, maybe 4 balls better. Not a motherfucker in the world is playing at this level."

Jimmy was in sync with Cav now, and it felt unbelievable.

"This Frenchman is as good as it gets in pool action—none better. And you, boss man, are playing miles above him. Who can beat you? Tell me. There's nobody in the world that can post $20–$30 million in pool. The pool world will owe us a debt of gratitude if we pull this off. When we pull this off!"

Cav joked, "Where do I sign, Jimmy? $20 milion, $50 million in a week's time? Are you fucking kidding me? Let's get it on! Fuck Marco, we're done with that shit, it's over. We've been his mule for far too long, and it's time we fade to black on that business. After what we just went through at LaGuardia, I'm bailing out. Fuck all that. Had those federal agents not been ordered out of their positions, we would have been fucked. It's like God had bigger plans for us."

Jimmy crossed himself.

29

Jimmy and the Billionaire

Jimmy put in a call. "Mr. Le Blanc."

Gustave answered, "This is he who is speaking."

"Jimmy here. I believe Rhode Island Red..."

"Nice to hear from you, Jimmy. They said you would be calling. I understand you would like to wager up $25 million on a match with Junjun. You will come to Monaco, of course, and we will televise the match live from here. I will need to arrange this with Junjun. Has Cav played Junjun before?" Gustave asked.

Jimmy was eager to respond.

"Well, sir, I believe they played in a tournament some time ago but I'm not crystal clear on the details." This was the truth. Their memory of Junjun was vague at best. Could they pick him out in a lineup? No way. "And yes, sir, your numbers are correct, $25 million. I've done some preliminary searches for flight availability and hotel space."

Gustave was very motivated and matter-of-fact. "No need, Mr. Jimmy. My agent will take good care of you. We have everything just about organized. The only thing missing is a contender with enough gamble and a bankroll—and that sounds like you. Will three weeks be soon enough for you gentlemen?"

Gustave had Jimmy salivating. "Yes, sir, that sounds about right. Let's figure three weeks."

Gustave eagerly laid out the details. "Fine, I will plan the match for the 17th of next month. My associate, Lonnie—he goes by 'Odd-smaker'—will make all the special arrangements for you on this end. Oddsmaker will be there to meet you upon your arrival. You will be booked to stay here at my property. I have a VIP suite in mind for you. It faces the Mediterranean, very nice view. I think you will enjoy it. My property is world renowned as a five-star resort. I believe you will feel right at home. A company car and driver will be provided. You should take the time to enjoy our beautiful part of the world—the French Riviera and the Sovereign Principality of Monaco. I will block out 10 days for your stay.

"As soon as your funds are verified on this end, I will immediately begin to organize everything. Press releases, notifications to all the gambling outlets around the world, interviews. I will build a media center and billiard room in our small arena for the press and dignitaries along with local celebs and my VIPs."

Jimmy's response was rock-solid. "Sir, if you would please include all your banking details, I will go to my bank today and wire those funds so there are no delays."

Gustave's enthusiasm was unfeigned. "Jimmy, you sound like a man of your word and someone I look forward to doing business with. I will get busy immediately; this is the spirit I wanted to hear."

Jimmy felt better than Cav pocketing the 9-ball on the break to win a match.

"Sir, the feeling is entirely mutual. My banker will relay the Fed wire number issued to our bank here upon confirmation that our money has been sent. We can send this to you or someone in your accounting department, and that should be within the next four hours."

Jimmy savored the moment.

"Mr. LeBlanc, I hope you appreciate the amount of trust we have put in you from this end. Your reputation is second to none in the high stakes gambling world. Our transfer of funds will significantly exceed the $25 million initial wager. Me and Cav, just like yourself, love the action. You reach this level, it's not easy to find a worthy opponent."

Gustave agreed. "We couldn't get action on the $10 million offer I sent out around the world some time ago. You have restored my faith in humanity. Let me connect you with the lady who handles these matters for us on this end, Fleur Toussaint, our account executive in the accounting department. I will put you in her trusted hands. She will be handling all the banking side of things."

He paused for emphasis.

"Well, Jimmy, we are off to a great start. The pool world is about to get a giant boost. Safe travels, and I look forward to welcoming you and your player to Monaco. Au revoir!"

It was a dirty, nasty little hustle Jimmy and Cav had just played on Mr. Billionaire right there. An insurance policy of sorts that might just come in handy down the road. Jimmy and Cav needed to know who was in the chain of command at the Casino on the banking side. Was Ms. Toussaint the account executive exclusively certifying funds transferred? Was verification also furnished to Mr. Big at the top? Jimmy and Cav could not confirm if it was or not. So, was it possible to fire an "air barrel"—an imaginary amount of money on a wager—to super-max the bet during the heat of battle in the middle of the match? Such things are common in high-dollar pool if trust has been established between both sides. It would be a free swing perhaps, but "fire away" was Jimmy and Cav's business model.

Jimmy returned to the billiard room brimming over with good news. "Cav, this guy wants to televise the match around the world, live from his House of Versailles Hotel Casino. You're gonna be a star. I can see it now, in the bright lights: Cavalier McTavish versus Junjun, 9-ball heavyweight title championship of the world. Dig this, he has us pimped out in a VIP suite. BOOM! He is providing everything, car and driver, food, first-class flight, a two-bedroom suite overlooking the Mediterranean in his 5-star hotel. What a blessing this is, to get the fuck out of that trap with Marco, and really make some serious money doing what we were made for. I shipped it all bro, $30 mill, all we had left.

"Are you bullshitting me again, Jimmy? That's a wet dream on steroids."

Jimmy put a brotherly hand on Cav's shoulder. "It's 100% solid, bro. I'm headed to the bank right now to initiate the wire to his casino. He's already started rolling out the red carpet."

"Marco's going to blow a head gasket," Cav said with a sly grin.

"Let him."

"Jimmy..."

Jimmy was getting a little testy. "Hey, Cav, this is getting old. We're done, and we need to just tell them that. We've built a fortune for us and him, and now we can put it to good use. We've got that bank account all pimped out. We're flush. Fuck him. This is the deal of the century."

"I'm just saying, Jimmy, Marco is powerful."

Jimmy snorted. "Powerful how, Cav? He's a hundred thousand miles away from the French Riviera! Fuck him."

"If we tell him we quit, it's gonna piss him off even more. I believe if he wanted to kidnap us, he could, Jimmy. Give me some insurance."

"Listen to me, Cav. Kidnap, schmidnap, he ain't gonna jack us, bro. Marco's got you shaking like a blonde faggot at a weenie roast."

"You say you can't buy me any peace of mind, with my own money? Fuck you. I make you the richest man on the planet, maybe you'll buy me a velvet-lined casket."

Jimmy spread his hands in a conciliatory gesture. "I ain't too cheap to buy my racehorse some insurance, Cavalier. I'll just have to walk on tiptoe. Say nothin' to nobody until I know exactly who we can trust. Here, let me rack those balls for you."

***

Cav looked at his phone ringing. "It's him, the prince of darkness calling. Hi, Marco."

"How's my American partner?" Marco's voice was weak over the bad connection. "We're preparing your next shipment, getting it ready for you."

Cav laughed. "See, Marco, that's why I had to speak to you. Me and Jimmy have decided to take a short vacation and we will be there on the 25th."

The word "vacation" sent Marco off the rails on a crazy train. He snapped, "I will tell you when you take a fuckin' vacation! I've worked overtime to prepare your next shipment in light of what happened at LaGuardia. That will never happen again. You have my word on that."

"Your word?" Cav chuckled. "Your word wouldn't have gotten me out of jail without a bond. No Toomay, no Mr. Anderson. And what about that UN Ambassador getting assassinated, shot down in cold blood right in front of us? What's the value of your word to a pair of Turkish terrorists? Let that sink in."

"As if I could control all that shit," Marco scoffed.

"As if you could control anything. We were damn lucky we didn't take a bullet in the spine and serve our prison term in the prison hospital as a pair of paraplegics."

"A pair of paraplegics," Jimmy repeated, doubling over with laughter.

Marco's comeback was not a masterpiece of diplomacy. "I have personally invested millions in you two broke-back fucks. My wife and I have done everything to make you rich."

Cav laid into him. "Marco, you have personally invested sweet fuck-all in what I care about most, which is staying alive." The connection went dead.

Cav sent his phone skidding across the pool table. "The son of a bitch hung up on me." The phone came to rest near a corner pocket.

"Decent shot," Jimmy remarked. He handed Cav the phone. It rang a minute later.

This time it was Marcella. "Cav, please don't do this to us. To me. You know Marco loves you like a son. And I love you like... like... you know what I'm saying."

"Keep talking," Cal encouraged her, feeling a slight tingle.

Marcella did. "Marco's on the edge. He covered your $400,000 pool match losses. He's bending over backwards for you and Jimmy."

"The bastard hung up on me," said Cav. "All I told him was that we'll be there on the 25th. What's wrong with the 25th? If we miss one slot, it's going to break him?"

"I'll cool him down. Are we firm about the 25th? Yes? Please don't let me down, honey."

"Couldn't be firmer," said Cav, with real warmth. "One hundred percent. And I'm sorry for putting you in this spot. We haven't taken a break since we started. Thanks, it means a lot to us."

They hung up. "Jesus, what a prick-tease. I'm not sure that sick fuck deserves her."

"They deserve each other, believe me," Jimmy replied. "You kept your cool, brother. Too bad there isn't an Academy Award for bullshit."

The phone rang again. Marcella's number. "I cooled him down," she breathed. "He's bought into the 25th. Please don't make me regret trusting you."

"It goes both ways," Cav said. By way of insurance, he added, "It's a bit mysterious what happened to us in New York, and no one's discussing it. I remind you, that mistake could have cost me and Jimmy 25 years in the slammer. No one seems to care down there, like it never happened. So, consider the sacrifices me and Jimmy have made, yes for us, but also for you."

"See you on the 25th."

Cav hung up and stared at the phone for a full minute. "She barely acknowledges what happened to us in New York. These people are cold-blooded killers. They don't give a fuck about us. We're about to jump ship."

Cav and Jimmy had discussed a backup plan long before, a conspiracy that would involve Fredrico. A very dangerous move. If Fredrico were to blow the whistle and turn on Cav and Jimmy, they would be wanted men. On the flipside, pure brilliance! Fredrico would bag enough cash to retire. Not that he would want to.

"Jump ship where, the South of France?"

Cav nodded vigorously.

"It's a hell of a plan," Jimmy said wistfully. "Everything will be set up, flights booked, hotel, bank wire."

"I'm ready to go unleash," Cav said. "I will say this about this Junjun, from everything I hear he's one of the top elite players. A 10-speed, as they say. He hasn't seen the new and improved Cav. He'll get a glimpse pretty soon."

"Only a glimpse?"

Cav laughed. "I'm going to beat him all day, and I'm going to beat him all night. We've been ghosts in the pool world for a long time, Jimmy; they forgot all about us.

"We're coming in clean, and way underrated. He and his Junjun must think we're going in as huge underdogs, which is perfect for us. A thousand ways to trap them."

Jimmy said, "We got a couple of weeks to prepare. You need a sparring partner to perfect your skills so when you arrive in Monaco you will be ready to undress this Junjun. I've called up Texas Ted. He will be here to spar with you starting tomorrow until we split for France. Perfect your chops, my man. Texas Ted is eager to work with us. I've been talking to him the past few days. He's rock-solid on our plans and just wants in on the action with side betting. I've gone over some numbers with him. If you wanted anyone better to spar with for the next two weeks, I can't imagine who it would be. Texas Ted is playing his best right now and can be trusted to keep his mouth shut."

For two relentless weeks, Cav and Texas Ted immersed themselves in the billiards room, sparring ten hours a day without fail. Ted mostly sat and watched Cav beat down near impossible runs night after night in a trance.

Ted was shocked at how far Cav had improved, and how fast.

"You are some kind of ET motherfucker," joked Ted. "This is some supernova shit I'm seeing here. If you play like I have been seeing, there is no one, I mean no one, that can compete with you. I'll mortgage my house right now to throw down on your side action."

"No need for that," Jimmy assured Ted. "Whatever you want to throw down, you're covered. Any amount."

In between games, Jimmy role-played Ted on keeping his mouth shut about the phenomenon he had just witnessed. Not that anyone would really believe it until they saw it for themselves.

And nobody would see it until Cav and Jimmy wanted them to—after the bait was taken and the hook was set.

30

Los Angeles to Monaco

Jimmy and Cav entered LAX to find Gigi, a stunning Asian lady, holding a sign that read, "Mr. Cav and Mr. Jimmy." They walked over to her; Cav made the introductions.

"Welcome, gentlemen. I will be your personal assistant for pre-boarding. I'm Gigi. Let me show you around." She led them to a dedicated first-class terminal, the St. Cloud Lounge, and left them to enjoy some eats and drinks. They discussed in depth the treasure chest that awaited them in Monte Carlo.

About an hour later, Gigi rejoined them in the St. Cloud Lounge and announced that their flight was ready. At the gate, Gigi introduced Cav and Jimmy to the first-class flight attendant. "This is Odette. She'll make sure that everything is to your liking. Safe travels, gentlemen." Gigi departed.

Odette said in a beautiful French accent, "I'm your flight attendant at 50,000 feet." Odette graciously escorted them onto the plane, offering a personalized tour of the luxurious amenities.

"Here, you'll have access to your own shower. The Kaleidoscope Bar is over here. Allow me to present Chef Chevalier," she said, gesturing toward a master chef impeccably attired in chef whites.

Chef Pierre bowed graciously. "Bonjour messieurs—gentlemen. I am Chef Pierre Chevalier. I have prepared a special feast for the first-class passengers. You may choose between the French beef bourguignon or the superb Chateaubriand."

Jimmy responded, "Pardon me, Chef, but they both sound so good. May I propose an assortment of both?"

"Excellent choice, as you wish," confirmed Chef Pierre.

"Now," Odette added, "perhaps you would like to upgrade to a bottle of Napa Valley's Screaming Pheasant. It's one of the most famous cabernet sauvignons in the sky. It's a $1500 upgrade."

"Yes, please, Mademoiselle," Jimmy replied. "We would like to upgrade—twice, twice as nice. Two bottles, please."

Odette seated them with a warm cloth and a glass of chilled Perrier.

The boys got settled into their own private luxury cabins, each one complete with sliding doors; a custom leather, hand-stitched armchair; and a double bed, exclusively for first class passengers. Cav couldn't wait to compare notes with Jimmy.

Cav tapped on Jimmy's door and walked in, blown away. "Bro, this is top shelf here. Can you believe this shit? Tell ya what, if a dude were ever to get a mile-high club membership, this would be the plane for that. It's the best setup I have ever seen."

Jimmy asked, "What the hell is a mile-high club membership?"

"Seriously?" Cav laughed. "Oh, it's when you get laid in the friendly skies. Boy meets girl, girl takes boy to Loveland at 50,000 feet. They say those airline hostesses are the horniest. I saw Odette checking out your ass when you were walking in front of her." Cav paused for effect and they both burst out laughing.

Cav got down to business. "So, okay, we meet Lonnie, aka Oddsmaker. He is our contact on the ground there and lives in St. Tropez. All our rooms have been arranged by this Mr. Big dude. LeBlanc. He is doing a live broadcast around the world in Europe, Dubai, Asia, Australia, and North and South America. This should be a whole new level for pool, I hope."

"I believe you're spot-on," Jimmy replied. "Yes, Oddsmaker is our go-to guy. He has us all set up, apparently every detail has been covered!"

They wined and dined and rested through the remainder of the flight.

31

Welcome to Monte Carlo

The captain's voice echoed through the cabin: "Folks, we are beginning our final descent to Cote d'Azur International. Welcome to the South of France. On behalf of my flight crew and the cabin crew, we hope you have had a restful and enjoyable flight. We will be landing shortly."

The boys gazed out their windows at the majestic views of the Mediterranean Sea. Below was the coastline of the Côte d'Azur—the French Riviera—with its cliffs, sandy beaches and coastal towns. Luxurious yachts were in abundance. These aerial views captured the spirit of the glamorous Mediterranean destination, designed and built for the rich and famous.

They were met and swiftly escorted through immigration and customs, and led straightaway to a heliport where a casino staff member greeted them.

"Welcome to the Riviera. This is a brief 30-mile flight to Monaco, about 15 minutes, aboard our custom Versailles helicopter. You will enjoy a beautiful view of Monaco en route."

With their luggage loaded, they boarded the chopper and departed for Monaco. The pilot banked a little to show off the natural beauty of Monte Carlo from the air.

They set down at a heliport in Monaco and were met by a sharply dressed man who introduced himself as Oddsmaker.

"Gentlemen, there is just a short drive from here to our Versailles Hotel and Casino. I'll alert Mr. LeBlanc you have arrived."

They retrieved their luggage and made their way towards a waiting Rolls-Royce. Jimmy asked Oddsmaker where he was from in England, because his accent sounded British but unfamiliar. Oddsmaker replied that it was called a "Cockney" accent, and that he was "an East Ender from London town." He seemed smart and classy and endlessly enthusiastic about life in general.

Upon reaching the Rolls, Oddsmaker introduced their driver. "This is Peter Thompson, who will be your driver for the duration of your stay."

Mr. Thompson welcomed Jimmy and Cav, got their names straight, and as soon as they were settled in he immediately put them at ease with a joke about his driving record. It was delivered with an impeccably posh Oxford English accent, a distinct contrast to the working-class sound of Oddsmaker.

"I once had a bloke tell me I couldn't drive a hot dog to a bun. I simply responded, 'I would, but my zipper is stuck.' He piped down— it was a French bloke." They all burst out laughing.

32

A Cool 20 Million

Upon arriving at the Versailles Hotel Casino, Cav and Jimmy began to grasp the enormity of this global event awaiting them.

A half-dozen paparazzi swarmed them, cameras flashing in a frenzy, yelling and screaming for a pose. Oddsmaker immediately rescued them, and took them on a short tour around the casino. A small, luxurious billiard arena had been constructed to showcase the event, a state-of-the-art media/broadcast center was adjacent, and in the center of the arena stood a beautiful 9-foot pool table constructed exclusively for this contest.

Oddsmaker cheerfully informed them of their next surprise. "Gentlemen, we would like you to enjoy a night out, compliments of Mr. La Blanc, at the Chez d'Azur, our finest French restaurant. Mr. Le Blanc arranged this personally for you. Let's get you settled in, and we will accompany you whenever you're ready. This is the card for Peter Thompson, your personal driver. The Rolls is yours around the clock to take you shopping and sightseeing—whatever you like."

Oddsmaker handed Cav his card. "Here is all my personal contact information. I'm not sure if you're aware of the enormous efforts the casino has made to get this event complete and ready in such a short period. It's going to be broadcast live to North America, South America, the United Kingdom, Asia, Dubai, Bahrain, and throughout the Middle East, Africa, Australia, New Zealand, the European Union—in fact, the entire world, my friends." He pointed at Cav and said, "You, Cav, will soon be a household name on a global level."

Cav reached out and shook Oddsmaker's hand. "Very fine work, my friend. Very impressive. And, yes, I fully appreciate the magnitude of the spectacle we are witnessing. Please extend to Mr. LeBlanc our most sincere thanks and let him know we applaud his very amazing work in such a short amount of time."

Oddsmaker bowed. "Okay, gentlemen, I'll hear from you later whenever you're ready. We're all set for a night of luxury, the experience at one of the finest French restaurants in the world. Whereas there is a three-month waiting list at Chez d'Azur, Mr. LeBlanc reserves his special room there year round and tonight, my friends, it's reserved for you."

Jimmy responded appreciatively for both of them. "Oddsmaker, Mr. LeBlanc sounds like a class act. My impression of him over the phone was that he was straight business, no messing around, yet a proper gentleman. I look forward to meeting him tonight."

This was said by the man whose actual intentions toward the honorable Mr. LeBlanc were to scalp him.

Cav and Jimmy got settled in their suite, relaxing until they had an unexpected visit. Four men, claiming to be casino employees, dressed in perfectly tailored Italian suits, knocked at the door, and Jimmy, unaware, let them in. The last man to enter placed a "Do Not Disturb" sign outside the door and locked it. Not casino employees. Another helped himself to a very expensive bottle of Courvoisier from the bar, opened it, and poured drinks for Cav, Jimmy and the man who appeared to be the leader of this group, who invited Cav and Jimmy to take a seat. Together, the four of these men formed a threatening presence.

"I'm Casimo, and this is my Italian support group," he declared arrogantly, exuding confidence. Cav figured they were about to get kidnapped or robbed. Cav raised his Courvoisier glass in a toast, as if he didn't give a fuck, as if it were all theater to him.

Casimo continued his rant: "It's confusing, and I apologize for that. You see, I alter sports history, in a sense. We bet in all the casinos, and we have a big stake in your match with Junjun. We need you to lose." He gestured to his men, all wearing pretty much the same scowl.

Cav kept his cool. "Jimmy, you want to weigh in here?"

Jimmy did. "I'm Jimmy, the CEO and chairman of this motherfucker. We came here to bet a lot of money and already risked our lives to get that fuckin' money to bet it all on this match!"

One of the thugs grabbed Jimmy and lifted him in the air. Cav instantly grabbed a wine bottle by the neck to use it as a weapon. Casimo waved his thug off, and the thug put Jimmy back down and stepped back.

Casimo made his pitch: "I will give you $20 million cash to lose. Put on a good show but in the end, I need you to lose the match."

Jimmy held his ground. As if addressing a child, he explained, "We didn't come here to win $20 million. We came to win $10 billion! I don't know who you are...."

Another thug interrupted Jimmy: "We don't understand English."

Jimmy's attention remained fixed on Casimo. He explained, very matter-of-factly, in his face: "The money behind our opponent, as you know, is huge. It's a hell of a lot more than $20 million. Allow me to share a little insider trading information with you, Casimo. We're going to win. Take that $20 million and bet on Cav here. Bet all you got on Cav."

Casimo leaned in and whispered, "Gentlemen, think about the consequences. We have powerful interests at play here. Lives, fortunes, and reputations are on the line."

Casimo stood up, preparing to leave, and suddenly blurted out his best imitation of the Italian dictator, Benito Mussolini: "Non creare nemici che non puoi gestire!" (Don't create enemies you can't handle!)

The four hoodlums tramped out of the room. Jimmy closed and locked the door after them.

"That's some cold-blooded shit. I'll have to remember to use that one," Jimmy said, trying to lighten the mood.

Cav wasn't amused. "Call Oddsmaker, get him up here now!"

Jimmy picked up the phone and dialed. "Hey, Jimmy here. We just had some visitors from the local Cosa Nostra demanding we throw the match. They offered us $20 million. Oh, they also opened a $5,000 bottle of your Cognac, Frapin Cuvee."

Oddsmaker, unfazed, replied, "Let me guess, was it Casimo?"

Jimmy confirmed, "Yeah, and three goons."

Oddsmaker asked to be put on speaker so Cav could hear. He stated firmly, "Gentlemen, I will put those punks on notice. You have nothing to worry about. I told you about these hooligans. There is a pecking order here in Monaco. I will put them on notice that if they get within 10 feet of you, they are marked men. Marked men in this town have a poor relationship with breathing, and they bloody well know it! I'll take care of it pronto!

"Meanwhile, lads, please call me when you're ready, and I will arrange for the car to take you to the restaurant. We're all set whenever you're ready, no rush. It's Monte Carlo's finest. I don't think I could do any better. You are in for some very fine French hospitality. Mr. LeBlanc has prepared a true French experience for you to enjoy. Call me if there are any other surprises."

Within the hour, Cav and Jimmy stepped out of their room, all dressed up and with somewhere to go. Two pool bums from Kansas with $30 million in the casino vault. Money was no obstacle. Life was good.

The moment they entered the casino, they were stunned by the class and sheer elegance of the French-style casino. It was world-class in every direction. The clientele comprised the super-rich from Russia, Kuwait, Dubai, Europe, America, Africa and Asia. You were here because you were an exceptionally high-net-worth individual with significant gambling financial means. If you didn't have deep pockets, you just were not welcome here.

Joelle, the charming French floor manager, greeted them with elegance and authority.

"Welcome to our casino, gentlemen. We've been expecting you." She guided them to the VIP section where the high-stakes gaming tables were positioned. "Enjoy your evening, and if there's anything you need, feel free to let us know. We're here to make your experience unforgettable." With that, she stepped away to let them explore.

Jimmy called her back "Joelle, if you wouldn't mind telling Oddsmaker we're here, and that we're ready whenever it's convenient for him and our driver. We're going to wander over beside the billiard arena. Thanks." She assured Jimmy she would attend to it straightaway.

Jimmy and Cav found the billiard arena to be a class act. They were impressed at the dedicated space Mr. LeBlanc had created for this event. Pure magic.

Cav showed Jimmy images of Junjun on his phone. "Man, I know this guy," he said. But Jimmy was so star-struck by the remarkable details of the arena that he didn't seem to hear.

33

Official Announcers' Booth

While Cav and Jimmy were admiring the arena and waiting for Oddsmaker, just a few yards away the first official TV coverage of the competition was getting underway.

Dressed in a sleek black blazer, Lilou exuded elegance and authority as she took center stage in the Media Broadcast Center announcers' booth. Lilou received a "you're on" nod from the director and made her first announcement.

"Ladies and gentlemen, valued guests, and passionate participants, welcome to the grandest pool match in the world, unfolding at The House of Versailles Hotel and Casino in the heart of Monaco! I am Lilou, and it is my great pleasure to stand before you today as we kick off the most thrilling event in our 25-year history here in Monaco. Our praise goes out to Gustave LeBlanc, our host, and to all the staff here at The House of Versailles that have made this historic event possible. A first of its kind on the global stage. Brace yourselves for an unparalleled experience at the world's largest 9-ball shootout and online gambling extravaganza ever."

Massive images of Cav and Junjun were displayed in the background. Lilou continued, "Let the excitement echo across borders and oceans—welcome to The House of Versailles, and welcome to the future of pool! As we say in Monaco, 'Bon Courage!'— good luck!

"And now, it is my absolute delight to present my fellow broadcaster on this voyage. Please join me in a warm welcome for Miss Coco!"

Coco acknowledged the introduction with a beautiful smile. "Thank you, Lilou! It's an absolute delight to be here in Monaco at The House of Versailles. Get ready, everyone, for a 9-ball match that will go down in history!"

The feed transitioned to a split screen featuring Lilou and Coco in Monaco alongside correspondents Dison Abubukati in Las Vegas and Sir Anthony Nosy Parker in London, showing off the global scope of the event.

Coco continued, gesturing towards the split screen. "We've got correspondents live from the Las Vegas Strip and the heart of London. Sir Anthony Nosy Parker, what's the vibe in your location?"

The feed shifted to Sir Anthony Nosy Parker in London, a renowned snooker and billiard expert. Sir Anthony prepared to make his mark on the global stage:

"Good evening to our global audience and welcome from London, the snooker and pool capital of Europe. It's a pleasure to be part of this international broadcast. We're in for an explosive, highly competitive 9-ball match with billions wagered from around the world. The top 15 casinos and bookie shops here in London and throughout the European Union are reporting explosive excitement on this match with Junjun and Cav—the best numbers they have seen in 10 years. The betting has reached its highest numbers from the whales in Dubai, the Saudi Kingdom and the entire Middle East. A group of African billionaire pool enthusiasts have arrived in London to Bookmaker William Hill, with an expected 8-figure wager, minimum bet. Coco, I must add, we haven't seen this much action in London since the last World Cup or, to put it another way, 'since Moby Dick was a minnow.' Sending it back to you live from London, Nosy Parker."

The feed transitioned to split screen with Lilou and Coco in Monaco, and Dison Abubukati live from Las Vegas.

"Ladies, you might mistake this for a heavyweight title fight if you didn't know any better," Dison shouted over the noise. "Monte Carlo, you may have been upstaged. Vegas is the gambling hub of the world," he said cheerfully, "and the sports betting floors are reporting wagers that outshine the largest sporting events to date. Whales are flying in at record numbers from LA and back east to catch this live broadcast. Standing room only, hotels are sold out for the duration of this match. It's reminiscent of a modern-day Ali/Frazier world heavyweight title fight. A pool party on the Strip, and everyone's invited!"

Coco said, "Thanks, gentlemen. There you have it, without a doubt one of the largest and highest-stakes sporting events of the 21st century. What started as a $10 million dollar wager between two players has now more than doubled to a cool $25 million, in-house. The hotels are sold out here in Monaco, no vacancies, and we're backed up to Cannes. This is Coco reporting live at the French Riviera's finest gaming destination, The House of Versailles Hotel and Casino."

***

As the Rolls pulled up at the entrance to Chez d'Azur, two doormen stepped forward and opened the doors of the limo, and escorted Cav and Jimmy towards the imposing entrance, adding a special touch of class to the moment. Mr. LeBlanc had made sure the paparazzi were there to cover Cav and Jimmy's stroll down the red carpet into legendary Chez d'Azur.

In their Brioni suits, the elegant young hustlers looked right at home in the posh, 900-year-old museum-like restaurant.

The female owner greeted them in a thick French accent: "Messieurs, welcome to Chez d'Azur. I am Faustine, the proprietor."

She presented her hand formally for the boys to kiss. Cav accepted it smoothly, pressing her fingers to his lips, giving the star-struck Jimmy an extra few seconds to pull himself together.

Faustine exuded confidence and superiority with her seductive French accent. As they entered the restaurant, it became evident that they were not merely patrons but admired VIPs, given the level of attention and service.

The interior of Chez d'Azur was a masterpiece of graceful simplicity. Faustine, the empress of this culinary retreat, had arranged the evening with pure elegance. She led them to Mr. LeBlanc's private room, which offered a sweeping view of Monaco's dramatic Mediterranean coastline.

In the privacy of the luxurious dining room, Cav and Jimmy were introduced to two elegantly graceful ladies, Neige Laurent and Solange de la Fayette, their pre-arranged escorts for the evening's enjoyment. The ladies resembled nothing short of world-class high-fashion models. In a gesture that conveyed both warmth and a sense of polished charm, Neige Laurent extended her hand to Cav. Similarly, Solange de la Fayette presented her hand to Jimmy.

The private setting and these stunningly dressed ladies hinted at an entirely different component for the evening.

The culture shock the boys had experienced in Brazil, eased by the careful guidance of Esmeralda and Gisele, served as a crash course in adapting to new cultures and customs. However, France was an old-world challenge, a culture so refined that it could afford to be gracious even to a pair of louts.

The styles of French customs, the elaborate dining rituals, and this high-society environment were uncharted territory for Cav and Jimmy. What Esmeralda and Gisele displayed at Marco's party had set Cav and Jimmy on a needed learning curve. The ladies back in Rio did their best to enlighten these pool bums, but in France, it was taken to another level.

As the evening progressed, they were not mere guests but became participants in a carefully tailored experience that exceeded the boundaries of ordinary luxury.

Commanding the attention of the room, the sommelier arranged a stylish presentation of port wine.

With studied charm, Faustine personally poured the first glass of port, filling the moment with a touch of formality. As she did so, she extended a wish, "May this bring you good fortune," with the Monaco phrase "Bon courage" (good luck).

The chef entered the room and spoke with ceremony. "Mesdames et messieurs, please indulge in the assortment of flavors that awaits you tonight. We commence with iced poached oysters."

The oysters were presented with artistic precision, inviting Cav, Jimmy, and the ladies to appreciate and enjoy. And the sommelier returned with two bottles of superb, very rare, white wine to further elevate and enhance the experience.

The meal unfolded with more courses of fine French cuisine and rare wines, served with military precision throughout the evening.

Meanwhile, Neige Laurent and Solange de la Fayette, the exquisite escorts, quietly observed the exhibition. As the boys stumbled through the evening, attempting to grasp the difficulties of French customs, it became a humorous contrast—the Kansas charm colliding with the sophistication of the French. The French escorts, well-versed in the art of blending in, found amusement in the boys' genuine attempts at this cultural assimilation, or lack thereof.

Surprisingly, Neige and Solange, in addition to their mastery of their native French language, were conversant in English, Russian, and Arabic. This language versatility added to their highly intelligent resume. Familiar with elevated degrees of the high-society environment, they skillfully engaged in dialogue with Cav and Jimmy. The boys, somewhat out of their element but maintaining their signature charm, managed to find common ground bantering with Neige and Solange.

As they concluded their time together and got ready to depart, Faustine presented them with a parting gift: a rare bottle of French Chateau. This event and experience at Chez d'Azur had established a level of hospitality on a scale the boys had never experienced.

Cav, Jimmy, and the ladies made their way from Chez d'Azur towards the waiting Rolls. But as they crossed onto the cobblestones from the red carpet and started towards the car, Casimo and two associates leapt out from behind a parked van and rushed towards Cav, Jimmy and the girls.

What happened next made it clear that LeBlanc was a man of his word. The response was swift and deadly. An armed security detail appeared out of nowhere with silenced automatic weapons and instantly neutralized Casimo's two henchmen. Casimo, miraculously untouched, turned to run, but froze as two security guards closed in with weapons leveled at him.

It was a miracle, Cav thought, that he and Jimmy and the girls were okay. But he was furious at Casimo's attack. He ignored the security guards and grabbed Casimo by the shirt, and furiously yelled in his face: "What was that horseshit you were telling us? 'Know my movements'? How about those movements?" he yelled, pointing to the two dead thugs. He slammed Casimo down onto the cobblestones and threatened him. "Know this move: if you ever come anywhere near me and my friends again I will kill you with my bare hands." And with that he kicked Casimo in the crotch.

Humiliated and writhing in pain, Casimo struggled to his feet, almost doubled over in pain. But he suddenly darted forward a few feet and leapt into the van at the curb and raced away before the security team could grab him.

Mr. LeBlanc's chief security man approached Cav and mildly expressed "regret" for the disturbance, as if it was just some minor setback. But he reassured Cav, "Don't worry about it. I am a witness, and we have it all recorded. Please, go enjoy yourselves." He then instructed Thompson, the chauffeur, to immediately leave the area with Cav, Jimmy, and the ladies.

Thompson got his four shaken passengers into the Rolls and sped away, just as several police cars and an ambulance arrived on the scene with sirens blaring.

Paramedics quickly zipped the two dead thugs in body bags and carted them off in the ambulance. Several policemen cleared the area, making sure everyone was okay, and then listened with interest to the security chief's discussion with the paparazzi, who were looking none too pleased with things.

Of course the paparazzi had witnessed the entire attack and captured all the action, countless photos and videos. But all this visual evidence along with important details of the incident never made it onto the news, online or print, anywhere. Ever. All the evidence mysteriously disappeared.

There's possibly a reason this happened. Crime and crime scenes are rare in Monaco. The authorities and public are aware of this fact.

In a near crime-free city that depends almost entirely on tourism for its existence, events like this are swiftly and quietly hushed up from the public. The reputation of Monaco is spotless and it is not allowed to be smeared.

Oddsmaker's prediction had proved accurate—they did manage to approach Cav and Jimmy within 10 feet and they did stop breathing. Unfortunately, the shooters missed Casimo, the prime target. And as it turned out, he cheated death and escaped.

Junjun and Cav were regarded as highly valuable assets to The House of Versailles Hotel and Casino. Mr. LeBlanc stood to make an enormous amount of money from this event, especially with the online gambling associated with his casino. Cav and Junjun were worth their weight in gold to Mr. LeBlanc. His motto was, "Do not fuck with my money!"

When Oddsmaker briefed Mr. LeBlanc about Casimo's surprise invasion of Cav and Jimmy's room and the threats to their lives, and then the subsequent foiled attack at the restaurant, a mad fury overtook him.

"These punks got some neck to barge into my house barking orders and threats to my VIPs."

He immediately called his friend, Police Commissioner Francois Milligan. Wants and warrants were issued immediately on Casimo.

To Oddsmaker, Mr. LeBlanc said darkly, "You know what I say. Don't ever fuck with my money. I will have those motherfuckers on a guillotine if I have to do it myself."

In the Rolls, Jimmy and Cav were trying to shrug off the effects and aftershock of the violent encounter, but it was no good. They were both still freaked out. Their two escorts, however, displayed remarkable composure. They maintained an air of professionalism and seemed relatively unfazed.

More paparazzi caught the group arriving at the hotel, and the desk clerks welcomed them as they crossed the lobby and headed up to their room.

Before long, Cav came back down and crossed over to the arena to put in some practice, preparing for tomorrow's match. As he racked the balls and assembled his cue, a small crowd began to gather to watch the star player practice.

Cav broke, made a couple of balls off the break, and started sinking the remaining balls. The audience gawked in admiration as he effortlessly executed one incredible shot after another.

Jimmy and the ladies arrived and joined the impromptu audience. The girls' surprise was evident when they saw Cav's image posted in the arena as the star of the event. They also noted the enthusiastic applause from the onlookers as they admired Cav's athletic and powerful skill at the table. Jimmy especially enjoyed the girls' exchange of looks as they realized they'd been in the company of true greatness all evening and didn't have a clue.

34

Game Night, Light the Fuse

The gambling world was moments away from seeing history unfold. Numerous dignitaries, tycoons, A-list patrons of the casino and local celebrities were introduced by the Master of Ceremonies in French and English. The incredible prize money up for grabs had become the talk of the town as well as the talk around the pool and gambling world. Chat rooms, gambling blogs, pool forums, all the social media platforms, were lit with excitement. As the pre-game momentum and excitement built, legions of gamblers from all parts of the world, from London to Vegas to Asia and beyond, were pouring into town in record numbers.

Cav and Jimmy were at lunch in the main dining room when Jimmy was called away for "a brief and informal meeting" with Mr. Gustave LeBlanc, apparently at a nearby table. Within moments, Jimmy was back, smiling.

"Hey Cav, they want to bump it up to $30 mill! We're already in their heads, bro!"

It was a proposition to raise the stakes an additional $5 million, raising the total to $30 million.

Jimmy and Cav understood this move. They had been in this spot a hundred times for a lot less money, but it was the same basic move. This move opened the floodgates to far bigger opportunities.

Cav's cocky response was, "One small step for man, one giant step for some good hustling, something like that, I heard Jasper say it once."

All cocky as well, Jimmy said, "It's us against the motherfuckin' world, and we got them by the nuts."

With a smile and a nod, Cav replied, "Who are 'they'? 'They' who? I wanna meet this Mr. Big dude."

Jimmy pointed out the group. Cav and Jimmy confidently strode over for the meet and greet, ready to negotiate. The boys stood confidently in front of Mr. Gustave LeBlanc and his right hand man, Oddsmaker.

Cav opened the discussion. "I'm Cav."

Oddsmaker took over and did the formal introductions very properly. They all shook hands.

Cav lit the fuse with a bold statement. "In all fairness, we want to gamble. Why is there so much hate in the world? Why is everybody against me and Jimmy? I know we have a hill to climb to beat your boy Junjun. We just want a fair game and fair odds. We will bump it another $5 million. Give us 10 to 1 and let's do the $30 million. We understand you're the favorite. I'm supposed to lose. We know you're favored to win. You clearly have home court advantage, and the entire world favors your boy to win. I'm the underdog here, you and the world know it. We like the action, and that's why we're here. So you got me, do the 10 to 1 and we're good on the $30 million."

Mr. LeBlanc maintained his composure. "There is no guaranteed winner here, Cav, and you know that. I have no monopoly on who wins, no crystal ball. It's gambling, and it can go either way. Cav, I'll give you 4 to 1 if you bet $30 million."

Cav carefully confirmed and clarified Mr. LeBlanc's proposed terms.

"So, you're proposing our $30 million to your $120 million. If we lose, you take the $30 million. If you lose, we take $120 million. Is that what you're proposing, Mr. LeBlanc?"

"Yes, that is correct, Cav," Mr. LeBlanc confirmed. "Should I lose, you may collect your bounty at the casino vault. You will be issued uncirculated FRNs—a tranche of $120 million. I have a $500 million slush fund at my casino vault." Oddsmaker nodded in confirmation.

Cav and Jimmy asked to be excused to discuss the terms privately. They were surprised, but then, not completely stunned, at the revelation of the $500 million in a private vault. After all, it was one of the wealthiest and most expensive places in the world, a country renowned for gambling before Las Vegas was even dreamed of.

After a calculated Hollywood pause, they returned.

Cav and Jimmy exchanged confident glances before nodding in agreement, sealing the terms of the bet. "You got action, sir," Cav confirmed with Mr. LeBlanc. He followed with a question. "By the way, you mentioned uncirculated FRNs? What's that? I mean, you're talking dollars, right? Sorry, a little confused."

Mr. LeBlanc reached into his pocket, pulled out a crisp $100 US banknote, and showed it to Cav, pointing out the words "Federal Reserve Note" on the bill.

Cav, still curious about one more detail, asked Mr. LeBlanc about the meaning of uncirculated. Cav pulled out a wad of cash, pointing to it, "It's the same shit, right?"

Mr. LeBlanc, amused with Cav, explained, "Yes Cav, 'same shit' but uncirculated, brand new in the box, never used, unspent." Mr. LeBlanc pointed to Cav's wad of cash and said, "Circulated."

Smiling, they all shook hands again, and departed.

Cav and Jimmy had a good laugh about the concept of uncirculated Federal Reserve Notes. Cav pulled out his wad of cash again waving it dramatically: "Circulated FRNs. It's a bottomless pit of money in this joint. You heard him, he has $500 million to blow—plus plus. Oddsmaker told me he's worth at least 25 B—B as in Billion!"

With this new understanding, they continued their preparations for the high-stakes match, fully aware of the enormous financial possibilities and the global attention on this match.

The anticipation of the crowd was getting more intense. The arena was already packed, and the French sports/news anchor Lilou, with her sidekick Coco, prepared for the broadcast.

35

The Prince of Monaco

The formal ceremony began with the announcer introducing the foreign dignitaries and local leaders in attendance, leading up to the Sovereign, His Serene Highness Albert II, Sovereign Prince of Monaco. The audience was treated to a very special formal introduction in true French style to His Highness at the podium.

"Ladies and gentlemen, distinguished guests, it is with great honor and privilege that I introduce to you His Serene Highness, Prince Albert Grimaldi, the Sovereign Prince of Monaco. Please join me in extending our warmest welcome to Prince Albert, a true statesman and leader." His Serene Highness received passionate applause.

Prince Albert then addressed the audience: "Ladies and gentlemen, admired guests, and sports enthusiasts from around the world, it is with enormous pride and great honor I stand before you today. As we gather to celebrate the spirit of sportsmanship and competition, let us also embrace the values of unity, respect, and excellence that these events raise among us. Recently, my friend Gustave LeBlanc approached me with an idea that not only caught me by complete surprise but also left me humbled, sparking a curiosity I hadn't felt in years."

The Prince paused for dramatic effect, and then continued: "He and I agreed that we honor my mother, Princess Grace, born Grace Kelly. A celebrated icon of the silver screen turned royalty; American film legend and later the Princess of Monaco. Today, we endeavor to enshrine Princess Grace, immortalizing her not just as a figure of elegance and majesty, but as a beacon of inspiration whose grace and benevolence illuminated the world.

"In a gesture of timeless praise, a plaque is hereby dedicated to the enduring memory of Grace Kelly. This emblem shall be preserved in a place of distinction. It shall invite those who pass by to pause and remember her, ensuring that the grace and beauty that she personified remains an eternal inspiration."

The prince unveiled the bronze plaque, and the arena erupted with thunderous applause and a standing ovation. This celebration of Grace Kelly created heartfelt acclamation with online viewers around the world.

Prince Albert continued: "Monaco, though small in size, is enormous in its passion for sports. Today, we continue this proud tradition by hosting the 9-ball billiards match of the 21st century. Joined by guests in 130 countries sharing 30 languages, I salute our contestants, Cav and Junjun, for their courage and fortitude, and wish the best for both players. As we now proceed to our national anthem, a symbol of our nation's unity and strength, let us stand together."

As the national anthem played, the national flag was raised. Resounding applause followed the flag raising, and Prince Albert proclaimed: "Let the games begin!"

The MC then declared with great drama, "Ladies and gentlemen, allow me to present the stars of this event. Representing the United States, from Lawrence, Kansas, Cavalier 'Cav' McTavish!"

To a round of applause, Cav rose from his seat a few feet from one corner of the brilliantly lit pool table, bowed graciously, and waved to the enthusiastic crowd.

"And hailing from our very own Cote d'Azur, a warm welcome for Junjun!"

Junjun rose from his seat near the other corner and acknowledged the applause with a humble bow.

As he sat back down, the crowd went nuts, cheering and clapping for their chosen combatants for over a minute. The announcer had to break in, and continued: "Ladies and gentlemen, welcome to the world's most-watched billiards match in modern history. What started as a phone call and a $10 million dollar wager has tripled overnight into a global event of $30 million U.S. dollars in-house.

"Wagering around the world on this world-first match is estimated to be in the hundreds of millions or even billions of euros, dollars, rubles, every one of dozens of currencies are in play. And this live event is being broadcast to a record number of countries and fans worldwide.

"As most of you know, the game is called 9-ball, because there are only nine balls on the table, numbered 1 to 9. Here's how it works—the first player attempts to sink or pocket all the balls, in order, from 1 to 9. Sinking the number 9-ball wins the game.

Even if a player sinks the first 8 balls but misses the 9-ball, the opposing player wins the game if he can sink that 9-ball. Each game goes back and forth until one of them sinks that vital, all-important 9-ball, the moneyball.

"This match is a race to be the first player to win two of three possible sets of 25 games each set. A set is won by being first to win 25 games. The entire match and prize money is won by the first to win two of these three sets—wins and all the prize money!

"I repeat, the first player to win two sets claims the ultimate prize of $30 million U.S. dollars."

The announcer paused briefly while the local audience and millions more around the world digested the details. He then leaned into the microphone and intoned:

"Gentlemen, you may begin your match!"

Cav and Junjun rose from their seats in their elegant, tailor-made 3 piece Hugo Boss tuxedos. Mr. LeBlanc had ordered these tuxedos personally from Hugo Boss to show a flawless, polished appearance, adding a first-class visual for the world to see. The 2 players removed their jackets and hung them beside their chairs. The air in the room was charged as they stepped forward to lag for the break. The referee entered, dressed in a tuxedo and white gloves, and handed each player a cue ball. They walked up to the table, exchanged a handshake, and then lagged for the break very formally.

The announcer explained to the audience that the lag was a crucial part of determining who got the first break. At about the same time, each player strikes his cue ball down the length of the table, intending it to bounce back from the far rail and return as close as possible to the near rail. The one finishing closest to the near rail wins the honor of the first break.

The room hushed as the two players carefully prepared for the lag. Junjun won the lag and broke first with an impressive start, running four racks. On the fifth rack, Junjun had a difficult shot and played a safety on Cav, hiding him behind another ball (snookering him). Regrettably, Cav's shot was weak, resulting in a foul, and Junjun captured an opportunity with a free shot. The referee retrieved the cue ball, handed it to Junjun, and declared, "Bad hit, foul." The cue ball must contact the next ball in the rotation and hit a rail—1-ball, 2-ball, 3-ball, and so on up through the 9-ball—each being referred to as the "object ball." Additionally, the object ball must either be sunk, or it, or the cue ball, must touch a rail, or it constitutes a foul. A foul awards the opponent a free shot, which means he can place the cue ball anywhere on the table for his next shot.

Junjun continued his strong performance, extending his lead to seven games. Cav staged a remarkable comeback, running six consecutive racks and closing the gap to 6-7. The momentum shifted as Cav demonstrated his skill and ability on the table. On Cav's next break, he suffered a small setback when his powerful break forced the cue ball off the table, resulting in a foul. Junjun was awarded a free shot. The concentration of both players was electrifying, keeping the audience on edge. Junjun dominated the first set, securing a commanding lead of 22-15.

Needing only three more games to win the first set, Junjun cruised to a 25-15 victory. The audience roared their approval. As the first set concluded, Cav, visibly affected by the loss, took a moment to regroup with Jimmy. Like a prizefighter's ringside trainer, Cav consoled Jimmy. They were a rock-solid team and had been through many battles together. A noticeable change occurred in Mr. LeBlanc after winning the first set. He was joking privately with Oddsmaker, confident that they were about to win the prize. One set away from the cash!

The second set got underway, and the tension in the arena escalated. Cav won the lag and started strong, breaking and running to a +7 games advantage. It was an opening statement of strength and power. However, the momentum shifted as Junjun rallied back. They traded the advantage back and forth for hours. Cav had slowed Junjun's momentum from the first set. The score became a close battle, with Junjun barely holding the edge at 17 to 15. The crowd was on the edge of their seats, witnessing a fierce battle. Every shot, every move, seemed crucial as they fought for the decisive games that could determine the outcome of this monumental match.

Tying up the match at one set apiece was an option, but that would eliminate a powerful hustle. Cav chose to give Junjun and Mr. LeBlanc a false sense of security.

This was where the true hustler, the money player, zeroed in on his actual opponent—Mr. LeBlanc, the money man. Had he and Jimmy accurately evaluated Mr. Big? Had they effectively penetrated LeBlanc's mind? Had they won the Frenchman's trust? If the answers were all "yes," it was time to go all-in.

If they didn't supermax this play, if they settled for the $120 million pot, he and Jimmy would forever regret the gigantic, enormous, super score that got away.

The future lay before Cav with great clarity. He would risk everything to double the existing $120 million-plus plus. Mr. LeBlanc would decide in the end and dictate the terms. This hustle, practiced over a lifetime, remained fundamentally the same, whether playing for five hundred dollars, ten thousand dollars, or millions—same hustle, different numbers. Oddsmaker, the man in the shadows writing the odds and the behind-the-scenes tactics, was as crucial to this hustle as the players themselves. All the answers lay in the next move. Had the boys effectively earned Oddsmaker's trust and accurately calculated his role?

A seasoned professional in the world of money pool had two critical skills. First was the ability to play world-class pool, performing exceptionally well or failing, playing bad to make his opponent think he has an advantage and make it all believable. Second was understanding the financial details. If a backer was involved, as opposed to a player using his own money, different tactics came into play.

The question was whether Mr. Big, absorbed in what he believed was free money and the excitement of the action, had lost sight of actual reality. Was he like most gamblers, working off of a hunch, lost in the greed and the action? Cav and Jimmy strongly believed so. They believed they had gotten into the Frenchman's head, and Oddsmaker's too.

Cav turned to Jimmy and said, "It's time to make a move, brother." Jimmy responded with a grin, signaling that it was "go time." Jimmy added, "I'll start at 10 to 1 to Mr. Big and go down from there."

The boys knew from Mr. LeBlanc's own words that the billionaire had $500 million sitting down in the vault. They knew Mr. LeBlanc would give 4 to 1 odds, but would he do 10 to 1 odds at this stage of the match?

The boys knew that whatever odds Mr. LeBlanc gave would be strictly on his own terms. Junjun needed 8 games to get to the cash, and Cav and Jimmy needed 35 games to get the cash. Heavy odds were favorable for Mr. LeBlanc and would be confirmed by any bookmaker or financial wealth consultant. It looked good from the outside, but was it really? Cav summoned the referee and Oddsmaker, requesting a 60-minute break. The announcer declared, "Ladies and gentlemen, Mr. McTavish has requested a 60-minute break starting now." The match had been going on for hours, making it the natural moment for a break— and the ideal moment to execute this hustle. Junjun 17 to Cav 15 in the second set.

36

The Window of Opportunity is Now

Jimmy and Cav huddled with LeBlanc and Oddsmaker, and Cav let Jimmy do the talking, at least to start with.

Jimmy proposed adjustments to their wager. He skillfully maneuvered from a disadvantaged position in the overall match to a potentially winning position—a gambler's dream and the height of this ultimate hustle.

Jimmy's first triumph had been getting Mr. LeBlanc to give the boys the 4-to-1 odds. The second stage was pressing the greed button and pushing for higher odds. Jimmy had opened the door to Mr. LeBlanc at 10 to 1 odds.

Mr. LeBlanc responded with skepticism. "Are you completely insane, Jimmy?" he asked.

Jimmy scratched his head. "Yes, probably, sir. I'm in a foreign country, in your house, at your property. We need 35 games to win the cash, and you need eight games to win it all. Eight games and out. Maybe I've fallen under your spell with all the beauty, all the luxury. But I've never had a hunch this powerful."

Cav joined in and added to the negotiation with his own bravado. "Mr. LeBlanc, may I be honest with you? We came here to gamble and bet high, far beyond $30 million. We have the cash, and I will put my $50 million Beverly Hills mansion, my Lambo, my Ferrari, all of it on the line if I run out of cash, which is going to take a while. If I have to hand over the keys to my Beverly Hills mansion, if that is what it costs me, we are prepared to go all-in."

It wasn't a complete lie. Yes, Cav and Jimmy owned a Beverly Hills mansion, a Rolls Royce, a Lambo, and a Ferrari, but everything was on a signature. They had put up $10 million on the house, but a foreclosure would swallow that $10 million up in a New York second. All of these assets had their names on them, but the truth was, they were technically owned by the bank. They didn't even realize they were paying interest on all the assets, the house, the cars, everything done on a signature loan. But they had bragging rights, leveraged out of sheer creativity.

Jimmy made a gesture as if to hold Cav back. "Slow down, Cavalier," he said. "What if he's hustling us?"

Cav turned to Mr. LeBlanc and challenged him directly: "Are you hustling me, Mr. LeBlanc?"

The question hung in the air. Mr. LeBlanc responded with a sneaky smile, grinning as if he had these two right where he wanted them. If the boys played it correctly, Mr. Billionaire was figuring out how to get more money, not play it safe and take the $30 million. He wanted more. He must have been thinking, *How much can I get out of these two Kansas country bumpkins?* This was how the boys circled for the kill. The next move would seal his fate.

When the boys profiled and evaluated Mr. Gustave LeBlanc, they only had to look at him and his casino business. Forget the hotel side of Versailles: each hotel room served as a fancy high-dollar prison cell to trap the compulsive gambler. His cash cow was the casino. He waited for whales, huge-bankroll gamblers, high-net-worth individuals to come into his casino and lose millions, all day, all night. This was his daily routine more or less in a nutshell. Mr. Big was the big fat whale, in the boys' minds.

In his greedy mind, Mr. LeBlanc believed he was arranging the hustle, while the boys were executing their own hustle. The winner in this would be the one who walked away as the supreme hustler—the brightest, smartest, and the best at this elaborate con game. If Mr. Big took the bait, he would lay down the rules and the exact wager, on his terms, the exact way he wanted it. Mr. LeBlanc had to dictate the terms, and if he did, then the boys would have hustled him.

Could Cav and Jimmy potentially lose? Of course. Would it kill them? Probably not. And there was always a fallback—a job back at the salt mines in Rio, with Marco.

Mr. LeBlanc led out. "Okay, Jimmy, here is my offer, take it or leave it, I don't care." He answered the $250 million dollar question, unable to resist. "Jimmy, I'll give you 5 to 1 if you bet another $20 million. Your $50 million to my $250 million."

Ka-ching, they had gotten in his head! If they had influenced Mr. Big, Oddsmaker would be a lay-down. Now all they had to do was take it down and win the 35 games.

Jimmy fluffed his ego: "Mr. LeBlanc, you got moxie, I'll give you that."

Cav broke in. "Could we have a moment to discuss this matter privately? Please give us a minute."

This was all part of the act. They walked away for a couple of minutes, leaving Mr. LeBlanc and Oddsmaker to enjoy the thought of stealing the boys' $50 million, hoping and praying the boys would accept Mr. LeBlanc's offer. It was one of the oldest cons in the book.

Returning to Mr. Big and Oddsmaker, Cav broke the silence. "I have no objections."

Jimmy gave them a curt nod of agreement.

Their performance was played to perfection. You would think Cav and Jimmy had graduated at the Actors Studio along with Paul Newman and Marlon Brando.

Oddsmaker confirmed once more exactly what the terms were. "Okay, we have a $50 million wager with Cav at a disadvantage of minus 1 set and a 2-game loss at the current score, 15-17, in the second set. The winner of the best two out of three sets claims all the cash. The odds are 5 to 1. If Cav stages a comeback and wins, he walks away with $250 million. In the event of a Cav loss, $50 million goes to Mr. La Blanc."

Oddsmaker continued: "Does everyone understand the wager?" They did. A $50 million-$250 million wager on a handshake, leaving the weight of the high-stakes wager hanging in the air, unannounced to the world, kept between them.

Risky as hell, but the boys had let Mr. LeBlanc take the initiative with his ultimate offer. The boys knew it had to come from him for this hustle to work. It didn't matter if Mr. Big said $100 million or $900 million. As long as he dictated the terms, the boys were golden. They had ginned it!

This was the genius boss move. Cav would have to win the second set, but he just needed ten more games for that. Then the clock would go back to an even match 0—0. Both players would start over, and the first to get to 25 games of the 3rd set, the last and final set, would win the cabbage—in their case, $250 million for the boys.

It was risky as hell and a dangerous move. They were well aware of the fact that for this hustle to work, Mr. Big had to feel like he was in control; all that mattered was that "he dictated the terms." As long as it was played in that exact sequence, the boys were golden, and they knew it.

The boys also knew that if there was an issue with POF (proof of funds) for the additional $20 million, Mr. Big or Oddsmaker would have mentioned it. Mr. Big or Oddsmaker would have mentioned it either at the time of the raise of the bet or when the boys walked away to think about it. The boys' "walkaway to think about it" was a move, a hustle. If Oddsmaker or Mr. Big had any issues or realized they were being hustled out of $20 million, it would have been brought up right then and there. The boys were counting on Mr. Big and Oddsmaker being so consumed and pre-occupied with this event, the construction, the broadcast rights on six continents, the players, the staff in his casino, the huge amount of money coming and going. A thousand distractions in a thousand directions, away from the fact that Jimmy and Cav could not cover the $20 million. In pool speak, it was a $20 million dollar air barrel. If Einstein were there to do the math, he would say, "$E=MC^2$ grade bullshit!"

If they were asked to prove the $20 million, this hustle wouldn't work, but they had ginned it!

Their confidence was bolstered by the fact that the boys had been hearing Oddsmaker bragging about the casino rake (money intake) since they arrived. The casino profits were through the roof. Mr. Big was making millions a day on his casino, at full capacity, triggered by this event. His attention was scattered in a thousand directions, as was Oddsmaker's, and this was what the boys calculated with.

Chapter 37

Anyone happen to have a spare $20 million?

Mr. LeBlanc's excitement and greed dominated the moment, and he failed to realize that Cav and Jimmy only had $30,000,000 to their names. That amount represented their entire fortune under the sun, moon, and stars—all tucked away in that casino vault at The House of Versailles Hotel and Casino.

In true, classic pool hustler style, they had placed it all on the line for this hustle. If they lost, they would not only end up penniless but also face the grisly possibility of deadly consequences. The mansion, the shiny cars, everything done with a signature, all on auto pay. Since they never saw the money, who cared? They owned nothing; it was all on borrowed money. That $10,000,000 equity in the crib would be liquidated to pay lawyers, realtors, and sold at a quick foreclosure sale of the property at a reduced price and on and on. Bust!

Hey, did anyone happen to have a spare $20 million? Because Jimmy and Cav sure the fuck didn't. It was a free swing at $250,000,000 for $30,000,000. This risky gamble was the lifeblood of how to super-max your money—simply make it up.

They skillfully played Oddsmaker, as a victim in their con, on the side of POF—proof of funds. Oddsmaker left this to Mr. LeBlanc. After all, it was his money, not Oddsmaker's.

Oddsmaker naturally assumed that Mr. LeBlanc would have verified Cav and Jimmy's bankroll. Meanwhile, Mr. LeBlanc assumed that Oddsmaker would have, of course, had his back and checked their financial status. Elementary, right? There was never a doubt or question about Cav and Jimmy's access to the funds.

This intricate web of assumptions and misdirection was the nature of this hustle—the artful maneuvers just like it was done in Kansas City.

Oddsmaker, ever the greedy bastard, had bet a ton of cash on Junjun. Don't think for a second that he wasn't eager to grab a piece of this seemingly free, easy, loose money. The cash was flowing at Mach 10—lightning speed—and being passed around like Girl Scout cookies. His greed blinded him, sending Oddsmaker into dreamland. The boys were well aware of this flaw in Oddsmaker's judgment.

One other fun fact to this brilliant hustle: when Cav and Jimmy wired their money to the Casino, they carefully identified who at the Casino verified the POF (proof of funds) transfer. They discovered, in fact, it wasn't Oddsmaker nor Mr. Big; it was a lady in accounting, Fleur Toussaint. This minor detail made it possible that they could make a wager in the dark, off the books of the accounting department, on a handshake.

On paper, it all added up to $30 million, no alarms, no eyes wandering. With a raise to $50-$250 million not on any official radar, Cav and Jimmy were golden, in the clear. Only four men on the planet knew about this latest bet.

Most likely Jimmy and Cav were still in the clear, even if there was somehow a leak on this latest mega monumental wager. None of the staff would speak up for fear of being fired or sent to Siberia. Staff knew Mr. Big had a short fuse and not to ever fuck with his money or, in this case, his reputation.

If Mr. LeBlanc wanted the $50-$250 million wager concealed and secret, that's how it would be.

In the kingdom of high-stakes gambling and pool hustling, trust was a fragile currency. Jimmy and Cav had clearly made it to another level. Who would have the matzo balls to attempt a hustle on such an epic scale?

The lines between associate and opponent blurred upon such schemes. If the stars aligned and their timing was right, if events were strategically set in motion correctly, they were in for a thrilling, explosive climax.

The only thing left was for Cav to play 9-ball at his AAA game on an epic level and win the match. If they ginned it and won the match, they'd be set for two lifetimes.

Cav retreated to a quiet, private place and made a call to his princess, Esmeralda. She softly expressed her concern. Cav reassured her with confidence that he was going to win. He reminded her of the Rio pool hall robbery, of his promise that they would be okay, reminding her that the Rio statement applied here as it did there. She recalled. Cav insisted, "I'm going to beat him all day, and I'm going to beat him all night."

Esmeralda, after a few moments, broke the silence and spoke. High above the world in her ivory tower, she gently said, "Hey, Cav... it's your world right now, this is your moment. There are just a few moments in life that matter. One moment of perfection counts for more than a lifetime of 'quite good'."

Esmeralda knew exactly what to do to get her man's mind right, to turbo charge Cav into another dimension, and she succeeded. Esmeralda's voice steadied him, as it always had. She was the voice that cut through the chaos and reminded him why he played.

Cav went quiet for a few moments. "Yes, you're right. This is my moment," he stated with the *ne plus ultra* of confidence. A lot had been sacrificed to get him there, and now it was all on his shoulders. Would he prevail?

Cav added a touch of humor to the conversation. "Hey, gorgeous, were you and Gisele able to get those bets made?"

Esmeralda responded, "Yes, Gisele and I bet it all, up-high." She paused. "We're watching you on TV you know. You look fantastic."

Cav playfully remarked half-jokingly, "Thank me later. Please do not blow it all at Harrods."

"You know me," she said.

"Listen to me, gorgeous. We sent all the money we had and placed it all on this match we felt so sure I could win. It's all we got and it sits in the casino vault in Monaco. We got Mr. Big to give us odds and five people on Planet Earth know about what I'm about to tell you. We got him to give us odds on a fifty million dollar bet to win $250 million. You're one of the five that know this."

In a super-ninja, high-voltage state he declared, "Ok, good! I'm going in there, and I'm gonna take this down. Ciao, I love you!"

As Cav re-entered the game room, radiating confidence like a Greek god, the crowd sensed that something had changed during the break—a newfound confidence and self-determination had come over him. The buzz in the air was electric.

Cav knew something that nobody in the world knew except him and Jasper, and he had known it since the enlarged likeness of Junjun had appeared next to him in the arena.

One cold, quiet winter night in Lawrence, Kansas, two foreign hustlers had shown up at Jasper's, and had clipped and scalped Cav and Jasper to the tune of $15,000. Cav was just finding his place in the world of gambling and high-stakes pool. It was his bitterest memory, unless you counted the ones involving his father.

The hustler who took him down back then was known as Bongbong. Bongbong—or Junjun as he now styled himself—had robbed him once.

From the moment he saw that picture, this had become a grudge match, a chance to settle an old score.

The $15,000 lost back then was about to come back with interest, to the tune of a quarter billion. The pool gods were smiling on him.

It was payback time, motherfucker. This wasn't just about money; it was about rewriting history. Every hustle, every loss, every sleepless night at the table had led to this moment.

The culmination of Cav's life flashed before him. Jasper, Kansas, Poughkeepsie, Rio, Marco, Marcella, so many images flashing. Now was the time to clear it all out and play 9-ball, focus on the game. Enter the zone.

He was ready.

The announcer inquired of the players: "Are we ready to commence, gentlemen?" With Junjun patiently waiting at the table, Cav gave the nod; the stage was now set for the final act.

38

So this is what
$30 million looks like...

The announcer's words re-emphasized the global scope and importance of this event. The applause from the crowd, the excitement in the air, and the broadcast spanning six continents underscored the magnitude of this final act. Mr. LeBlanc's strategic move to broadcast the event globally showcased his mastery in maximizing revenue and publicity for The House of Versailles Hotel and Casino.

Several African countries staged a boycott and banned the broadcast. In his brilliance, Mr. LeBlanc fired up his media machine to capture the controversy and turned it into a public relations masterpiece, maximizing every minute of free media and gaining even more publicity for his global event.

Mr. LeBlanc's complex worldwide financial web ensured that every dollar wagered on the spectacle passed through his casino, contributing to the record-breaking revenue generated by this historic match. The House of Versailles emerged as a financial powerhouse regardless of who won the match, benefiting Versailles in billions of revenue and widespread publicity, all while enjoying the benefits of Monaco's status as a tax-free haven.

As the players chalked up their cues, all attention was riveted on the scene of the final shootout.

The announcer proclaimed: "Ladies and gentlemen, we now proceed to the conclusion of this match. We are in the second set, and the players stand at Junjun 17 games to Cav 15 games. We begin with Cav breaking."

Cav broke and strung, running five racks. Cav's next break came up dry, with no balls pocketed. Cav now stood at 20 games. Junjun took over and won five games, passing Cav to take the lead at 22 to 20. Cav needed five games to claim the second set, Junjun needed 3 games. Junjun broke weak, pocketing a ball but getting snookered, hooked. If he risked hitting the object ball and missing, Cav would get a free shot. Junjun opted to reduce his risk and roll out on the first shot after the break, in accordance with the rules. He left Cav a jump shot, a disaster for Junjun, Cav stared at the table, envisioning every possible shot and counter-play. Cav executed a remarkable jump shot to gain control of that game and ran the table. Cav evened the score to 22-22 and broke, pocketing the 9-ball on the following break. Now Cav led 23 to 22 over Junjun.

Cav needed two games to win the second set. Winning would set the stage for a final set for the prize. Cav executed a near-perfect break and ran that rack, needing one more game to clinch the second set. He broke, pocketing two balls and the cue ball went airborne but remained on the table in a very dramatic fashion, straight up and down. Cav very carefully surveyed and studied the table, considering his options. Cav knew if he missed now, it would likely cost him the match and $250,000,000. The world froze around him in complete silence. He saw a carom shot. It was a very difficult shot, especially under this much pressure. He could go for the win or play a snooker and hook Junjun, leaving it up to chance. Cav elected for magnificence, nailing the shot and pocketing the 9-ball to claim the second set. The crowd rose to its feet, applauding both players for such an outstanding performance under tremendous pressure.

The announcer called for a 45-minute intermission, mainly to allow participants around the world to place their final bets on the final set.

39

For All the Money

The announcer said, "Ladies and gentlemen, we are about to begin the final deciding set for the winner. We have arrived at the peak of this breathtaking contest between two of the world's titans, where dreams are made and legends are born, right here this evening. A fortune will change hands tonight: a fortune so vast, it will change lives forever. Let us salute Cav and Junjun with a warm thank you and extend to them both our wishes for good luck in this final set." The audience rose as one in a thunderous ovation.

Two gorgeous females made a great show of rolling a cart full of cash into the room, $30 million worth, with glitter and confetti, with music, with the audience going ballistic. Few world events attracted such a prominent, in-your-face, grandiose display of affluence as those in Monaco. Even the Prince of Monaco, viewing from ringside, was clearly enjoying the spectacle of sumptuous wealth.

Mr. LeBlanc allowed himself a modest peek at the cart, assuming it was all his.

It was "go time." All the bets were made, and all the chips were in; there would be no further interruptions or intermissions.

The announcer intoned: "Gentlemen, you may begin your final set."

The players lagged for the break. Junjun won the lag, broke, and pocketed the 9. On his second break, no balls found the pockets, leaving Cav snookered. He evaluated his options and chose a risky, strategic move. According to the rules, Cav had the option to shoot the cue ball anywhere on the table, giving his opponent the option to take the first shot after the break or force Cav to shoot it. Cav rolled out, creating a scenario that favored one of his most spectacular skills—a jump shot.

The referee announced "Option," indicating that Junjun had the choice to take the shot or pass it back to Cav. Junjun, not liking his chances, declined, giving it back to Cav.

This decision turned the tide in Cav's favor. *I am in control here*, he asserted silently, with all the force of his will.

Cav elevated his cue and struck down with force, sending the cue ball in the air over a ball to hit the object ball. He pocketed that ball and drew the cue ball back the entire length of the table. The crowd erupted in riotous applause.

Cav positioned himself perfectly for the next ball and continued his crusade, break-run, break-run. Junjun mounted a serious challenge of his own, making difficult shots one after the other.

After hours of play, Junjun and Cav had reached a tied score at 15 games apiece. It was a race to ten games for the win.

Cav, shooting, was confronted with a very dangerous, highly technical shot that carried a high risk of failure. Unruffled by the intense pressure, Cav calculated the trajectory from a position outside space and time.

Elevating his cue stick almost vertically, Cav struck down on the cue ball with precision. The result was a very dramatic, rare shot.

As the cue ball struck the 7-ball, the 7-ball soared over the 8-ball, landing cleanly to set up a dramatic combination shot that sent the 9-ball rolling into the pocket, securing the game-winning shot. The crowd exploded in wild applause, and even Junjun bowed his head in admiration.

That single shot won Cav the confidence of the audience and delivered a well-placed blow to Junjun's self-confidence. It was a power shot calculated to get inside Junjun's head more than anything, and Cav knew it had succeeded. Wear down, overwhelm your opponent. Risk and reward. The scales had tipped in Cav's favor.

Cav could have attempted the three-ball combination 7-8-9, but the balls were too far out of line. Sometimes, in the heat of battle, a player just "feels" such a shot, but Cav's instinct and skill shone through in this very rare moment.

Cav entered a state of heightened focus, oblivious to the surrounding noise and distractions. Junjun could see that Cav had tapped into a level of play beyond what he had already shown.

As they battled back and forth, Junjun demonstrated remarkable tenacity, seemingly all but invincible. By throwing every possible roadblock at Junjun, Cav clung to a slight advantage.

Then Junjun overtook him at 20 games each. Either player was capable of stringing five racks together.

By the grace of the pool gods, it was Cav's break, and he unleashed a break from hell, pocketing six balls on the break, including the 9-ball. The crowd was speechless, and Cav was now only four games away from claiming the monumental prize.

Cav, clearly in the zone, relied on everything Jasper had taught him and everything he had mastered over all his years. It all came down to these last four racks of 9-ball. Cav went on a rampage, playing as if his life depended on it.

Break after break, run after run, he relentlessly played every shot with precision. Cav was flawless. As he stood on the brink of victory, he broke the balls and ran the final rack down to the 9-ball. With one easy shot remaining for the win, Junjun stood up and conceded defeat by tossing a white towel onto the table. Cav looked at Junjun, sharing a smile, and proceeded to pocket the 9-ball, clinching his triumph in the match of the century for all the money.

40

Triumphant

The arena exploded in an uproar of cheers and applause as the referee declared Cav the winner of "game, set, and match," holding up his arm high for the world to see.

The crowd, overjoyed, rose to their feet, showering Cav with their admiration. Confetti filled the air, and the lights intensified, marking the conclusion of an extraordinary two days.

Junjun, with sportsmanship and grace, approached Cav, offering a handshake and congratulations on the hard-fought battle. The two shook hands, and Cav leaned in to thank Junjun for a hard-fought match.

Prince Albert was afforded the first congratulatory handshake with Cav and Junjun. He approached with his entourage and praised both players with class and dignity.

Meanwhile, the paparazzi and press surrounded Cav, capturing his moment of triumph. Lilou and Coco, the sports/news anchors, positioned themselves to interview Cav and Junjun.

As the cameras focused on Cav, he took a moment to address the world. His first words were a heartfelt thanks to Esmeralda, acknowledging her significant role in their shared victory. He sincerely thanked all watching the broadcast, "including those that bet against me."

The broadcast cut to a live feed in London to Esmeralda and Gisele at a pub. Versailles correspondent Sir Anthony celebrated their successful bets with the crowd enthusiastically. "Overjoyed" would be an understatement. Esmeralda and Gisele tossed wads of Euros and pounds in the air, reveling in their triumphant gamble.

The global impact of this monumental win echoed across the world of sports and gambling, leaving a lasting mark on The House of Versailles Hotel and Casino and its proprietor, Mr. LeBlanc.

Cav, celebrating his victory, posed with his new friends Lilou and Coco. The prospect of the massive winnings seemed to have Cav in a trance. When Coco asked him about his plans for all the money, Cav responded with a laugh, "If you only knew." He then playfully added, "Hell, me and Jimmy are the worst at money management, I'm gonna give it to Esmeralda and let her deal with it." Looking into the camera, he addressed Esmeralda: "We did it, gorgeous!"

As the celebration continued, Cav called out for Jimmy, who waved and turned away from the publicity. Meanwhile, Mr. Big, witnessing the entire spectacle, shook his head, laughed, and exited the building, seemingly unfazed.

Despite the staggering $250 million loss on the bet to Cav and Jimmy, Mr. LeBlanc reportedly raked in an astounding two billion dollars from online betting, with estimates of $20,000,000 on the floor of his casino during the few days of the event and another

$50,000,000 over the next few weeks as the crowd busted out and went home.

Every Euro, Pound, Dinar, Dollar and Dirham contributed to Mr. LeBlanc on a monumental scale, driving his global online gambling frenzy. All funds were transferred through the XRP digital platform directly to The Versailles Hotel and Casino, adding to the impressive gains the casino had already enjoyed.

The financial success didn't end there for Mr. LeBlanc. The prestige gained from the publicity surrounding this epic pool match ensured future revenue from re-broadcasts and related ventures. Additionally, the Versailles was projected to generate billions in the years to come, fueled by the success and reputation established by this high-profile event.

To cement his financial gains and maintain control, Mr. LeBlanc had the players sign a nondisclosure agreement (NDA), by which the players would not receive any revenue from online gambling or re-broadcasts, and granted the casino free use of their images.

Junjun found himself well compensated for his incredible performance, enough to retire comfortably. This financial windfall provided him with the freedom to pursue a life of leisure. He made it into the pool and gambling history books.

For Cav and Jimmy, the victory went beyond immediate financial gain. The generational wealth they accumulated from this match undeniably altered the course of their lives and secured a place for them in the archives of both pool and sports betting financial history.

In the grand scheme of things, the $250 million gamble made by Mr. LeBlanc to Cav and Jimmy turned out to be a relatively

small price to pay for the massive financial gains and global recognition Mr. LeBlanc achieved.

Mysteriously, the only loser among this group of hustlers, this
fabulous four—Cav, Jimmy, Mr. Big, and Oddsmaker—was a guy
named Oddsmaker.

As the curtain fell on this unforgettable night in Monaco, Lilou
and Coco bid farewell to their worldwide audience. This historic
pool match and its surprising twists of fortune would echo through
the grand halls for many years. The intense showdown concluded
with Lilou and Coco signing off from Monaco with a simple, "Ciao."

Cav and Jimmy retreated to their room to celebrate.

Cav shouted, "Are you kidding me? We're quarter billionaires!
Fuckin' hell!" He took out his wad of cash and threw it in the air.

Jimmy yelled, "We killed the bull! $250 million! We scalped
the billionaire, the biggest pool score in history. You did it, bro!"

Cav phoned Esmeralda and had her put Gisele on speaker so
they could all celebrate the moment together. They made plans to
catch up, and Cav explained they had the room for another week
and insisted they come to the South of France and join them. All
the plans were set; they would fly down the following day. Cav,
Jimmy, and their driver would pick them up at the airport.

A strange phone call on the house phone interrupted their victory party. A female voice, identifying herself as "Sasha," extended
an invitation to the boys for a special night out to celebrate the win.

Cav, sensing something was off, declined the offer and hung
up. Jimmy suggested they pay one more visit to their new favorite
restaurant, Chez d'Azur. "Cav, we owe it to ourselves, one more
time!"

"What about the three-month waiting list?"

"You're right, Cav. I'll call Oddsmaker and see if we can even get in."

"Jimmy, I say you're spot-on, and yes, we need to go say goodbye to Faustine and her wonderful staff. What a class act!"

Jimmy contacted Oddsmaker, who made the arrangements.

The celebration carried on at Chez d'Azur, where Cav and Jimmy reveled in their extraordinary triumph.

Faustine, having heard all the amazing news, took the opportunity to make their evening still more special. As the boys celebrated, Faustine assembled her staff and they all raised a glass to Cav and Jimmy in a special toast. Faustine congratulated them with genuine warmth and presented them with a lifetime membership to their very exclusive wine club, where the Prince of Monaco was an honorary sommelier. In Monaco and indeed in France, this was considered a very special honor and distinction.

Cav and Jimmy were actually moved by this unexpected and very personal gesture. Their evening at the restaurant drew to a close, the honored guests said their farewells, and they left the restaurant overjoyed in a state of euphoria.

It was all too perfect to imagine. As Cav and Jimmy left the restaurant and started for the Rolls, Thompson was ordered into the trunk. Casimo and several of his thugs fell into step with Cav and Jimmy, clapped them in handcuffs and blindfolds, and forced them into a car. Casimo still wanted his pound of flesh. The mysterious phone call from a lady named Sasha should have been a clue. What would LeBlanc care if they went missing, never to be heard from again? It would be another $250 million back to him, that never really left him, still in the vault.

The car maneuvered through the city, eventually turning off to a gloomy pier, a secluded spot on an old section of waterfront on the outskirts of town—perfect for an execution.

Or perhaps not so perfect. Casimo was about to be upstaged by another set of goons, another lethal force providing security, more deadly and ruthless than Mr. LeBlanc's. They had a legitimate claim to Cav and Jimmy, who were collateral in a different transaction altogether.

41

A Tragic Loss to Such Large Gain

Cav and Jimmy recognized Casimo's voice as he ordered them out of the car in a violent rage. "You don't sound happy, Casimo," Cav said. "You must have bet against us."

"It's like I said, you fuck," shouted Casimo. "Conoscere i miei momenti di movimento. Know my movements. You had your chance to lose, and you fucked it up."

"What do you gain by offing us?" Cav asked him. "Our winnings are still in LeBlanc's vault."

"Personal satisfaction," Casimo whispered. "But first, you're going to enjoy a swift kick in your cheap American 'coglioni' (balls)."

For Jimmy and Cav, the smell of ocean water made them think it was probably lights out for them—thoughts of the end of the road, the finish line. They say your life flashes in front of you when you think it's over, and all those thoughts were going through their minds. Casimo and his henchmen had guns prodding their necks.

Suddenly everything changed. The boys heard a series of muffled pops from silenced weapons as Casimo and his henchman collapsed to the pavement one after another.

More silenced bullets pierced the glass of the getaway car and killed the driver trying to pull away from the dock.

Casimo didn't stand a chance, not a prayer. He was way outgunned and outmaneuvered. As if he'd brought a knife to a gunfight. As the commotion settled down, Cav and Jimmy found themselves in new hands. The new handlers rushed them into another vehicle, and off they went in a fury.

Cav and Jimmy had been snatched from the jaws of death, but by whom? Why? To what end?

Another driver took them to a new location, about an hour's distance away. Their new captors chatted away in Spanish or Portuguese—the boys had never been good at languages—and took them to what had to be an airstrip, because they heard the sounds of aircraft taking off and landing.

The car stopped and the boys were hustled onto a portable stairway and buckled into seats on a luxurious Gulfstream.

As the jet took off, the worry eased. At last their blindfolds and handcuffs were removed, and Cav and Jimmy were handed drinks by the Prince of Darkness himself.

Marco.

42

The Return of
Mr. Black Magic

"You see, I'm not all bad," said Marco. "The two of you have been headed to the death house, and I've saved your sorry asses, twice now."

Jimmy, overcome with gratitude, grabbed Marco's hand, shaking it vigorously, nearly in tears. "My God, man, how can I repay you? You just saved our lives."

Cav echoed his sentiments. "Marco, we owe you. We were dead meat." He shook his head, marveling at the close call. "How long were you following us?"

"My network kept me informed from day one. Your movements weren't exactly secret. I knew the Italians would call in a hit if you beat them. You would never have been heard from again. Ever."

"They grabbed us right in front of the restaurant," Jimmy said. "Right out in the open. How could that happen?"

Marco said laughing, "How could you not have the sense to hire any security? Couple of rookies."

"I appreciate you, boss," said Cav.

"You should. Do you have any idea how many times my competitors have tried to off me?"

"Plenty?" Cav asked.

Marco said proudly, "I've had five attempts on my life that I know of. I live, eat, and breathe treachery and deception. Do you think the plotting and whispering escapes me? I can't even count the number of men who would kill me to gain power and take over my operation, my trade routes, contacts, and on and on. My trade routes stretch from Brazil to Bangkok, my contacts run deeper than the ocean, and my influence reaches places you can't even spell. My business would be worth $25 billion on the New York Stock Exchange. If it was legal."

"When did you find out we were in Monaco?" Cav asked.

"On day one," Marco responded, chuckling. "Cav, Ray Charles could see this happening, splashed all over the world. Big score, huh? Guess you don't need me anymore?"

"No, Marco, you're still the top guy for us," Cav pledged. "We would have shown up right on schedule, just like we promised Marcella. A promise is a promise."

"I'd like to believe you," said a pissed-off Marco.

43

A Woman Knows

In a panic, Esmeralda called the concierge at The Versailles. "Has Cav checked out yet?"

"He has not, madame. Let me try to page him again."

Her countless attempts to reach Cav or Jimmy last night and throughout the day had met only frustration. The boys were still at the hotel as far as anyone knew, enjoying a private celebration.

"He's not like this," Esmeralda cried to Gisele. "He always texts or calls back. I know something happened. I just know it! I'm going crazy!"

Gisele was shaken too, but she kept her cool and did her best to calm her best friend's fears. "They know how to handle themselves," she said. "They're probably just dodging the paparazzi."

"They're probably ducking Marco," Esmeralda said. "He didn't like them taking any time off, and he knows everything by now. How could he not?"

"See if Oddsmaker knows anything," Gisele suggested. Esmeralda called The House of Versailles Hotel and Casino. "Is there a Lonnie or Oddsmaker I could speak to, please?" she asked the concierge.

The concierge said, "Let me page him; just a moment, madame." Silence on the line for a long minute. "Madame, I have Lonnie on the line. Let me connect you."

"Put him on speaker!" said Gisele.

"Lonnie here, how may I be of great service?"

Esmeralda forced herself to be calm. "Are you 'Oddsmaker'?"

"None other. And whom do I have the pleasure..."

"This is Esmeralda."

"Of course," said Oddsmaker. "Cavalier's girlfriend. I've heard wonderful things about you."

"Is he alive?"

"As far as we know. The French police have given us a sketchy report. I'm headed over to the station now to get all the information they have."

"Tell me everything you do know!" she exclaimed.

"OK, Esmeralda. Cav and Jimmy were last seen leaving the Chez d'Azur restaurant between 9:00 and 9:30 last night. Security cameras outside the restaurant captured footage of three men apprehending them in the parking lot and driving away with them."

"Driving them where?" she demanded.

"Out of town, apparently. But the vehicle was followed."

"Followed by whom?" said Esmeralda in terror.

"We don't know, but the new vehicle is tied to a mysterious private flight arriving at the Nice Côte d'Azur International Airport late yesterday afternoon. Police had flagged the flight as suspicious. Study of the flight plan revealed that it was a last-minute scheduling, which is always a red flag. A clever detective captured the license plate numbers of any vehicles departing the airport in haste. They found a match on the vehicle that subsequently followed Cav and Jimmy's abductors."

"Where was this private plane coming from?" Esmeralda demanded.

"Brazil. Rio de Janeiro."

Both ladies mouthed the name at the same time: *Marco.*

"Police lost contact with the two vehicles as they drove out of town, but reported that the plane was wheels-up by 0:100 hours, 1 a.m., leaving French airspace. The aircraft's tail numbers were registered to the South American Emerald Mining Company," Oddsmaker concluded.

"Lonnie, you've been amazing," said Esmeralda. "Call me at this number anytime, day or night." She threw the phone down on the couch and hugged her friend.

"Thank God they're alive," said Gisele.

"That's the good news," said Esmeralda. "The bad news is that Marco assumes Cav and Jimmy are his property—and they're dispensable. He'll only keep them alive until he gets his hands on their winnings."

"It's a better chance than they had last night," Gisele answered. "What's the soonest we can be back in Rio?"

"I will charter a private plane for our immediate departure, and we will be back in Rio within 15 hours," said Esmeralda. She picked up her phone and speed-dialed Juan, her brother in Rio.

"Juan, on my way home from London. I have an emergency. Marco has kidnapped Cav and Jimmy in Monaco, and they are going back to Rio. Cav is in a lot of danger."

Juan, concerned, questioned Esmeralda, "How do you know he is headed back to Rio? Did he call you?"

"I trust my intel, and my intuition," said Esmeralda, in tears. "We'll have to intervene. Think about all the time we have spent discussing this insanity about Marco and Marcella. This time it's finally going to blow up right in our face, just like we imagined, Juan. It's about to happen. Marcella and Marco are sadistic cold-blooded killers. That monster is going to murder Cav and Jimmy."

Juan realized the seriousness of the situation. Though he had never met Cav or Jimmy, he was emotionally involved on his sister's behalf. He and Esmeralda had had long discussions about the drastic measures that might be called for with Marco, and the domino effect that would be triggered by such a course of action. His little sister had suffered enough heartbreak and misery at the hands of the mob boss. It was time to end it.

Juan understood the constant danger Cav and Jimmy had put themselves in, blinded by the money. He knew Esmeralda's commitment to Cav was unwavering, just as he knew that Cav's love for her was unconditional, though he could be thoughtless at times. Her hand was a much sought-after prize, but she had always held out for the love of her life, and she had found him. Cav would never know how many hours of sleep she had lost in fretting about his welfare.

Juan told Esmeralda, "OK, allow me to prepare my team. I will organize this immediately. Be safe and hurry home."

Esmeralda replied, "I'll be there within 15 to 20 hours. Expect this to get extremely violent. We'll have to act fast and ruthlessly."

As Esmeralda rushed to secure a flight to Rio, her anxiety became grim determination, then certainty that her team would prevail. She found a private jet service with service to Rio, ready to depart. She booked the flight, and she and Gisele raced to the airport and were in the air shortly after arriving.

Her uncertainty that Cav would survive the ordeal continued to torment her. Eighteen helpless hours in the air over the Atlantic Ocean left Esmeralda fighting against worry and uncertainty. She tried to prepare herself for the loss of the one person she cared for most in her life next to her family. Her sacrifices, her patient relationship-building could all be lost and buried.

44

The Return of Marco and The Boys

Two limousines awaited Marco at the private airstrip in Rio. Marco had arranged a meeting place inside the airport for them to discuss the plan going forward.

Marco was fast becoming unstable. "You know, Cav, you and Jimmy really disappointed us," he shouted. "Your decisions have left us in a very difficult position. Is this how you treat decent people?" His clenched fists shook.

"Jimmy and I have always treated you fairly," Cav responded. "Listen to me, Marco. You know I'm a pool player, and you know I love pool. Is that a crime? I had a brilliant opportunity in Monaco, and Jimmy and I needed a little break, so it's all good, right? I live for pool, I love the game and the action. You wanted us to live, eat, and breathe the coke trade, and we've done that for a long time. We've made you and ourselves a lot of money."

Marco couldn't argue with that. He saw a change in Cav and Jimmy, though. They had woken up to the fact that they were being played, and those days were over. They didn't need his money, and without that incentive, he could never get compliance by force alone.

The thought that his mules didn't need him terrified and enraged Marco. He feared his empire in America was about to crumble, with his most valuable trade route in the world about to go dark.

It was a credit to Marco's genius that he had found the perfect partners to do his dirty work so professionally. His job placement skills were top-notch. What Cav and Jimmy had done for Marco and Marcella required a very special kind of courage and personal ability. Their ability to run blow so successfully, for so long, was almost superhuman.

The personnel side of the smuggling business emerged as all-important. Cav and Jimmy had the perfect temperament and attitude. Nobody before them had even approached their level of success. They had perfected the process to an art form.

Above all, they had proven themselves both loyal and trustworthy.

Bullying them just wasn't going to work.

The way Marco had developed this operation was sheer genius. He started by risking $200,000 to find the perfect talent for his North America operation. He brought them down to Rio on the pretext of a high-stakes pool match with Fredrico. In reality, it was a casting call and a job interview.

The two hundred grand was a very low stake for the Prince of Darkness. Marco got to meet his proteges face to face and conduct a TTM (tabletop meeting). The perfect hustle. Over the years, those two Kansas boys had made him well over $500 million.

Esmeralda had always seen Marco and Marcella as cold-blooded killers. Her parents and the news media had painted them as monsters. One reporter had dubbed them the "Bonnie and Clyde of Brazil." That reporter hadn't lived much longer after that. Had Marcella ordered the hit? She didn't attempt to discourage the rumor.

This was how Esmeralda, Gisele, and their brother Juan grew up, seeing these images of Marco and Marcella as cold-blooded killers.

Esmeralda braced herself to secure Cav's freedom at all costs. She knew it was a tough road ahead; likely a life or death showdown. Could her brother Juan pull it off? The federales were worthless; Marco owned most of the police. She knew that Marco would have conducted extensive background checks on Cav and Jimmy before they ever left L.A. to join him in Rio. He would have run profiles on them so deep that the FBI couldn't have done better. Marco had very powerful connections in Langley, VA, too.

***

On the ground in Rio, Marco had the boys driven to his resort.

They'd been through a series of shocks and were pretty shaken. First they cheated death at the restaurant, then were kidnapped and cheated death again, then kidnapped again by the Prince of Darkness, forced onto his plane, and abducted to another continent.

Casimo's thugs had stripped them of phones, passports, money, everything. They felt helplessly exposed. All they could do was wait for Marco or Marcella to come settle the business once and for all. Marco set them up with rooms at the resort, where they could relax and reflect on recent events and hopefully reconcile their life plans to realign with Marco's.

They settled into their suite and discussed ideas about how to get out of there and back to Monaco. An impossible task without outside help.

The following morning, they made their way to the hotel restaurant, still without meaningful options and with no word yet from Marco. Their dependence on him was demoralizing. The absence of mobile phones and no way to even pay for burners left them isolated and helpless. In an attempt to regain a sense of normalcy, they visited a clothing shop in the hotel, acquiring basic walking-around clothes and supplies, like toothbrushes and deodorant and shaving gear, and charged it all to their rooms.

As they were crossing to the elevators, Esmeralda and Gisel burst into the lobby in a panic.

"You guys are in serious danger," Esmeralda called as she ran towards them.

No greeting, no hugs, all business—and in a mad hurry.

"I thought you two were in London! How did you know we were here?"

"Save it. What did Marco instruct you to do and when?"

"Marco gave us no instructions at all," Jimmy answered. "He left us at some airplane hangar with a limo and took off in another one, totally pissed off."

Esmeralda grabbed Jimmy by the shoulders. "Listen, you guys need to get out of here now; he is going to murder you. Let me take you to another secluded property."

Cav walked over to Esmeralda and laid his hand on her shoulder. "If he wanted to kill us, he's had 24 hours and endless opportunities to do it! And anyway, if we're in as much danger as you say, running would probably seal our fate. I would be looking over my shoulder for the rest of my life. We have to handle this now. Listen to me. I got us into this, and I'm going to get us out of this."

"Don't you see? Marco doesn't forgive. He'll make you pay for this—one way or another." Esmeralda was furious. "No, you listen to me," she insisted. "Of course you have the balls, nobody doubts that. What you don't have is information. There's no time to discuss it now. Trust me and Juan, do exactly what we say, and you might have a chance."

Esmeralda said she'd be back before long, and she and Gisele left to meet her brother. That night, still waiting for a call from Marco and hearing nothing, Cav and Jimmy began to consider Esmeralda's warning.

Cav broke the silence.

"She is right, you know. Marco is a criminally insane man. Think about it. We've made him countless millions, and you saw him. He's so obsessed with control, playing deadly games with people's lives. It's not about money anymore."

"So we call his bluff," Jimmy said. "Say we're done and shake hands on it."

"Maybe."

"Hey, look, we'll see him soon, and that will be the end of it," Jimmy said. "It's been a good run, hasn't it?"

"A good run," Cav agreed. "If Mr. Big pays us what he owes. Does he even know we're alive?"

Jimmy, now dead serious, added, "Esmeralda's comments are weighing on me. What kind of information does she have? What does her brother have to do with it? Why should we wait for her to save our asses?"

"Because she can," said Cav. "I say we trust her."

The room phone rang. Jimmy picked up and Marcella started barking orders. "Marco will see you tomorrow. I will send the car around noon. Be ready." She hung up.

"Man, that woman is unhinged," Jimmy said.

"What did the bitch say?" Cav asked.

"She'll send a car for us at noon tomorrow. Marco will see us. That was all."

The phone rang again, and Cav answered this time.

Esmeralda pressed him urgently: "Cav, when is your meeting with Marco?"

Cav replied, "His car picks us up at noon tomorrow. Are you clairvoyant, gorgeous?"

"Thank you." She hung up the phone.

Cav was immediately concerned. "That was Esmeralda. She wanted to know what time the meeting with Marco is. I know she'll try and interfere. But how the fuck did she know about a meeting?"

"Maybe she's psychic?" Jimmy said. "Anyway, we can't let her interfere."

Cav countered, "We can't stop her either. Let it play out. Whatta ya say? I think we'll need all the help we can get with this mad fucker."

The phone rang again. Cav answered, listened, and hung up.

"Esmeralda. She's on her way over, with Gisele. Said to sit tight until she gets here."

45

Esmeralda's Sad Story

"Go ahead, go ahead and tell them. Everything." Gisele sat back and waited.

Esmeralda shook her head, "It's too much!" And then, looking at Gisele, she nodded okay.

The girls had arrived shortly after Esmeralda's call. They were sitting in the boys' suite. Jimmy and Cav waited to hear what she had to say.

Esmeralda turned to the boys, paused, and took a deep breath. There was a story to be told, but telling it wasn't going to be easy.

"Nearly seven years ago, my best friend Sabrina—who was also my first cousin—was..." Esmeralda's voice broke, tears streaming down her face, "...was killed. Murdered in cold blood by that bastard you call Marco." More tears. "And Marco? That's not his real name."

Gisele reached over to squeeze Esmeralda's hand. "Go on, go ahead."

"She was a newscaster, a network reporter, she was famous for her reporting on the so-called 'Bonnie and Clyde of Brazil'—yes, we saw the movies here. We know who they were."

The tears stopped, Esmeralda took another deep breath and lowered her voice almost to a growl.

"Luis Fernando Da Costa Jr. That is his real name. And Marcella? Nobody knows the real name of that murderous bitch calling herself Marcella. She's the real brains of the pair."

Esmeralda paused. Again more tears. Gisele reached over and squeezed her hand for support. Cav and Jimmy were already terrified at this story.

"Sabrina was my cousin, we grew up together, played at our country estate, riding horses, and swimming. She even got me started with archery. We went on our first real dates together with boys that were, like, approved by our parents."

"You two were always hanging out together, I remember," Gisele said. Esmeralda nodded, and took a deep breath to continue.

"So I went off entering beauty contests and modeling after I got bored with the local rich boy snobs and horses and even archery..."

"Yes! Esmeralda was a national archery champion and Olympic hopeful," Gisele said.

"...and then Sabrina went into television news reporting, going after crime and corruption. For several years she was after your 'Marco' and Marcella, right up until her death. It all ended when they killed her."

The boys were hypnotized, in a trance at this claim, and listened intently as Esmeralda continued the story, pausing at the tough parts, and never too far from tears or anger.

"Sabrina did a six-part series on TV on the 'infamous pair of thugs' or whatever she called them. She became a household name, praised for her reporting on the Marco-Marcella saga, the drugs, the money laundering, the cold-blooded murders of anyone stupid enough to double-cross them.

"It was Sabrina who coined the name 'Bonnie' for Marcella and made them the modern day Brazilian Bonnie and Clyde. Word was that Marcella was infuriated, it just got right under her skin, it got to a 'tipping point.' You know? That's when you better watch out!

"Marcella often could be seen at the resort watching what was being reported about her by the hated TV news reporter, the alternate magazines with her picture splashed on the front page, the alternate newspapers with articles about her and Marco 'acquitted yet again for crimes normal citizens would be put to death for.'"

Esmeralda now just let the story flow. "The two crooks became household names across the country. Marcella and Marco went on for years after the series by Sabrina. The infamous duo escaped charges that would have put them away. It was known that Marco and Marcella had a heavy connection to a few corrupt Brazilian government figures, crooked judges and politicians, high up in the state police. They were all bought and paid for, beholden to the two criminals.

"Marcella is the brains of their operation, cunning and relentless. She's the one who orchestrates their escapes and eliminates anyone who stands in their way. People underestimate her—and they shouldn't. Every now and then, a new report from Sabrina, hammering home the idea they just got away with cold-blooded murder again. And people did just disappear, never heard from again. And the cops did little to nothing trying to find them."

Esmeralda and Gisele, both thriving as models, remained close friends with Sabrina and met whenever Esmeralda was back from Europe or the Far East. Their girls' night out became legendary, like unofficial public holidays amongst their tight-knit group. Sabrina knew she could razzle and dazzle her good friends on the latest goings-on with the thugs Marcella and Marco. She'd tell her tales of crime and corruption, captivating them with her fearless insights to the delight of Esmeralda and Gisele and a handful of their closest friends. These parties were always at Gilberto's, the famous hill-top restaurant overlooking the stunning skyline of Rio and the beaches.

But then, one early morning when Sabrina was leaving home to go to work, tragedy struck. A group of thugs shot her down in cold blood. They were caught on her home security camera but all wore masks and black clothing.

At this point, Esmeralda couldn't contain herself. She gave in to the grief and loss. The masked killers, never brought to justice, and only one couple obviously to blame. This was the moment when Esmeralda had reached her "tipping point" and swore to avenge that brutal murder. It was a dark moment in the life of Esmeralda, and Gisele and their friends were part of that story.

"The funeral service was a national event aired on television," Esmeralda said. "All the politicians speaking and making 'sworn statements' about how they would 'fight corruption and graft' and all the typical bullshit politicos do with little ever being done and crooked business as usual!"

Esmeralda concluded the story with fury and anger. "Investigations wore out over time, nothing was ever found, no one was ever arrested, and the investigation just quietly ended!"

What didn't wear out was Esmeralda's resolve to find some way to ensure that her best friend Sabrina did not die in vain.

"I have never forgotten. Every day, I wake up with one goal: to ensure Sabrina didn't die in vain. I don't care how long it takes or what I have to do—I will make them pay. I made a promise, a 'sacred oath to myself,' to get those monsters once and for all. And when I heard you were working for them, I just... well, I couldn't accept it."

"Why have you waited so long to tell me, to tell us?"

"I'm sorry, Cav, I was just unwilling to look back at all the hell and misery. And I thought maybe you and Jimmy would be able to straighten it all out and leave that chapter of your life behind you. You know, get on with something new and useful and legitimate." She was near tears. "I hope I haven't screwed things up between us!"

"That is never going to happen, ever," Cav said. He put his arms around her and they clung to each other. "Listen to me, gorgeous. I'll never let you carry this burden alone. We'll handle Marco and Marcella together—whatever it takes. This isn't just your fight anymore, Esmeralda," Cav said, his voice unshakable. "It's ours."

46

The Final Settlement

The car picked them up promptly at noon and transported them to the old shabby mine building. The driver led them to the office, where Marco sat, shabby and visibly sleepless. A couple of thugs sitting at the far end of the office pretended to be doing things with their phones.

"Take a seat," Marco whispered.

The boys sat and waited while Marco composed his thoughts. "Firstly, I wanted to assure you that your efforts have not gone unnoticed."

"Thank you," said Cav. "And we want you to know how much we appreciate the opportunity and all the money. But it's the guilt that has been torturing us inside."

"Guilt?!" Marco was shocked, instantly infuriated. His eyes were bloodshot; they looked like the road maps of Los Angeles. "What's that supposed to mean?"

"You don't know the word 'guilt'?" asked Jimmy.

"Don't talk down to me, motherfucker!" Marco yelled.

"Let me speak, Marco," Jimmy said. "We're leveling with you now. As unbelievable as it may sound, Cav and I have never stopped to weigh the cost of this business in terms of human lives through all the killing."

Marco covered his face with one hand, rubbing his eyes in frustration. "I make you two bums rich and I get lectured to?"

"Forget it," said Jimmy. "Let's just say Cav and I have decided to move on."

Marco lost it.

"You think you can just waltz in here and preach to me about right and wrong?" he screamed. "I gave you two fucks millions and made you rich beyond your wildest dreams, and you come down to my house and disrespect me like this? I'm going to teach you a lesson, and when I'm done, you're going to have some respect for me, by God."

"The word was 'guilt.'" said Cav. "I choose my words carefully."

"Well, fucking choose this," Marco shouted. He ordered his two thugs, "Grab those two broke-back fucks and take them outside."

The henchmen grabbed Cav and Jimmy and dragged them out to a small open area behind the building. Marco had them both tied up to a "slave post" in the middle of the yard. Still in a rage, he picked up a bullwhip and snapped it a few times.

Laying the whip aside, he stepped close and with a spring-blade knife, sliced the back of Cav's shirt from waist up to the collar and violently yanked the shirt open. He did the same to Jimmy's shirt, and then threw the knife into the dirt. His face was twisted in hate, spittle at the corners of his mouth. He moved back a few feet, and then swung the whip with full force, striking Cav's back with a loud crack. Cav shouted in pain and jerked against the ropes. A long, bloody wound stretched across his back.

47

The Prince of Darkness Goes Dark

Some 60 feet away from Marco, crouched behind a pile of boards and shipping pallets, Esmeralda watched with a fierce expression. In her hands she held a hunting longbow. A quiver of razor-sharp hunting arrows hung from one shoulder.

When Marco ripped the boys' shirts open and grabbed his whip, she loaded an arrow onto the bow. As he lashed out with the whip at Cav, Esmeralda leapt to her feet and in the same motion drew aim at her hated nemesis and screamed out Marco's birth name, his real name:

"Fernando!"

Marco spun toward the voice, panic flashing in his eyes, terrified at being caught in the act of his sadistic ritual with the whip that he so enjoyed privately. For a fleeting instant there was recognition of Esmeralda on Marco's face, just as the bowstring thrummed and the arrow cut through the air at 250 feet per second, the impact of the arrow and the thump of penetration straight into his chest, the sound of ribs splintering like a gunshot, the force driving him back a step as his lungs collapsed around the sharp intruder with a last rasping expulsion of breath. It was a perfect kill shot, less than a second from bow-string to death. Marco dropped to his knees, silent, and then fell backwards into the dirt, motionless, eyes staring blankly at the sky, the deadly arrow protruding from his chest.

Marco's thugs stood frozen for a heartbeat, eyes wide with disbelief as their untouchable boss went down and they saw the blood and Esmeralda's impossible arrow. Panic, disbelief, primal rage and fear—their pistols came up, hands trembling, gunfire shattering the stillness, firing wildly, aimlessly, bullets ricocheting off trees and biting into the dirt.

Hearing the shots as she sat inside, oblivious that her empire was crumbling by the second, Marcella assumed that her husband had just whacked Cav and Jimmy.

The thugs were swiftly neutralized by military sharpshooters firing silenced rifles from nearby cover. It was all over in seconds. Two soldiers ran over and checked that the two henchmen and Marco were neutralized. Another cut the ropes holding Cav and Jimmy against the post and helped the men to their feet.

Jimmy and Cav stood stunned, struggling to process the whirlwind of events unfolding before them.

They'd been able to see and hear most of what was happening and it was confusing, especially what sounded like Esmeralda's voice shouting a name a few moments ago and then a hail of gunfire. Now here was Marco and his two thugs lying dead in the dirt, an arrow sticking out of Marco's chest, and uniformed soldiers running around with rifles. Adding to what they'd already been through in the last 72 hours, it was almost too much to take. And as if that wasn't demanding enough, Esmeralda came running up out of nowhere with a tall man also armed and wearing a military uniform.

Cav was thrilled to see Esmeralda. But what the hell was going on?

"Cavalier, Jimmy, I'd like you to meet my brother, Colonel Juan Carlos Bolivar."

Things started to get a whole lot clearer!

Cav gripped Juan's hand firmly. "Juan, let me shake the hand that shook the world. Fine job, sir," and he waved his hand to include the dozen or so soldiers still checking the area, "and to your men."

Jimmy stepped forward to offer his own thanks. "Colonel, we'll always be indebted to you," he said, shaking Juan's hand. "And that goes double for you, Esmeralda."

Esmeralda managed a smile, and Cav squeezed her in a tight hug. She was careful not to touch the whip wound on his back.

Cav walked over and felt Marco's pulse. "He's gone all right. Perfect shot."

"If she had missed..." began Jimmy.

"My sister doesn't miss," Juan Carlos said. "She was the South American title holder for many years, first flight, a national champion. Almost made the Olympic team."

"Shhhhh," Esmeralda hushed them all, and turned Cav around to inspect the bloody whip wound on his back. She used shreds of his shirt to dab at the wound.

"It's okay, thanks," he said. "Just kind of pull it together and I'll tuck it in." Which she did, but carefully. Then she helped Jimmy do the same.

"Okay," she said. "Let's go inside and clean house. We still have someone else to attend to."

Esmeralda took a pistol from her brother Juan, cocked it, and turned off the safety. Juan directed some of the soldiers to check the entrance and clear the way of any hostile threats. With an all-clear from the men, Juan led Esmeralda, Cav and Jimmy through the back entrance and into the building. A dozen employees stood by their desks. Several backed away in fear at the sight of armed soldiers.

Juan loudly announced in Portuguese: "The Brazilian military now controls this property. Everyone stay right where you are."

Marcella came rushing into the area and stopped in shock at the presence of the military, Jimmy, Cav and Esmeralda. Her face was a mask of bravado trying to hide her fear, which was compounded by the absence of Marco.

Her eyes darted here and there, looking around. No Marco. Her fear turned to terror.

"Where is Marco?" she demanded. "What do you think you are doing? You have no right to invade my property. Where is my husband?"

Esmeralda ignored her. "There is nothing to worry about," she said to the employees in Portuguese. "Your lives are not in danger."

The employees stood uneasily, glancing back and forth between Marcella, who was obviously in shock, and the Colonel and his men.

Juan gestured to two soldiers and pointed at Marcella. The two men quietly apprehended her, and Juan informed her she was no longer in control. They escorted her into Marco's office and ordered her to sit and remain seated. One soldier was posted just inside the door to guard her, his weapon at the ready.

Esmeralda told Cav and Jimmy to sit and relax for a bit while her brother and his men searched the premises. The military strategically surrounded the office with complete control and authority from every angle. They began searching the entire facility for potential threats and anything that seemed like incriminating evidence.

All the office employees were gathered in the main office and asked to remain seated. Their faces revealed a mixture of relief and hope, but not fear. Marco and Marcella had had them walking on eggshells for years on slave wages. Now the reign of terror appeared to be over.

The legality of the military operation would be up to the Brazilian authorities to sort out. Esmeralda and Juan were counting on the fact that Marco and Marcella had burned most of the bridges with any officials who might step up to support them.

The employees had waited years for the bosses to get their comeuppance, and the day had finally come. They had been forced to watch over the years the cold-blooded killings and torture that Marco casually inflicted on anyone who crossed or displeased him.

Cav and Jimmy were subdued by the succession of shocks over the past 72 hours—one kidnapping and murder to the next kidnapping and murder and now this—an execution by bow and arrow and thugs dropped in their tracks by a lethal military kill force. They had witnessed it all first-hand, two pool hustlers from

Kansas, guys now sitting semi-stunned more than anything else by the sudden emergence of Esmeralda the Conqueror—woman of Cav's dreams and architect of Marco's demise.

Sitting in Marco's empty office, watched by a soldier, Marcella knew she had missed something terrible outside. She'd heard the gunshots. She knew that Marco was no more. She also knew what was intended to happen to her, and refused to believe it. Arrest? Criminal charges? Trials?

How could anyone do this to her and her husband? Were they not invincible, totally protected by their connections?

Esmeralda, finally in her element after years of grief and anger over the death of her cousin Sabrina, walked to the office door and motioned with the pistol for Marcella to come outside. She wanted Marcella to fully absorb the grisly scene, to understand the finality of what had happened.

Marcella stepped through the door, and stopped just outside as soon as she saw Marco lying on the ground, the fatal arrow still protruding from his chest. She walked over and knelt beside her dead husband, and then did something very strange. She lay down on her back in the dust beside him, staring up at the sky, expressionless. No tears, no words. Some kind of communion.

To Esmeralda it was more than weird. It was eerie.

48

Put Your Wet Thumb Print Right Here

Esmeralda led Marcella back inside and seated her at Marco's desk. She ordered Marcella to sign over all their real estate holdings throughout South America and around the world, all hotels, resorts, mansions and bank accounts both in and out of the country, to a special trust set up in Esmeralda's name.

"You are also going to hand over all the secret codes and passwords for all the shell companies in the Cayman Islands and Panama."

She kept the loaded pistol steadily aimed at Marcella.

Esmeralda had hired the best private financial and corporate investigations company in the world to conduct an asset search for anything and everything under the sun, moon, and stars that were connected in any way to Marco and/or Marcella. She now pulled several sheets of paper from her shoulder bag that contained listings of all these holdings.

"Hand over all of it!" Esmeralda said. "And the courts may grant mercy. I wouldn't give much for your life at this point, otherwise. It's over. You're finished. Now open that safe." She pointed at the wall safe and then gestured with the pistol. "Now!"

With trembling hands, Marcella opened the safe and withdrew a huge pile of file folders and record books. With the contents spread on the desk, Esmeralda produced an ink pad and rubber stamp from her bag, pressing an impression on the first of Marcella's files. The stamp declared the property hereby deeded to "Esmeralda Inc." and certified the transfer of ownership which, with this thumbprint and signatures, certified and confirmed the validity of the document as true and factual—Marcella's legal transfer, done of her own free will under no duress. She then grabbed Marcella's right hand and guided her right thumb to the blue ink pad, pressed her thumb into the ink, and then onto the stamped image on the document. Esmeralda stamped dozens of documents, each bearing Marcella's thumbprint and signature alongside the declaration.

The blow business, the cocaine business, however, was reserved for something extra special. All of those global affiliates that once depended and relied on Marco and Marcella were now out of the cocaine business. It was time for those men up in New York, the customs officer Mr. Toomay, and the carrier Mr. Anderson, to lawyer up. The cocaine processing lab in New Jersey, complete with the Swiss chemist, was about to get a 4:00 a.m. rampage. SWAT teams, raids, and arrest warrants were all part of their future. The overseas banking networks in Thailand, Tel Aviv and Hong Kong were all finished.

The killing scene outside was left untouched until all the workers got a chance to see it for themselves—a reflection on this last chapter in a cold-blooded reign of terror throughout South America and the world.

Through the long process of finalizing all the paperwork, ensuring that her newfound authority was legally solidified, Esmeralda maintained a firm grip on the situation with Juan's automatic pistol never far from reach. The military personnel stood guard, ready to intervene should any resistance arise. With the transition of power complete, Marco's and Marcella's once formidable empire now rested in the hands of "Esmeralda Inc." She had no intention of keeping any of the wealth for herself. It was all being assigned to Sabrina's family and heirs, plus many other victims and assigns, along with a huge amount going to various charities for the poor and indigent.

Esmeralda placed the large stack of signed and thumb-printed records into a large portfolio, and handed it over to her brother. Juan took the portfolio for safekeeping in his military vault under guard. That single portfolio was worth countless billions.

Esmeralda, with cold fury, asked a final question to Marcella: "I ask you in the end, with blood on your hands from innocent children and countless thousands of people around the world, after all the murders, all the killings, all over this white powder: why?" And then again: "Why?"

Marcella was aware of her inevitable fate. She began to beg for her life. "I'm a good person! I give millions to charity! I go to church every Sunday! I do so many good things."

Esmeralda was unsympathetic. "It's the bad things you've done that far outweigh any good. But I am getting ahead of myself here. That's just my opinion. You will be happy to know that I called and set up a meeting for you with a higher power to decide your ultimate fate."

She picked up Juan's pistol from the desk, and removed all but one of the cartridges from the magazine, and put them into her pocket. She then pumped the last cartridge into the firing chamber and carefully placed the weapon on the desk, just out of Marcella's reach.

Pointing a finger heavenward, Esmeralda said, "We will let Him decide."

She turned and walked out of the office, motioned for the guard to come with her, and closed the door, leaving Marcella trembling with rage and fear, alone with the weapon and her sense of impending doom.

Esmeralda stepped away from the door and paused, as if waiting to say something to the office staff clustered near the far exit. A few seconds ticked off. Then BANG!

Everyone jumped at the pistol shot from inside the office. It signaled Marcella's decision to avoid trials and prisons and eventual capital punishment.

Esmeralda gestured for the guard, rifle at the ready at the sound of the pistol shot, to carefully check inside the office.

"Be careful, she's a crafty bitch," she said to the young soldier.

He nodded and tried the door. No reaction from inside. He carefully pushed it open, and peered inside. He stepped back and nodded, wide-eyed, at Esmeralda.

"It's okay," he said. "It's safe. But you may not want to go back in there."

***

The office staff could scarcely believe they were about to be vindicated and set free. No strangers to sudden violence and even executions, for years they had watched the disregard for law and order on that property, cold-blooded murders of Marco's and Marcella's enemies, real or imagined.

They chatted and laughed a little. One of them shouted "Libertação! Esmeralda!" Calling her name like she was their hero and provider of liberty and freedom.

A soldier who had found Marco's wine cellar was sent back for a few bottles and some glasses. Corks popped, and everyone toasted the new era. The staff had never been shown this level of respect in all the years they had been slaves for The South American Emerald Mining Company. All that terror and cruelty was now behind them.

The workers were in a state of near euphoria at the prospect of release from their bondage to Marcella and Marco. One of the workers looked at Esmeralda and asked, "Marco, is he...?" and he drew a finger across his neck.

They wanted reassurance that Marco, the head of the snake, was actually dead. They wanted to see it. Among all the chatting and excitement, Juan announced to the workers that he would like to treat them to a special tour outside to see the end of the reign of terror by a gangster and ruthless killer and his mules. He escorted them all outside to observe the dead Marco and his two thugs. They cheered and clapped. One man spat on Marco's lifeless corpse, and another, a middle-aged woman, picked up a handful of dirt and threw it over the body. This was the moment of closure they had all prayed for, and now their world was new.

They returned inside. Esmeralda announced, "Yes, you are all free. Consider this your early retirement." Her words met with explosive cheers and excitement. Esmeralda's declaration brought an end to an era of control and terror, marking the beginning of a new chapter for the workers' lives.

Throughout all this, Cav and Jimmy had been trying to stay out of the way and let Esmeralda and Juan and his men clean things up. When the pistol shot rang out in Marco's office, right after Esmeralda came out, the two exchanged glances as if to say, "there goes Marcella."

Cav discovered a substantial amount of cash in Marco's desk and began handing out wads of money to the workers. For many, it was like winning the lottery, though it was hardly compensation for the years of torment and suffering imposed by Marcella and Marco.

But at least the money provided them with the means to celebrate a new life, one that promised liberation from the shackles of the past and hopefully a financially secure future.

49

Light This Mother Up

After the staff had been paid off, the equivalent of several years' salary each, they cleaned out their personal areas. Everything else of value was being found, itemized and removed for transport to storage.

One staff member, an African-Brazilian worker who had suffered more than most, expressed his deeply felt relief at this turn of events. He stormed out to Marco's corpse, pulled out the arrow, and held it up high for everyone to see. "This bloody arrow," he proclaimed in Portuguese, "from this day forward, will represent to me our liberation here today. I will place this on my wall at my home, where it will remain for the rest of my days."

Esmeralda applauded enthusiastically along with everyone present. She then took charge, directing the staff to reveal all the secret hiding places and vaults. Everything of value had to be located, itemized, packaged and removed for transport.

The discoveries in the wine cellar included 100 bottles of some of the highest-priced rare wines in the world. They also recovered 20 bottles of the most collectible, rare bottles of single malt whisky. The rarest of all was a bottle of Macallan 1926, one of which recently broke auction records when it sold for more than $2.5 million. Only three bottles were known to still exist in the world.

The art collection reflected sound financial judgment on the part of Marcella or her advisors. Several rare pieces by Monet and Picasso were included in the haul. All were carefully packaged and removed for transport to a safe location.

The staffers led them to various hidden rooms and closets where treasure chests of wealth were stored. Everywhere they turned were more and more diamonds, emeralds, rubies, gold, precious metals and stacks of cash from numerous countries.

Cav seized the opportunity to quietly pilfer a sizable ladies' diamond ring.

One of the employees led soldiers to an arms and ammunition storage vault containing hundreds of high-powered rifles, handguns, hand grenades and small handmade bombs suitable for personal assassinations.

Another major discovery was the processing lab in the back of the property, previously unknown to Cav and Jimmy. This was where Marco processed all the cocaine for export. Stacks of white blocks from the floor to the ceiling waiting to be exported were now marked by the soldiers for destruction, along with everything in the opium den. Any cocaine and other drugs in odd areas, like Marco's office safe, were gathered and piled in the center of the office.

Anything else of any value, from the rare Persian rugs and office furniture to Marco's ultra-chic custom-built desk and Louis XV gilt bronze rock crystal chandeliers valued at millions, was loaded onto the trucks for transportation to the new Esmeralda Inc. repository for safekeeping.

Finally, the lifeless corpses of Marco, Marcella and the two thugs were placed in the center of the empty offices with the drugs, a horrific assembly serving as a death row conviction and execution for high treason punishable by death, same-day service.

"Okay! Let's get this wired for sound and light it up," Cav said joyfully. The atmosphere grew tense as the transition team began wiring the walls with dynamite, preparing for a massive explosion. All the invaluable, collected treasures were symbolic representations of Marco and Marcella's criminal empire.

With everything removed from the facility and the explosives set and primed, everyone gathered on a small hill a quarter mile or so from the buildings. They all felt united in the impending erasure of everything "Marco and Marcella."

As the countdown hit zero, a thunderous explosion erupted, consuming Marco, Marcella, the thugs, and all that cocaine and opium in a spectacular display of fireworks—flames, sparks and smoke that sent shock waves through the fragments of Marco's depraved empire of cruelty.

The workers had watched from a safe distance but close enough to provide a release, a complete and personal disconnection. Everyone cheered as the explosion blew an immense cloud of smoke into the sky, a testament to what had been and was now no more.

"The tyrants, once mighty, returned to dust, as all empires built on tyranny must."

Watching the fiery spectacle was like witnessing an act of symbolic liberation. Esmeralda, Cav, Jimmy, and the others felt a weight lifted from their shoulders. It was a perfect closure to a dark chapter in their lives. The explosion marked not only the end of Marco's reign but also the beginning of a new voyage for everyone present.

Any threat of revenge literally evaporated with the end of Marco and Marcella. They had no children, no parents or heirs. Marco had one brother, a religious man who would never accept what he called "dirty money." The man had learned at a young age to let Marco be Marco. He wasn't ever going to change.

No one knew who Marcella's family was or anything about her origins. But it was said that her family knew who Marcella was, and they had long ago disowned her for her involvement with the notorious Marco.

So it was certain that Esmeralda's acquisition of the Marco and Marcella empire would go unchallenged and would ultimately fade to black along with the memory of them and their nefarious lives.

50

The Final Curtain Approaches

Corcovado, rising majestically over the vibrant city of Rio de Janeiro, stands as a symbol of peace, welcoming all with open arms. Its iconic 99-foot-tall Christ the Redeemer statue, perched atop Corcovado, is shown in countless breathtaking panoramic views that capture the beauty and spirit of Brazil.

As the sun dipped below the horizon, the sky became busy producing a warm variety of colors, enhancing the city's natural beauty.

Cav, Esmeralda, Gisele, and Jimmy rode the tram high above Rio, enjoying breathtaking views on their way up to Corcovado. Upon arrival, they were greeted with the happy, playful energy of dogs running around.

A curious bloodhound pup made its way to Esmeralda. With a tender touch, she lifted the adorable pup into her arms. To her surprise, she discovered a small note attached to the dog's collar, bearing her name. Unfolding the note, she read the words, "Will

you marry me?"—her heart overflowing with jubilation. Overcome
with emotion, Esmeralda couldn't hold back her tears. Cav knelt
on one knee in front of her and the pup. With a heartfelt nod,
Esmeralda signaled her acceptance. A diamond ring, discreetly
liberated from Marco's dark stash of hidden treasures, found its
new place of freedom on her finger, sealing their commitment.

Jimmy and Gisele congratulated Esmeralda and Cav on their
engagement.

As the sun continued its descent, painting the sky in breathtaking colors, the couple stood on Corcovado, in a state of euphoria
at what had just happened, something that would forever have a
deep and profound effect on their lives.

51

Sunset At Copacabana Beach

The following night, beneath a glowing sunset at Copacabana Beach, Cav, Esmeralda, Jimmy, Gisele, and their local friends gathered for their final "settle the score" meeting with Fredrico. The distant waves, the ocean breeze, and the gentle surf, all seemed to promise relief, hope and good things to come. A celebration of triumph and newfound freedom.

Fredrico emerged from the shadows, accompanied by Davi, the manager from the pool hall—the thought-to-be-shot-dead manager! They acknowledged all the welcoming smiles and joined the party.

"We nailed it, brother," Cav said to Fredrico, handing him the duffel bag with the orange patch. Fredrico opened it, pulling out wads of cash on the beach. There were hundreds of thousands of dollars in the duffel bag.

Fredrico was shocked. "Man, this is way more than we agreed to, Cav."

"It's a small expression of my gratitude to you, Fredrico. You earned it, my friend. You were in far more danger than me and Jimmy." A humbling statement far from the truth.

"Cav, I can't thank you enough. You too, Jimmy. I'm real sorry I missed the fireworks. We heard you lit up that mine old-school," said Fredrico.

"Wait just a damn minute here," Cav began, but Esmeralda interrupted: "Honey, hush." She turned to Cav. "Cavalier, am I expected to believe that you, Jimmy, and Fredrico were behind this from the beginning?"

Fredrico attempted to play it down, "Yes, but..." "Don't you 'yes, but' me, mister." Esmeralda cussed Fredrico in Portuguese. She looked up at Davi. "And you're supposed to be dead, mister pool hall manager. I saw you die right in front of me. Am I to believe this whole thing was a hustle from the beginning?"

Davi just smiled and looked at Fredrico for support. But Gisele, heating up, loudly proclaimed, "Hang on here!" She turned on Cav and Jimmy. "You're telling me this was a hustle? And me and Esmeralda were pawns? And we risked our lives for your hustle?"

Cav responded matter-of-factly: "No, you were not pawns—just in the wrong place at the wrong time. Pure accident. The truth is, we came to Rio to play what we thought was a $200,000 9-ball match with Fredrico. Turns out it was a fake match, but we didn't know that until later. I spoke to Fredrico about a plan. It was sloppy, but it was a plan. Fredrico didn't tell us anything until the timing was right. I found out later the pool match was a front, pure theater for Marco's pleasure. Marco just wanted to see us face to face."

The whole group fell silent, listening intently.

"So when you two showed up at the pool hall," Cav continued, "we didn't know yet about the master plan. That came later. How many people go to that mine, do you think? The answer is no one. That mine was a hideaway and an opium den and a laboratory processing plant with millions of dollars' worth of raw materials, millions in finished product. Five people, any given day at that facility with all those millions. Add to that the harmless slave employees. You know Marco and Marcella were addicted to opium—they were freaking junkies. They had a 10-year stash of pure opium on that property—you saw it!"

"When me and Cav saw how cruel and heartless Marcella and Marco were to their workers at the so-called mine," Jimmy added, "that among other things made us turn against them."

Cav continued. "Our plan was a heist. We would put Marco, the mules and Marcella in quarantine on lockdown. Then we would jack, take the goods, empty the mine, take out all the valuables, and call it a day once we were back in L.A. No connection to us, no suspicion. We could call it 'Esmeralda Inc. Lite.' We sent our guys to Rio to scout out around the mine and paid them a ton. They spent two weeks in Rio working out the logistics. All we had to do was lock them down, move out the inventory and remove all the valuables, relocate the goods to a container to the Porto do Rio de Janeiro, and we get the bank wire the same day. Everything was inventoried and pre-sold. Marco and Marcella got lazy, arrogant, and cocky. Easy targets."

Jimmy explained, "Credit to Fredrico, he steered the ship through some rough waters. He didn't expect me and Cav to get carried away with the blow. It was never supposed to go that far. Once you showed up and Cav fell in love with you, I knew there was no turning back."

Esmeralda asked the million-dollar question: "How did you know the cavalry would come in at the last minute to save you?"

Jimmy tried to explain more: "Fredrico, knowing what he knew about you and your brother, Colonel Juan Carlos—a decorated soldier of fortune for Esmeralda Inc. in this case—it was pretty much automatic. Especially when you showed up at our hotel back from London, demanding to know our meet-up time with Marco. Me, Cav and Fredrico envisioned a divine military intervention as a possibility."

"Well, then you told us your story about Sabrina and Marco and Marcella," Cav said, "and there was no coming back from that. It was on for sure."

"That's right," Jimmy said. "We still were determined to confront Marco and give him the heads-up that we were done. We considered buying him out to be done with him, but we knew after speaking to him at the airport that it probably wouldn't work. Cav still hoped we could just make peace with Marco and get out. We thought there was a hope and a prayer that Marco just might come to his senses when we confronted him at the office. When we told you we would handle it and you insisted on taking care of it yourself, we figured you must have a trick up your sleeve. But we couldn't count on it. We had to act like it was all up to us, and that's the way we approached it."

Cav added, "Since we were sitting on $250 million, we figured, why not offer Marco $30 million for anything we might still owe him, and let us get on with our lives? But he was too madly insane to reason with. We never wanted you and Gisele involved. We really did think it was lights out when Casimo tried to put a hit on us. But for once, Marco came to our rescue."

"Yeah," Cav added. "It turns out Marco had been following us and knew from his connections in the underworld, in France and Italy, what was about to happen to us. The bastard bought us 72 hours and whacked the punks that were about to kill us so he could kill us later. There has to be some comedy in that somewhere."

Cav paused and then, with an embarrassed grin, said: "Hey gorgeous, I'm sorry I couldn't tell you sooner. But you and Gisele know we had to keep you safe. And look, it all worked out. We're all here, alive, fucking rich and free. On the bright side this gave you a golden opportunity to settle the score that was way overdue."

Esmeralda smiled but she was still irritated about getting played.

"Cav, you hustled me and Gisele—you, Jimmy, Fredrico, and even you, Davi—mister pool hall manager indeed!"

"You boys are pretty slick," Gisele nodded, poking Jimmy. She got a big smile in return.

"Long story short," Cav continued, "Marco was going to go down one way or another, deservedly. Who better than Esmeralda Inc. to settle the score, dispense justice and take the title over all those millions, probably billions—as my new wife? I liked the sound of that."

"What you and Juan showed us at the mine was such a magnificent performance," Jimmy said to Esmeralda. "Hollywood couldn't have scripted it any better. It was clean, it was needed, and you and Juan had the courage to do something about it. The both of you deserve some kind of medal, and I mean that from the heart, Esmeralda."

She still had something to say: "What you don't know, Jimmy, is how much the horror show of Marco and Marcella dominated our lives. We grew up reading in the newspapers and hearing about them on TV, an endless stream of senseless killings of good people. Judges, reporters, innocent people coming forward, decent people, all got murdered by these tyrants. My parents for so many years suffered watching these monsters run free and make an insane asylum out of our beautiful country."

"You're absolutely correct!" Fredrico said, passionately validating Esmeralda's description. "They both were tyrants! But then, Cav, you and Jimmy killed it in The Riviera, $250 million, greatest score in pool history and you almost got killed. You crushed all the pool books and records for a long time to come. The pool world owes you a debt of gratitude. Way cool. And Jimmy—hats off to both of you. You did the impossible. You should have seen the look on Marco's face when I leaked that match in Monaco with Mr. LeBlanc. He couldn't get there fast enough. He took off like a rabbit with sneakers. Smoke and vapor in his tracks straight to the South of France. Your total security in Monaco was assured at that point."

Jimmy yelled, "We got bank in Monaco! Esmeralda set us free. No more blow business, and the South American Emerald Mining Company has a new holding company— Esmeralda, Inc. Hey Esmeralda," Jimmy continued. "I'm just curious, why the arrow?"

"I did think long and hard about this, Jimmy. If Marcella needed some real shock value to push her into signing over the empire, and if I was ever to get her blue ink right thumb to paper with no resistance, I just figured I had one chance. I needed to really create an effect, something very dramatic, some theater, to move her emotionally."

Cav wondered what they were all thinking. "Why not just shoot the freak?"

Esmeralda shook her head. "I needed the shock value to make her apathetic. A gunshot would have been a wake-up call instead. I needed to make a kill shot with my bow and arrow for the theatrics. When we took Marcella outside for a last look at what was left of him, she was a mess. I knew at that stage I owned the bitch." Esmeralda was almost in tears reliving the moment. The others nodded respectfully.

Esmeralda continued, "Call me cold-blooded, but if we put the whole place to the torch, including Marco's remains and the other bodies, there would be nothing left to pin the killings on us. There would be no DNA sample left at the crime scene once Juan fired that neutron bomb up their asses."

Everyone was a little shocked at this revelation, and at the same time, impressed and in agreement.

"One more thing," she continued. "When I decided to use the bow and arrow, not a gun, I knew I needed a full frontal shot for my aiming. I could think of just one thing that would make him turn and face me. Just as he picked up that bullwhip to humiliate and beat my man, I yelled out his birth name. Which I knew he hated."

Fredrico goaded her to dramatize the action. "Show us what you did, show us how you did it!"

Esmeralda stood up, like she had her bow and arrow pointed with perfection. "I aimed my bow and arrow and I screamed his name, F e r n a n d o!!! and set my final aim again. I had just one second for my final aim, and I let the arrow fly straight to his heart!"

Her revelation was met with cheers of agreement from the group. Esmeralda allowed herself to accept the praise, prompting tears of relief.

Fredrico had a proposition. "Hey Esmeralda, you now own the pool hall. Its former owner is now a puff of smoke in the sky. Can I send Esmeralda Inc., an invoice for a complete makeover and renovation?" The crowd playfully booed and whistled. Fredrico and Davi were seriously interested in hearing her answer.

Esmeralda counter-offered, "How about I sell you the pool hall for one dollar and you may have your way with it, do anything your little heart desires? I am confident that the duffel bag and its contents should be more than enough for all-new pool tables, floors, walls with no bullet holes. Oh, and could you surprise us someday with a new bar please? That bar was one of the ugliest in Brazil. You should have more than enough in that green bag to transform that grubby, worn-out old billiard room into a nice, civilized, shiny new pool hall."

Fredrico and Davi lit up with smiles. "You have a deal, Esmeralda. In that case, we will turn it into a first-class pool hall, fit for a princess. Two princesses, you and Gisele. Thank you for your generosity."

52

Reflections

Esmeralda's mother was proud that the first thing Esmeralda did was establish trusts for the families of those who had been murdered or ruined by the thugs. Especially her cousin Sabrina.

So, naturally this became Esmeralda's first order of business.

The second item on her agenda was to arrange for her parents to meet her soon-to-be husband, the mysterious and handsome American named Cavalier.

Esmeralda had set this up for a few days from the beach party, and invited everyone.

Cav took her hand and asked, "May I go shopping tomorrow and get some new rags, some decent clothes? We've been wearing this resort holiday crap for three days. I'd like to be decent to meet my new in-laws."

He let go of her hand and reached into his pocket and pulled out a huge wad of cash. "I didn't have any money until we had that Marco massacre. Oh, but wait, this technically belongs to

Esmeralda, Inc. Hey gorgeous, can I borrow this? I'll pay you back when I get my hands on—" his voice rose to a shout—"my $250 million dollars!"

This got a laugh from the crowd, especially Esmeralda. "Oh but wait," he continued, "the cash was not in fact technically yours quite yet because you hadn't yet done that blue ink thumb routine, whatever that was. I've never seen anything so bizarre in my life. Marcella still had a pulse. So let's all be honest here. This loot is mine and Jimmy's. So thanks, Marcella!"

There was more laughter and clapping.

It felt like a dream. A couple of pool hustlers from Kansas rising to stardom by some random, off-the-wall wager with a slick billionaire blow merchant. They got involved in a major smuggling operation, in Rio of all places. They partnered with the billionaire, who provided them a means to accumulate untold millions, which led them to another dead end—and another breakthrough, with Cav's attainment of pool prowess that would make him legendary.

The pool gods rewarded him, and whether he deserved it or not, he sure as hell wasn't about to question their generosity.

The boys took all their newfound fortune to another part of the world, the home of rich and very famous Monte Carlo, where they hustled yet another billionaire. They combo-bet everything and parlayed the moment into another massive fortune of untold millions. Like magicians they created $20 million out of thin air and brilliantly hustled it into a $250 million fortune. They got kidnapped, were rescued within seconds of losing their lives, and then kidnapped by another higher power which led them halfway around the world back to another attempted torture and murder event, and then saved at the last minute by the woman of Cav's dreams and her military regime of the moment.

At La Guardia, the boys came close to facing a 25-year sentence for smuggling and an additional 25 years for the RICO Act, 50 years total, more or less a death sentence. And they faced death itself in Monaco. And then again in Rio.

The "nine lives of a cat" story came into play here, best summarized by William Shakespeare: "Three years he plays, three years he strays, and for the last three years, he stays."

The hustler, the world-beater, met the soulmate of many lifetimes in this go-round. She rose to international fame as CEO of a now legitimate empire built on the ashes of one of the most notorious and powerful crime syndicates in the Southern Hemisphere.

Esmeralda, improvising on a grand scale, busted the slave masters into small pieces and took command of an unimaginable wealth of treasures few people ever dream of: 23 posh ultra high-dollar five-star resorts, mansions, flawless emeralds and diamonds, foreign and domestic bank accounts, and an art collection befitting the world's most prestigious museums. Esmeralda did it on her own, with her own brand of hustle and brilliance.

The hustlers, having outplayed and outsmarted the ringleaders, now emerged with generational wealth and new frontiers before them.

53

Let's Name Him Eddie

"All right, everyone— group photo time!"

With a mischievous sparkle in her eye, Esmeralda handed the camera to Cav.

The group lined up, some standing and the others kneeling in front. As Cav adjusted the camera to line up the photo, a banner was unrolled across the front of the group that read:

"Congratulations to Esmeralda and Cav On Their New Baby Boy!"

Cav froze in stunned silence, needing a moment to process the magnitude of this revelation. Then, bursting with joy, he tossed the camera onto the sand and wrapped Esmeralda in a jubilant embrace.

The group erupted in applause, celebrating the creation of a new 21st-century pool player.

With that heartwarming revelation, the story found its perfect conclusion, triumph, action, love, humor, and family, and the promise of a new world and new vistas.

« End »

Author Bio

From David Sutter's first encounter with pool at age ten in a small town in Kansas to the glamorous pool halls of Los Angeles, the author's passion for billiards has spanned continents and decades. After building a successful furniture import business, he traveled extensively through Asia. In 2017, he penned his first screenplay, which he later adapted into this novel—a story that weaves together his lifelong fascination with pool, gambling, and the artistry of the game.

www.ingramcontent.com/pod-product-compliance
Lightning Source LLC
Chambersburg PA
CBHW020602110726
47899CB00002B/337